Orders to Kill

a&b

Orders to Kill

EDWARD MARSTON

Allison & Busby Limited
11 Wardour Mews
London W1F 8AN
allisonandbusby.com

First published in Great Britain by Allison & Busby in 2021.

A CIP catalogue record for this book is available from
the British Library.

First Edition

ISBN 978-0-7490-2699-8

Typeset in 12/18 pt Adobe Garamond Pro by
Allison & Busby Ltd.

FSC
www.fsc.org
MIX
Paper from
responsible sources
FSC® C020471

The paper used for this Allison & Busby publication
has been produced from trees that have been legally sourced
from well-managed and credibly certified forests.

Printed and bound by
CPI Group (UK) Ltd, Croydon, CR0 4YY

To my wonderful son, Conrad

CHAPTER ONE

December, 1917

Days began early for Ada Hobbes. It was just past four o'clock in the morning when she let herself out of her house and felt the first blast of an icy wind. Head down and teeth clenched, she began the long walk over frost-covered pavements that did their best to bring her crashing down on the stone slabs. But she was far too watchful and sure-footed to slip and fall. Now in her fifties, Ada was a short, skinny woman, wrapped up in a moth-eaten fur coat that had been through three generations before it had reached her. The scarf around her neck also covered her mouth and her hat was pulled down over her face. Though she looked frail and defenceless, she was quite the opposite. Scarred by loss and tested by recurring misfortune, she had survived both. Ada was a fighter.

To reach the offices where her working day started, she had to walk the best part of two miles, leaving the drab, cheerless, overcrowded district where she lived before arriving in a more affluent area. Her destination was an imposing Victorian residence converted into offices by an insurance company. Those who worked there expected three things on their arrival. They wanted their waste-paper baskets to be empty, their desks to be polished and fires to have been laid in their respective grates. Ada never let them down.

She was quick yet thorough, cleaning each office in turn and leaving it spotless. After putting everything away, Ada went on a final tour of the building to make sure that nothing had been missed. Then she picked up the envelope on the hall table and slipped it into her handbag. There was no need to count the money. Her employers trusted her enough to give her keys to the property and she trusted them. Ada was soon letting herself into a house less than a hundred yards away and tackling another set of offices. Tireless and methodical, she went through the same routine. A second envelope was dropped into her handbag.

Her third assignment that morning was her favourite. It was in a detached house that stood in a tree-lined avenue. Ada only had to satisfy the needs of one person this time instead of whole groups of them. Her employer was specific. When she entered the house, she found his instructions awaiting her. After making a mental note of them, she bustled along the passageway, went into the kitchen and through into the room beyond it. Expecting to find all that she needed, she reached for a sweeping brush. Then she realised that there was an unexpected visitor in the room.

Opening her mouth in horror, she staggered back against the wall, then slid down it until she hit the floor and passed out.

CHAPTER TWO

No sooner had they arrived at Scotland Yard that morning than they were sent out again. Inspector Harvey Marmion climbed into the rear of the police car with Joe Keedy. It sped away from the kerb and dodged through traffic.

'Where are we going?' asked the sergeant.

'Edmonton.'

'Why?'

'We'll find out when we get there.'

'Didn't Chat tell you anything?'

'It's a gruesome murder, Joe. That's all we need to be told.'

'We always get the messy cases,' complained Keedy.

'That's because we usually solve them.'

'There's more to it than that. Chat has been throwing his weight around ever since he got promoted and we are his main targets. Other detectives get nice, easy, open-and-shut cases involving batty old women who commit suicide with an overdose of pills. The moment a severed head or a mutilated body is involved, we get lumbered with the investigation.'

'I don't see that as a punishment,' said Marmion, easily. 'In his own peculiar way, Superintendent Chatfield is paying us a compliment. And you must never sneer at batty old women. When people are driven to kill themselves, they deserve our sympathy. It may seem small beer to you, but it involves motives far more complex than those that make someone commit murder.'

'That's a fair point,' conceded Keedy.

'Remember it.'

'What's the name of the murder victim?'

'George Tindall.'

'What did Chat say about him?'

'Very little.'

'He must have given you some details.'

'He told me the one thing that was important.'

'What was that?'

'Tindall was a doctor.'

Keedy was shocked. 'Somebody murdered a doctor?'

'So it seems.'

'That's terrible. At a time like this, we desperately need people like him.'

'He worked at the Edmonton Military Hospital.'

'Then he was doing a vital job. Wounded soldiers sent there have the most appalling injuries. The wonder is any of them survive – yet they do, somehow.'

'That's because of the medical team.'

'They're real heroes in my book.'

'I agree, Joe.'

'I take my hat off to them.'

He was speaking metaphorically. In fact, he kept his hat on at its usual jaunty angle. Even though wrapped up in his winter wear, Keedy contrived to look smart. Marmion, by contrast, was as untidy as ever in crumpled clothing that never seemed to fit him properly. After a couple of minutes staring out of the car window, he turned to Keedy.

'As for batty old women, there's something you should remember.'

'Is there?'

'When you finally marry our daughter,' said Marmion with a grin, 'you'll become part of the family.'

'So?'

'For a start, Ellen and I will be happy.'

'And?'

'Imagine what may happen in due course.'

'I don't follow.'

'You may one day have a batty old woman as your mother-in-law.'

War had changed Ellen Marmion's life completely. It had imprisoned her in a routine that she did not even notice at first. Her day began with making an early breakfast for her husband and herself. After waving him off, she washed the plates and cutlery in the sink and left everything to dry on the draining board. She then did a sequence of chores that never varied. When she had finished, she took down the framed photograph of her son from the mantelpiece and began to rub it with a duster even though it was gleaming. Ellen then had her long, daily, ruminative stare at Paul.

Mixed emotions stirred inside her. Pride was uppermost. Dressed in army uniform, Paul was smiling at the camera, glad that he had joined up in a moment of patriotic fervour. He was the wonderful, confident, happy-go-lucky son his mother had adored. But unfortunately he no longer existed. Paul had been one of thousands injured at the Battle of the Somme and shipped back to a hospital in England. Temporarily blinded, he also had afflictions that seemed worryingly permanent. The cheerful extrovert of the Marmion family had become morose and confused. He could not understand why so many of his close friends had been killed in action while he had crawled away alive from the battlefield. Paul felt guilty and bereaved in equal measure.

The family was warned that it might take him a long time to adjust to home life, but he showed no inclination even to try. Ellen made allowances for him but even her patience was tested. Instead of getting better, her son got steadily worse, revealing a nasty streak she had never seen before and behaving in ways that shocked her. Her husband was away from the house for much of the day and her daughter, Alice, no longer lived at home. For the most part, therefore, Ellen was left alone to cope with Paul and his increasingly dangerous moods.

Then, suddenly, he disappeared without a word of explanation. They had no idea where he was or what his intentions were. Marmion organised a search for their son, but it was fruitless. When they did finally discover where he might be, Paul had vanished before they got there. Looking now at the dutiful son she had once loved, she felt the photograph was like a ton weight in her hands.

When they arrived at the scene of the crime, the detectives were relieved to see that they would not be hampered by a large and intrusive crowd. That would certainly have been the case if they were somewhere in central London with people swarming about. Instead, they were in a quiet avenue of detached properties. Standing outside the one owned by George Tindall was a burly uniformed police officer. When he saw them approach, he raised a hand.

'There's no need to introduce yourselves, Inspector,' he said. 'I've seen photos of you and the sergeant in the newspapers many times.'

'Our fame is spreading,' said Keedy with a smile. 'What's your name?'

'Constable Fanning, sir.'

'Are you on your own?'

'No, sir, I'm with a colleague, Constable Rivers.'

'Where is he?' asked Marmion.

'He's in the house next door,' said the other, indicating it. 'When we got here, Mrs Hobbes was in quite a state.'

'Who is she?'

'The cleaner.'

'Why did Dr Tindall need a cleaner? A house this size would surely run to a servant or two.'

'That puzzled me as well.'

'Who raised the alarm?'

'Mrs Hobbes did – when she recovered, that is. She was so upset by what she saw, she fainted. When she came to, she remembered that there was a telephone in the house.'

'Yes, that would be essential for a doctor. The hospital might have needed to summon him at short notice.' Marmion flicked a hand. 'Go on with your story, Constable. Tell us why you took her next door.'

'We needed to get her out of there, sir. She was shaking like a leaf and who could blame her? I've seen gory sights in my time, but nothing to touch this. I'd warn you to be prepared.'

'I'm grateful for your warning,' said Marmion, 'but it doesn't apply to the sergeant. He used to work in the family undertaking business

13

and often saw dead bodies in a deplorable condition. He learnt to take everything in his stride. Nothing unsettles him.'

'Well, it unsettled me, sir,' admitted Fanning.

'Then you'd better stay out in the fresh air.'

'Where is the victim?' asked Keedy.

'He's in the room at the back,' said Fanning. 'Go through the kitchen.'

'Thank you.'

Marmion led the way into the house, pushing open the unlocked front door. He went along the passageway to the kitchen, then stopped in front of the door to the room off it. He studied it warily.

'Perhaps you should open it, Joe,' he suggested.

'Is that a challenge?'

'No – but you've got a stronger stomach than I have.'

'You're not going to faint, are you?' teased Keedy.

'Get on with it.'

Grabbing the handle, Keedy opened the door and looked inside the room. George Tindall lay sprawled on the floor in the remains of his pyjamas amid a jumble of brushes, mops, buckets and other cleaning paraphernalia. Blood was everywhere. The victim had been tied up and gagged before being hacked to death. Marmion forced himself to look and wrinkled his nose in disgust. Keedy ran his eye over the multiple injuries.

'Someone enjoyed doing this,' he said.

Thanks to a cup of tea and the kindness of the neighbours, Ada Hobbes was feeling much better. She was sitting in the lounge next door with Stanley and Enid Crowe, an elderly couple who had been shaken by news of the murder. Standing by the door was Constable Rivers, a tall, thin, willowy man who kept shifting from one leg to another. Ada kept apologising to all three of them for causing so much trouble.

'I'm ashamed of myself for passing out like that,' she said. 'I always prided myself on being able to cope with any problem.'

'You shouldn't blame yourself,' said Enid Crowe. 'It must have been a terrible shock for you. Simply hearing about it has frightened the wits out of me.'

'That goes for me as well,' confessed her husband.

'Besides,' said Rivers, taking a step forward, 'you deserve praise for what you did. As soon as you recovered, you had the presence of mind to pick up the phone and call the police.'

'You did the right thing bringing Mrs Hobbes here, Constable,' said Crowe.

'Thank you, sir.'

'You're welcome to stay as long as possible, Mrs Hobbes,' said Enid.

Ada gave her a smile of thanks. She had only been cleaning Dr Tindall's house for a month or so. Like her, the neighbours could not understand why anyone would want to kill such a decent and dedicated man. Ada looked up at Rivers.

'You will catch whoever did this, won't you?' she asked.

'Yes,' he replied, confidently. 'We'll catch him, Mrs Hobbes, and when we do, he'll pay for this crime with his life.'

While they waited for the Home Office pathologist to arrive, Marmion and Keedy searched the house for information about its owner. Even in the study there was little of real use. Drawers in the desk had been left open, showing that someone had been there before them to remove items such as a diary and an address book. All that they could find was correspondence relating to patients at the hospital. It was when they went into the master bedroom that they had some insight into what had happened. As they opened the wardrobe, Keedy gasped in admiration at the suits hanging up inside.

'These are top quality,' he said, opening a jacket to read the label.

'Why did he have so many?' asked Marmion. 'Two is enough for anyone.'

'He lived in a different world from us.'

'Yes – and on a far better income.'

Breaking away, he walked slowly around the room and looked carefully at everything. Marmion stopped beside a landscape painting on the wall. He scrutinised it for over a minute.

'What do you think of this, Joe?' he asked.

'I hate it.'

'Why?'

'It's so dull and uninteresting.'

'It's also completely the wrong colour for the room. It doesn't match anything. You can see from what is in his wardrobe that he was a man with taste, yet he puts this unsuitable painting in here. There must be a reason for that.'

'What is it?'

'Who knows?' said Marmion. 'Perhaps it's hiding something.'

Lifting the heavy frame carefully off its hook, he revealed a safe set in the wall. Keedy stepped forward to grab the handle and discovered that it turned easily.

'It's not locked,' he said, opening the door and peering inside. 'And the safe is empty.' He snapped his fingers. 'That could be the motive behind the murder. Dr Tindall was burgled. Perhaps he made the mistake of catching the man in the act.'

'There wasn't only one man,' explained Marmion, lowering the

16

painting to the floor. 'It would have taken two of them to overpower him and truss him up like that. In any case, he was not killed here because there's no sign of a struggle. The butchery took place downstairs. Why did they choose there?'

Keedy shrugged. 'Search me.'

'And there's another thing that puzzles me.'

'What is it?'

'When we examined the body, I noticed that Dr Tindall was wearing a wedding ring. What happened to his wife? Why aren't her clothes in the wardrobe?'

'Perhaps she died.'

'Then why aren't there any photos of her on display? If she died before her time, he would surely want to preserve her memory. Yet there's not a single photo of Mrs Tindall anywhere. I find that weird.'

'Maybe the burglars took all the photos away.'

'Why?' asked Marmion. 'What possible interest would photos hold for them? They came to kill him and helped themselves to the contents of the safe while they were here. That is how it looks to me, anyway.' He rubbed his chin. 'All of a sudden, this case has become a lot more interesting.'

CHAPTER THREE

Before the conversation could continue, they heard a car pulling up outside the house. They crossed to the window and saw a short, stubby man coming up the drive.

'It's the pathologist,' said Marmion. 'I'll handle him, Joe. You go next door and take a statement from Mrs Hobbes. With luck, she's had time to recover and may be more coherent.'

'Right,' said Keedy, following him out of the bedroom and down the stairs. 'Will you want to speak to her yourself?'

'There's no need. Just remember to be gentle with her.'

'I will.'

As they reached the hall, the pathologist was coming through the front door.

'Good morning, Harvey,' he said, cheerily, 'and the same to you, Sergeant.'

'Good morning,' said Keedy, going past him. 'You'll have to excuse me.'

'Joe has gone to interview the poor woman who found the body,' explained Marmion. 'We're surprised that she didn't have a heart attack.'

'Is the victim in that bad a state?'

'You need to brace yourself, Tom.'

'Nothing will shock me,' said the other with a chuckle. 'I've just come from examining three people who were killed when a German bomb landed on their house. It's frightening to see what tons of rubble can do to the human body.'

Thomas Harrison was a middle-aged man with a puffy face and a habit of lowering his head so that he could look over the top of his glasses. He and Marmion knew each other well. They went through to the kitchen. When the pathologist put his bag down, Marmion opened the door of the room where the body lay. Harrison remained calm.

'That's what I'd call a comprehensive murder,' he said, quietly. 'The killer certainly went to extremes.'

'We believe that two people might have been involved.'

'Your guesses are usually right.'

'They're based on instinct.'

'That comes with experience,' said the other, studying the corpse with a practised eye. 'It's about the only virtue of getting older. Ah, well,' he went on, taking off his coat. 'I'd better get busy, I suppose.' Marmion was about to reply when he heard the telephone ring.

'Do what you have to do, Tom,' he said. 'I'll have to answer that.'

Going quickly back to the hall, he picked up the receiver.

'Hello …'

'Can I speak to Dr Tindall?' asked a crisp, male voice.

'I'm afraid not.'

'I'm ringing from the hospital. He was expected here over an hour ago.'

'Yes,' said Marmion, heaving a sigh, 'I daresay that he was. I have bad news, I fear. It's my sad duty to tell you that he won't be able to come today – or on any other day, for that matter.'

'What do you mean?'

'I am Detective Inspector Marmion of the Metropolitan Police Force. I'm investigating the doctor's unexplained death.'

Keedy was pleased to meet Stanley and Enid Crowe and grateful for the way that they had looked after Ada Hobbes. The cleaner seemed to have recovered well from her grim discovery and was eager to answer any questions. She explained what had happened when she entered the house, scolding herself for passing out.

'I should have been more careful,' she admitted.

'What do you mean?' asked Keedy.

'Well, whenever I've finished cleaning the house, I collect an envelope from the hall table. My money was in it. I should have noticed that the envelope wasn't there today. If I'd done that, I'd have been warned something strange had happened. Dr Tindall was very particular, you see. He'd never have left the house without putting my money on the table.'

'How often did you go there?'

'Twice a week.'

'Didn't he have a servant who could have done what you did?'

'Dr Tindall was a very private man. He preferred to live alone.'

'It's true,' said Crowe, intervening. 'He moved in next door almost three years ago. His wife died and he wanted to get away from the house where they lived. Yet, strangely enough, that is not what he did. He brought her with him. There were photographs of his wife everywhere.'

'She was beautiful,' said Ada. 'I should know. I had to polish the frames every time I came. That was always on his list of instructions. There was a photo of him and Mrs Tindall on his desk in the study.'

'Well, it's not there now,' said Keedy.

'Really?' She was scandalised. 'Do you mean that it's been stolen?'

'Probably.'

'That's dreadful!' exclaimed Ada.

'Let's go back to your job there. Who cleaned the house before you?'

'It was Kathy Paget, who is my sister. She had arthritis but kept going until the pain was too much to bear. Kathy knew I clean offices not far away. She asked me if I'd like some extra work. I told her I did so she spoke to Dr Tindall, and he took me on.'

'We remember Mrs Paget,' said Enid. 'We used to see her hobbling up the drive. I'm surprised Dr Tindall didn't recommend something for her arthritis.'

'He wasn't that kind of doctor,' Crowe reminded her. 'He was an orthopaedic surgeon.'

'I'm still trying to understand how he managed without a servant or two,' said Keedy. 'Who did his shopping? Who laid the fire? Who prepared his meals?'

'He was quite capable of making his own breakfast, Sergeant. That seemed the only meal he ever had at home. The hospital made great demands on his time. I know that he often ate there. Sometimes he even stayed the night at the hospital.'

'In all the time we've known him,' added Enid, 'he only once accepted an invitation to come here for dinner.'

'Yes, it was a rather awkward occasion.'

'Why was that?' asked Keedy.

'There was the age gap, for one thing,' said Crowe. 'We were at least thirty years older than him. I am a retired bank manager and he was a highly qualified doctor. We didn't talk the same language.'

'He just sat there in silence most of the time,' recalled Enid. 'The only thing he really talked about was his late wife.'

'That's another thing I should have spotted,' said Ada, slapping her knee. 'Her photo was missing from the hall table. It had pride of place there and was the first thing he saw when he came into the house. It should have been the first thing I saw as well when I let myself in, but I didn't. Dr Tindall would never have moved that photo from the table.'

When Alice Marmion and Iris Goodliffe set off on their beat, a steady drizzle was falling. It was one of the few times when they were grateful to be wearing their uniforms. One of the setbacks of joining the Women's Police Force was that their dark blue jackets and ankle-length skirts were very unbecoming. It was something that Iris complained about regularly, fearing that no man would look at her twice because of the way she was dressed. Proud of her hair, she hated wearing a hat that all but obscured it completely. She was glad of it now.

As the drizzle turned to rain, they stepped into a shop doorway for shelter.

'Do you think this will turn to snow?' asked Iris.

'I'm not sure,' replied Alice.

'When I was a little girl, I prayed for a white Christmas. Now, I'd hate it.'

'Why?'

'We'd be sitting targets for snowballs.'

'The city has to be policed, Iris.'

Alice was an attractive young woman with an air of vitality about her. Though she sorely missed the children she taught before the war, she felt that she was doing a more important job now. It meant that she, her father and her fiancé were all in the same profession. Iris envied her. Big, chubby, and decidedly plain, she wished that she had some of Alice's good looks and assurance.

'Have you had many Christmas cards?' she asked.

'Yes,' said Alice. 'Quite a few.'

'I don't suppose …?'

'No, we haven't had one from Paul, but we never expected to. We had no birthday cards from him either. We don't even know if he's still alive.'

'He must be. You said that he was very fit.'

'He used to be, Iris. He joined up with the rest of his football team for which he played. He loved exercise of every kind. One of the sad things was that the war squeezed most of the energy out of him.'

'At least he didn't come back with hideous injuries,' said her friend, 'or with a limb missing. On my way home last night, I saw that soldier who lost both of his legs. He was sitting in his wheelchair, trying to play the accordion. I put sixpence in his hat.'

'Paul hasn't reached the stage of begging yet – I hope not, anyway.'

'It must feel odd, not having him home for Christmas. How do you cope?'

'We pretend he's there.'

Alice was fond of her colleague but, as a rule, she kept her very much at arm's length. Aware how desperate Iris was for a closer friendship, she usually refused any invitations to go out together in the evening. Today was different. Alice suddenly felt a pang of guilt at the way she treated Iris and she felt a need to atone for her behaviour.

'We have a day off tomorrow,' she said.

Iris laughed, 'You don't need to tell me that.'

'Do you have any plans?'

'No, Alice. I'll probably end up working for my father.'

'You can't waste a day off by serving in a chemist's shop.'

'It's better than sitting at home and moping.'

'I've got an idea,' said Alice. 'I still have presents to buy. Why don't we go to the West End for the morning?'

'Yes, please!'

'We can go around the department stores. You are always saying you'd like to cheer yourself up by buying a new dress. Get one tomorrow.'

'I will,' said the other. 'Thank you so much, Alice.'

'It's not often we have a day of freedom. Let's make the most of it.'

'We will.' Iris hugged her. 'You've just given me the most wonderful Christmas present.'

During his career, Marmion had attended many murder scenes. The majority had been in isolated locations where contact with Scotland Yard was impossible. This time it was different. He had access to a telephone. When the initial phases of the investigation were over, therefore, he felt able to ring Claude Chatfield. Predictably, the superintendent was critical.

'Why didn't you get in touch with me earlier?' he demanded.

'There was a lot to do, sir.'

'I need to release information to the press.'

'I'm aware of that,' said Marmion, 'and I've taken the trouble of drafting a statement for you. Do you have pen and paper at hand?'

'Of course, I do. I'm sitting at my desk.'

'Then here it is.'

Reading from his notebook, Marmion dictated the statement slowly so that the superintendent could write it down. He could hear grunts of approval from the other end of the line. When he had finished, he closed his notebook.

'You've got the salient facts there, sir,' he said, 'but we're not giving too much away. I do not want newspapers speculating wildly about this case. It's far more complicated than they'll imagine.'

'Who discovered the body?'

'It was a cleaner by the name of Mrs Hobbes.'

'I suppose she was a gibbering wreck.'

'Then you are quite wrong, sir. The lady is very resilient, according to Sergeant Keedy. Mrs Hobbes was able to give him a clear account of what she discovered and provided useful details about the victim.'

'How will she bear up under pressure from reporters?'

'I'd rather keep her name out of it altogether. After taking her statement, the sergeant got our driver to take her home. It was the least we could do for her. Mrs Hobbes was helpful – and so were the next-door neighbours, a Mr and Mrs Crowe. We can hide the cleaner from the howling mob from Fleet Street, but it will be impossible to do that for the neighbours. They will be fair game. Sergeant Keedy warned them to say nothing whatsoever about Mrs Hobbes.'

'That was a wise move.'

'Yes, sir.'

'It's time for details, Inspector,' said Chatfield, fussily. 'What have you found and what have you and the sergeant deduced?'

After clearing his throat, Marmion gave a fuller account of what had happened since they had been there, telling him what the pathologist had said and how the body had now been removed. Chatfield got a clear, concise, measured synopsis. What he was not given were a few things that Marmion preferred to keep to himself.

'Where's the sergeant now?' asked the superintendent.

'He's making door-to-door enquiries, sir, to see if anyone heard anything unusual during the night.'

'What time did the murder take place?'

'Tom Harrison couldn't give a precise time. His guess would be somewhere between midnight and four o'clock.'

'Did the doctor have any known enemies?'

'That's what I'm hoping to find out.'

'He sounds like a strange fellow. Why live in a house entirely on his own? It is a rather spartan notion of life, isn't it? You'd expect him to have servants, surely.'

'Dr Tindall lived for his work, sir.'

'I live for mine but that doesn't mean I punish myself. My wife and I could not manage without a maid. One is entitled to some luxuries.'

Marmion said nothing. Unlike the superintendent's wife, his own would have been insulted at the idea that she could not cope without help. Ellen made light of the drudgery involved. She did what most mothers in London did and accepted her lot.

'What's your next move?' asked the superintendent.

'I'm going to the hospital where he worked,' said Marmion. 'His colleagues deserve to know more than I've told them over the phone and I want to find out exactly what sort of man Dr Tindall really was.'

'In a word, how would you describe him?'

'Mysterious.'

When she was offered a lift home, Ada Hobbes at first turned it down but Keedy had insisted. He knew that people who had witnessed horrific sights could not simply shrug off the memory. Though she seemed calm enough, the cleaner would be haunted by the event on the long walk

26

home. As she sat beside the driver, Ada realised that it was the first time she had been inside a car since her husband's funeral. An untimely death had once again earned her the bonus of a lift.

Keedy had warned her to say nothing to her friends and neighbours about her experience that morning. If she spoke freely about it, he said, she would make herself a target for press interrogation. Ada took his advice. When she arrived home in a car, she was bound to arouse curiosity. She therefore rehearsed the explanation she would give to everyone. Inside the vehicle, she felt safe and comfortable. When she was dropped outside her home, however, she felt her legs give way slightly.

Reality had caught up with her.

Keedy worked his way along one side of the avenue, knocking on each door in turn and explaining why he had done so. Ordinarily, a couple of detective constables would be doing the repetitive chore, but manpower was limited at Scotland Yard. Keedy was not dismayed. He felt that he could do the job quickly yet thoroughly. When he reached the house on a corner, he used the knocker firmly. Moments later the front door opened and an elderly, white-haired woman gave him a hostile glare.

'We don't buy anything at the door,' she said.

'I'm not selling anything, I promise you.'

'Then why are you bothering us?'

'I'm Detective Sergeant Keedy of the Metropolitan Police,' he said. 'There's been a serious incident in a house further up the avenue and we're anxious to see if anyone can help us.'

'Which house was it?'

'Number twenty-three.'

'That's Dr Tindall's house,' she said in alarm.

'Do you know the gentleman?'

'We know of him. He works at the Military Hospital. My husband and I look up to him.'

'Well,' sighed Keedy, 'I'm afraid you won't be able to do that again.'

'Why not?' Seeing the look in his eye, she gasped. 'Has something happened to him?'

'His body was taken away almost an hour ago.'

'Do you mean that he …?'

'Yes, I do. You'll now understand why I'm keen to find out if anyone heard anything unusual in the middle of the night.'

'Dr Tindall?' she said. 'I can't believe it.'

'Did you hear my question?'

'Yes, I did, young man, but I'm not the person to answer it. I sleep like a log, but my husband doesn't. You need to speak to him.' She raised her voice. 'Ronald!' she yelled. 'Come here at once, Ronald! It's the police.' She whispered to Keedy. 'You'll have to speak up. He's deaf in one ear.'

Deafness was clearly the least of his afflictions. When he finally appeared, the old man was shuffling along with his spine so bent that his head was almost level with his stomach. One blue-veined hand was holding a walking stick. His other arm was in a sling. He peered up at the visitor through watery eyes.

'Who are you?' he asked.

'I'll explain later,' said his wife. 'Tell him what you told me.'

'I told you lots of things, Mary.'

'Tell him what you heard last night.'

'I hear all sorts of things,' he said to Keedy. 'I have strange noises in my ears. There is nothing they can do. I have to live with them.'

'But you heard a particular noise, Ronald,' prompted his wife. 'You went to the bathroom and heard it very clearly.'

'Oh, yes, I remember it now.'

'What exactly did you hear, sir?' asked Keedy, leaning closer to him. 'You were in the bathroom, you say. Which side of the house is that?'

'It's around the corner,' replied the woman.

'And what was this sound your husband heard?'

'It was a loud, nasty, rasping sound.'

'Yes,' said the man, taking up the story. 'I'm not completely deaf. I heard it clearly. I mean, they should not have been out there at that time of night. It was against the law. They had no respect for other people.'

'Who didn't?' said Keedy.

'The two of them.'

'What my husband heard,' explained the woman, 'was the noise of two motorbikes. I do not think Ronald imagined it. When he opened the bathroom window, the sound was just beneath him. Then it suddenly stopped. If he says there were two motorbikes just around the corner, then there were.'

Keedy smiled. He had learnt something useful at last.

CHAPTER FOUR

The Edmonton Military Hospital had begun life as an infirmary for the adjacent workhouse. An iron fence stood between them. The outbreak of war in 1914 had brought huge numbers of casualties in its wake. Edmonton was one of many districts in London that soon acquired a military hospital into which an endless stream of wounded soldiers were taken. Built in Silver Street, it comprised a cluster of sizeable buildings supplemented by a series of large huts, hastily constructed in the grounds to house additional patients. When he was driven through the entrance, Marmion noticed the two red crosses painted on the gates.

The police car pulled up outside the main building and the inspector got out.

He turned to see an ambulance coming in through the gates. It was moving slowly, as if the driver was anxious not to shake up the wounded soldiers he was carrying. Marmion wondered from which battleground they had come. He felt a pang as he thought about the time when his son had been ferried back from France to a military hospital. He hurried into the building and was soon being conducted into the office occupied by the person in charge of the hospital.

Major Howard Palmer-Loach was a square-jawed, straight-backed man of medium height with a neat moustache decorating an impassive face. When Marmion introduced himself, the major shook his hand and motioned him to a chair.

'This is terrible news,' he said. 'Dr Tindall was a brilliant man. More to the point, he was indefatigable and worked more hours than anybody else on my staff. As a result of his death, we've had to cancel a number of crucial operations.'

'I'm sorry to hear that.'

'He's irreplaceable. There'll be a lot of tears when the word spreads.'

'What sort of man was he?' asked Marmion.

'The best kind for an emergency – committed and eager. When the war first broke out, he spent six months working in a field hospital in France, getting to grips with the scale of the horrors of war. I was lucky enough to get him shortly after we converted this place into a military hospital.'

'How many patients do you have here?'

'Our total bed complement is one thousand. Soldiers are sent here in pieces. We try to put them together again. Many manage to survive but we have our losses as well. It is not only physical wounds that need treatment, of course. Our patients usually come with mental scars.'

Marmion said nothing but an image of Paul had popped into his mind again.

'On the telephone,' recalled the major, 'you talked of an unexplained death.'

'Dr Tindall was murdered.'

The major gulped. 'How?'

'Unnecessary violence was used.'

Choosing his words with care, Marmion told him what they had found and how the safe had been emptied. He was careful not to release too much information. Palmer-Loach shook his head in disbelief.

'Why pick on George Tindall, of all people?'

'I intend to find out.'

'It makes no sense. He didn't have an enemy in the world.'

'That's what we've been told.'

'Can I help in any way?'

'Yes,' said Marmion. 'I'd be grateful if you could tell me more about him and what sort of work he did here at the hospital. The more information we have, the more able will we be to understand him. We know that he was still grieving over the loss of his wife, and it appears that he had almost no social life. Is that true?'

'I'm afraid so, Inspector. It was strange, really. He was a handsome, intelligent man with great gifts. Most of the nurses here adored him yet he hardly noticed them. As for what he did here,' said the major, rising to his feet, 'I suggest that you come and see for yourself. Dr Tindall was the heart and soul of this place.'

The prospect of going to the West End next day had lifted Iris Goodliffe's spirits. She could not stop thinking about it. Even when a ragged old man made a filthy gesture at her before scuttling away with a cackle of delight, she was neither upset nor annoyed. Iris walked on happily with her friend at her side.

'The rain has stopped,' said Alice.

'I didn't notice.'

'You didn't notice when you stepped in that puddle either.'

'Who cares about that?' said Iris with a giggle. 'I was too busy thinking about the dress I'm going to buy tomorrow. What colour should it be?'

'What colour would you like?'

'My mother always said that I looked best in blue but I'm not sure. Besides, I'm wearing navy blue all day long. I want a change.'

'Then I'd suggest a shade of green.'

'Really? That's a bit … daring for me.'

'Why?' asked Alice. 'You could carry it off easily. Green is a colour that would cheer you up whenever you looked at yourself in the mirror.'

'What about red?'

'That might be going too far.'

'I'll try on every colour of the rainbow,' said Iris with another giggle, 'then choose the one I fancy.'

'Yes, that's the right attitude.'

'What about you, Alice?'

'Oh, I'll be looking for a new dress as well.'

'You could get away with any colour.'

'Joe doesn't think so. He hates it if I wear anything with beige in it.'

'Why?'

'He says that it makes me look like my mother.'

'What a cheek!'

'Joe claims that it's the kind of colour you wear to hide behind.'

'That shows how much he knows about dresses,' said Iris.

'I told him that the best colour is the one we feel most comfortable in. We dress for ourselves – not for someone else's benefit.'

'What did he say to that?'

It was Alice's turn to giggle. 'I'm not telling.'

'What will you be looking for tomorrow?'

'I simply want something to catch my eye.'

'Will it be a dress for a particular occasion?'

'Not really,' said Alice, shaking her head.

'Then we're going to the West End for different reasons.'

'Are we?'

'Yes, I'm on the lookout for something special,' confided Iris, 'because it will be for a special occasion.'

'And what occasion will that be?'

Iris clicked her tongue. 'As if you need to ask me, Alice Marmion. It's for your wedding to Joe Keedy.' There was an awkward pause. 'I am invited, aren't I?'

Having recorded the old man's testimony in his notebook, Keedy soon found people who could corroborate the evidence. Once he turned the corner into the next road, he spoke to other witnesses roused from their sleep by the sound of two motorbikes. None could give him an exact time, but the general feeling was that it was somewhere between midnight and three o'clock in the morning. That was good enough for Keedy. It fitted in with the timescale given by the pathologist.

Marmion had been right, he accepted. There were two people involved. They had driven at low speed as far as the corner of the road, switched off their engines and parked their motorbikes. The pair had then turned into the avenue and walked along until they reached Tindall's house. Keedy had no idea how they had got into it, but he believed he knew why the killers had not driven up to the victim's doorstep. The sound of two noisy engines might have awakened the neighbours and even Tindall himself. Once they had done what they had planned to do, he decided, the couple had walked back to the place where they had left their motorbikes and roared away at full speed.

There were lots of questions still to be answered but Keedy nevertheless allowed himself to feel optimistic. He felt that he had picked up a trail.

As he led the way out of his office, Major Palmer-Loach turned to his companion.

'Have you ever been to a military hospital before, Inspector?' he asked.

'As a matter of fact,' replied Marmion, 'I've been inside two. The first was Royal Victoria in Netley, when we went to visit my son.'

'Where was the other?'

'Endell Street.'

The major's face darkened. 'The Suffragettes' Hospital,' he said with a note of disapproval. 'I don't think I could put my trust in a place run entirely by women.'

'Its doctors have a good reputation and I've never been anywhere that was so spotless. What I liked was the way they'd introduced a lot of colour to brighten the hospital up.'

'I don't question their medical expertise,' said the other. 'It's their political opinions that I can't stomach.'

'If a female doctor has the skill to save my life, I wouldn't care two hoots about any political opinions she held. You should have this conversation with my daughter,' added Marmion, smiling. 'Alice would enjoy locking horns with you.'

'Does she work at Endell Street?'

'No, she's in the Women's Police Force. But she has a friend who works as a doctor there and who took us both around the hospital. I was impressed.'

'I hope that you're equally impressed with what you see here.'

The major took him down a main corridor, acknowledging staff and patients alike with a curt nod. Marmion was struck by how many people were about. Legless soldiers were propelling themselves in wheelchairs and those with one leg used crutches to manoeuvre themselves along. A blind man was being led by a nurse as he took his first tentative steps. Some of the soldiers wore pyjamas and dressing gowns but a few were in saxe blue suits made of a lightweight flannel material. Marmion noticed their bright red ties.

'We try to get them outside whenever we can,' explained Palmer-Loach, 'but this weather is far too cold. Many of those who are convalescing will soon move on and make way for a new batch. They keep coming and coming.'

'They must be so relieved to be on British soil again.'

'Most of them are, Inspector, but there are some who wish they'd died in action. A Blighty Wound is not always a form of escape. When you are paralysed from the waist down and blind into the bargain, your future is going to be bleak. We have had more than one patient begging to be put out of his misery. It was another important aspect of Dr Tindall's work here.'

'What was?'

'He knew how to talk to men who felt they had nothing to live for,' said the major. 'It was extraordinary. He somehow gave them hope. It took time in some cases, but he usually succeeded in the end.'

They paused outside a ward and Marmion was able to glance inside. Rows of beds ran down both sides of the ward and all were occupied by patients with what appeared to be serious injuries. Some were almost invisible beneath heavy bandaging. A doctor was making his rounds with a nurse at his elbow. There was a sense of order about the scene. A faint smell of disinfectant lingered.

'Dr Tindall operated on some of these men,' explained the major. 'They're going to be horrified when they discover they'll never see him again.'

'He was obviously popular here.'

'That's an understatement, Inspector. He was revered.'

'We need to get in touch with his next of kin,' said Marmion. 'His neighbours told us that he had no children. What about his parents? Are they still alive?'

'Yes, they live in the north of Scotland somewhere.'

'Do you have an address for them?'

The major nodded. 'It's in my office.'

'Did he ever speak of relatives – brothers, sisters, cousins?'

'No, he didn't. If they exist, he saw them as irrelevant. As soon as he came into the hospital, he only talked about one thing and that was the care of his patients.'

'You make him sound as if he was a paragon.'

'In some ways, I suppose that that's exactly what George Tindall was.'

Marmion looked him in the eye. 'Then why did someone want to kill him?'

If Ellen Marmion wished to hear the latest news, she did not need to buy a newspaper. All she had to do was to visit the grocer's shop. Geoffrey Biddle, the grocer, kept abreast of current affairs. He seemed to pick up information that nobody else had access to and enjoyed passing it on to his customers. Biddle was a tall, skinny, red-faced man in his fifties with a bald head that looked as if it had just been polished. He had a quiet, confiding manner and a habit of tapping the side of his nose.

'Is there anything else you need, Mrs Marmion?' he asked.

'I don't think so.'

'How about sugar?'

'We've got enough to last until next week.'

'It might be safer to get more while you can,' he warned. 'German submarines are causing havoc with our food imports. They seem to be sinking our ships at will. Everything is going to be rationed soon. Sugar will be on the list.'

'But we can't do without it, Mr Biddle.'

'Coal has already been rationed. Sugar may be next, then meat, then butter, then something else we need. The Germans are trying to starve us to death, Mrs Marmion.'

'I thought our convoys were getting through.'

'Then where are our food supplies? Whenever I try to restock my shelves, I buy smaller amounts than usual. Lots of items are just not available. If things don't improve, everything will be rationed. We will have long queues of people getting more and more impatient. I dread it.'

'Perhaps I'd better have some more sugar, then,' she decided.

'Good thinking.' He took a packet from the shelf and put it on the counter. 'Is that the lot, then?'

'I think so. How much do I owe you?'

'Let me see.' He added up the figures and showed her the bill. 'Check it, if you like.'

She smiled. 'I know you well enough to trust you, Mr Biddle.'

After putting the bag of sugar into her basket, she paid the grocer and left the shop. Ellen did not get far before she recognised someone coming towards her. It was Patricia Redwood, a fleshy, middle-aged woman who belonged to the same sewing circle as Ellen. The two women had been friends until Paul Marmion had insulted Patricia's daughter, Sally, then gone on to pester her. It had destroyed the friendship between the two older women.

'Good morning,' said Ellen, politely. 'How are you?'

'I'm fine, thank you, and I've got some good news to pass on.'

'Oh?'

'Sally has met a young man,' said Patricia, proudly. 'That's an achievement when so many lads have gone off to war. Norman would have done the same, of course, only he damaged a hand in an accident. He's just what Sally needs. Norman works for that printer in the high street.'

'I know the one.'

'Then you'll know that it's almost opposite the jewellery shop where Sally works. He waved to her through the window one day. She was too shy to wave back at first. Sally's always been a bit of a shrinking violet,' she went on, releasing a sudden laugh. 'She takes after me in that respect.'

Ellen had to repress a laugh of her own. Nobody was less like a shrinking violet than Patricia Redwood. Whenever she came to the sewing circle, she dominated the conversation in a braying voice.

'I'm so pleased for Sally,' said Ellen.

'She and Norman make a lovely couple.'

'That's good to hear.'

'Meeting him has helped her to get over … well, you know what.'

Ellen winced at the mention of her son's involvement with the girl. Paul had treated her very badly and refused to apologise. His mother had suffered a fierce confrontation with the woman she was now facing.

'Is there any word of Paul?' asked Patricia.

'I'm afraid not.'

'Can he still be alive after all this time?'

'We don't know.'

'Most sons would at least let his mother know where he was,' said the other, pointedly. 'It's cruel to keep you in the dark – but then, he always did have a cruel streak, didn't he?'

'That's not true at all.'

'Look at the way he treated Sally.'

'I've apologised for that.'

'The memory of it still upsets my daughter. In fact—'

'You'll have to excuse me,' said Ellen, interrupting. 'I have more important things to do than stand gossiping here with you.'

Turning on her heel, she walked quickly away.

When he got back to the house, Keedy saw that Constable Fanning was on duty alone outside the front door.

'Is Rivers still in with the neighbours?' he asked.

'No, sir,' said Fanning. 'He's gone back to the station. It doesn't need two of us to keep people at bay. Inspector Marmion said it would be all right.'

'Then I've no complaint. How have you got on while I was away?'

'I've been busy. I don't know what you told people when you knocked on their doors, but it flushed them out good and proper. Dozens of them came to gawp at the house. One man dared to ask if he could peep inside so I gave him a flea in his ear. Then a woman strolled past, pretending not to look in this direction but she was just as nosey as the others.'

'That's the effect a murder has on a community,' said Keedy.

'I know, Sergeant. It becomes a sideshow.'

'I'm going back inside to conduct a more thorough search. When the inspector comes back, tell him where I am.'

'I suppose there's no chance of a cup of tea, is there?'

Keedy chuckled. 'You'll have to wait until I get thirsty.'

He let himself into the house and began a systematic search, going from room to room and opening every drawer and cupboard as he did so. What was clearly lacking was a woman's touch. Keedy imagined what Alice would say if she saw the curtains in the lounge. Dark green in colour, they clashed with the furniture and with the carpet. There was also a glaring absence of ornaments. Had she lived there, Tindall's late wife would surely have wanted some on the mantelpiece and the window sill. They would have been of personal significance to the couple. Looking around, Keedy concluded that Dr Tindall was determined to live in a bachelor domain. He might have kept photographs of his wife everywhere but there was nothing else to remind him of what he claimed had been a happy marriage. It was almost as if he had deliberately suppressed memories of her.

Keedy was upstairs when he heard a car pulling up outside. He assumed that it would be Marmion, returning from the hospital, but, when he glanced through the window, he saw two men climbing out of the vehicle. One was carrying a camera to take photographs of the crime scene and the other had a small case. His task, Keedy knew, was to collect fingerprints. It had been Sir Edward Henry, the Metropolitan Police Commissioner, who had founded the Fingerprint Bureau. During his time as Inspector General of the Bengal Police, he had seen the value of fingerprinting. It was now an important tool for Scotland Yard and Keedy had seen how effective it could be. He knew that there would certainly be fingerprints on the safe in the main bedroom and in the storeroom where the murder had occurred. If the intruders had a police record, their fingerprints would be on file.

He went quickly downstairs to welcome his colleagues and give them their instructions. When he opened the front door, he saw Fanning's face light up.

'Are you feeling thirsty yet, sir?' asked the constable.

Claude Chatfield was seated behind his desk when there was a tap on the door and the tall, elegant figure of Sir Edward Henry came in. The superintendent rose to his feet out of deference and the two men exchanged greetings. Ordinarily, the commissioner did not take a specific interest in most of the crimes with which Scotland Yard dealt. The latest case was an exception to the rule.

'I've just had a call from the War Office,' said Sir Edward. 'I gather that a surgeon at one of the military hospitals has been murdered.'

'That's true,' Chatfield told him. 'The hospital is in Edmonton.'

'The victim, apparently, was a man with rare skills.'

'So I was given to understand, Sir Edward.'

'I hope that you've assigned the best detectives to the investigation.'

'Inspector Marmion and Sergeant Keedy were despatched as soon as they arrived here. I've already had a telephone call from the inspector, giving me a statement to release to the press.'

'That's typical of him. Marmion always thinks ahead.'

Chatfield winced. He hated to hear praise of the inspector, especially when it came from the commissioner. While he recognised Marmion's efficiency, he always found ways to criticise him. The enmity between the two men went back years. Chatfield never let Marmion forget that he had been promoted to a higher rank in preference to his rival.

'I'd like to see the press statement, if I may,' said Sir Edward.

'Yes, of course,' replied Chatfield.

He picked up a sheet of paper from his desk and held it out to his visitor. The commissioner took it from him and read it carefully.

'Excellent!' he cried.

Clenching his teeth, Chatfield glowered.

'I'm glad that you picked the right man for the task, Superintendent. I'll ring the War Office and read this statement out to them. It may calm their jitters a little. They monitor activities at their military hospitals,' he went on, 'and quite rightly. If we ask young men to face appalling conditions in the trenches, we owe them the best medical treatment when they get wounded. Dr Tindall, I gather, was a leader in his field.'

'That's what I've been led to believe, Sir Edward.'

'When will you get a fuller report?'

'I'll have to wait until Marmion and Keedy return here.'

'Let me know what they've discovered.'

'I will.'

'A case like this will feature in all the newspapers,' said the commissioner. 'We must be careful to control the amount of information we give. Reporters always have voracious appetites. Feed them carefully. In fact,' said the commissioner as an idea came into his mind, 'it might be better if Inspector Marmion was responsible for the press conferences.'

'I disagree, Sir Edward,' said Chatfield, insulted at the suggestion.

'But he knows the situation in detail.'

'When it comes to detail, I have a gift for selecting how much to reveal. Besides, we both know that Marmion is at his best when he's out there in pursuit of the person or persons who committed a foul murder.' He thrust out his chin. 'That's where I intend to keep him.'

When they started out on the return journey, Keedy reflected that some of the most important conversations he had ever had with Harvey Marmion had been in the rear of a police car. They had always been close, but their friendship had been put under severe pressure when Marmion realised that his daughter was the latest in a long list of young women in whom Keedy had taken an interest. He did not wish Alice to be courted then discarded like her predecessors. It was a time when there were a lot of strained silences during lifts together in the car. When he saw that Keedy's commitment was sincere, however, Marmion eventually warmed to the idea of becoming his father-in-law. The ritual jibes that the sergeant received from the other detectives gradually died away. Joe Keedy had reformed.

He listened patiently to Marmion's account of his visit to the hospital.

'It was both depressing and inspiring, Joe,' said the inspector. 'My heart sank when I saw the state of some of those men. They were clinging on to life by their fingertips but what future could they have when they'd be severely disabled? Then I saw the way that the doctors and nurses were giving them hope and helping them to adapt. They treated every individual as a war hero and that raised morale. It really lifted my spirits.'

'Who was in charge?'

'Major Palmer-Loach.'

'I hate people with double-barrelled names.'

'He's doing a good job. The place is run with military precision. Thanks to the major, the hospital now has an X-ray department, and it also has a sausage-machine that can turn out the best part of a thousand bangers a day.'

Keedy laughed. 'We could do with one of those at Scotland Yard.'

'There's even a potato-peeling machine there.'

'What did this Major Thingumajig say about Dr Tindall?'

'He had nothing but praise for him, Joe,' said Marmion. 'As a surgeon, he was outstanding. Every doctor I spoke to told me the same. I was shown the operating theatre where Tindall should have been this morning. You should see the equipment there, streets ahead of anything you'd find in a field hospital in France or Belgium.'

'What about Tindall's family?'

'It seems to have been rather small. His parents were the only ones for whom they had an address. Mr and Mrs Tindall live in Scotland, apparently. They have no other children. I will have to ask Chat to ring the nearest police station so that someone can break the news to them. It's going to shake them to their roots,' said Marmion. 'They must idolise him.'

'Doctors are like policemen. They run in families. Maybe the father is also a doctor.'

'Judging by the address,' said Marmion, 'he's more likely to be a farmer or a fisherman. They live somewhere near Aberdeen. It seems as if Tindall preferred a career this side of the border.' He looked at Keedy. 'Anyway, tell me what you've been up to while I was away.'

'I was following your orders.'

Keedy described what he had learnt by knocking on doors, then talked about his search of the house. His impression was that the dining room and two of the bedrooms were never used.

'I think he spent most of his time in his study,' he decided. 'The shelves were stacked with medical books of one sort or another. There was nothing there you could read for pleasure. No wonder Mrs Hobbes enjoyed working at the house. She hardly needed to touch some of the rooms. They were always clean and tidy.'

'How strange!'

'Why did the doctor live like a hermit?'

'The Scots are a funny people, Joe.'

'I disagree. The ones I know love company, especially if there's plenty of booze at hand. They know how to enjoy themselves to the full. I reckon that Tindall was the odd man out.'

45

'The wonder is that he married.'

'Yes, it is.'

'My guess is that his wife might have been a nurse. They look so fetching in those starched uniforms.'

'Now, now,' warned Keedy. 'Calm down or I'll tell Ellen what you said.'

'Funnily enough, she thought about becoming a nurse once.'

'What stopped her?'

'We had children,' said Marmion. 'Right, let's put our thinking caps on and work out what we can tell Chat.'

'We believe the doctor was killed by two men who drove motorbikes.'

'What else?'

'Tindall spoke fondly about his late wife.'

'Most widowers do that, Joe. It's not a reason to murder him.'

'Well, those men obviously had a strong motive,' said Keedy, thinking it through. 'If he'd confronted them, they could have killed him with one thrust of a knife. Instead of that, they carved him up like a Christmas turkey then stole the most precious things he had – photographs of his wife.'

'That's where we start,' declared Marmion. 'We must find out who the woman was and how she died. Hopefully, his parents may be able to give us that information and there must be other members of the family we can track down.'

'If anyone has to go up to Scotland, I'll volunteer.'

'I need you here – and so does my daughter, for that matter.'

'I'd arranged to see Alice tomorrow evening.'

'Well, you'll have to cancel that,' said Marmion. 'We're going to be under great pressure from now on. Until we find the killers, your social life does not exist.'

Keedy's face fell.

CHAPTER FIVE

Ada Hobbes was in a quandary. She had been warned to speak to nobody about the way that she had stumbled upon a murder victim. At the time, she had agreed willingly, glad to block the experience out of her mind instead of having to relive it in front of a group of reporters. But it was not as easy to forget it as she had hoped. No matter what she did to distract herself, the image kept flashing before her eyes. She was terrified of going to bed in case the mutilated body of Dr Tindall reappeared in a nightmare. Ada wished that she had never worked for the man.

As she sat beside the kitchen table, the cup of tea she had made earlier stood untouched beside her. She had neither the urge nor the appetite to reach for it. Since she had come home, Ada had made no effort to take off her fur coat, hat, scarf and gloves. She just sat there, wishing that her husband was still alive to help, advise and simply hug her. Bert Hobbes, a sweep by trade, had been a chirpy, kind, hard-working man until his lungs became so silted by soot and cigarettes that he had coughed his way to an early grave. She had never felt his absence quite so keenly. Tears welled up in her eyes.

His death was not the only loss she had had to bear. Ada had somehow coped with recurring tragedies, adapting to a life on her own and learning to be proud of her independence. She could draw no strength from it now. Depressed, anxious and aching with fatigue, she felt utterly lost. At a time when she most needed the person who could offer love and support, she had been warned by the police to keep away from her. They had promised that Kathy Paget, her sister, would be informed of what they had described as an unforeseen development at Dr Tindall's house.

All that Ada could do was to stay alone at home and suffer.

They were in the superintendent's office. After reading the report that Marmion had typed out laboriously with his index fingers, Claude Chatfield looked up at the inspector and sniffed.

'I was hoping for more detail,' he complained.

'You know everything that we found out, sir,' said Marmion.

'There are too many gaps.'

'We'll do our best to fill them in.'

'You seem to have discovered so little about the victim himself.'

'Dr Tindall is to blame for that. He kept himself to himself. Even his closest colleagues said that they never really knew him. They described him as driven.'

'Yes,' said Chatfield, 'I know the feeling. I am driven as well. I am driven by the desire to solve this murder as swiftly as possible. The commissioner has taken a personal interest in this case. It seems that the

War Office have been on to him.' He glanced at the report. 'He'll have hoped for more information than this.'

Chatfield was a tall, thin, pallid man with a meticulous centre parting in his hair. Beside the chunky figure of Marmion, he looked undernourished. They had never liked each other but had somehow managed to work well together. Chatfield put the report aside.

'What is your next move, Inspector?' he asked.

'You have his parents' address. They need to be contacted immediately and informed that their son is dead. We are certain that the victim is Dr Tindall but identification by a family member is always important.'

'I agree.'

'All I can tell you is that Dyce is north of Aberdeen.'

'Then let us see if we can find its exact location.' He reached for a map book on the shelf beside his desk and leafed through the pages until he came to the index. When he found what he wanted, he turned to the appropriate page. Marmion stood behind him so that he could see the map of north-east Scotland as well.

'There it is, sir,' he said, jabbing a finger.

'All right, all right,' said Chatfield, testily, 'I can see it.'

'Dyce is close to Aberdeen. It might even be a suburb.'

'I'll find the number of the Aberdeen City Police and give them a ring.'

'Advise them to pass on the news gently,' suggested Marmion. 'They may be quite elderly and—'

'Don't tell me how to do my job. I know exactly what to tell them.'

'Yes, of course, sir.'

'What are you going to do?'

'Firstly, we're off to Edmonton again to speak to a woman named Mrs Paget. She was the cleaner at the house for years and knew Dr

Tindall far better than Mrs Hobbes. The two women are sisters, by the way,' explained Marmion. 'I was anxious that we told Mrs Paget what had happened instead of letting her sister do so. Given the circumstances, Mrs Hobbes has been remarkably composed, but she is bound to feel the full impact of the tragedy when she's alone. I didn't want her rushing around to her sister's house.'

Chatfield frowned. 'I'm not entirely happy about this, you know.'

'About what, sir?'

'Relying on the word of two cleaners. I mean, neither of them is going to tell you anything of real import. They just came to do a menial task and went on their way. From what you have told me, they hardly ever saw Dr Tindall.' He curled a lip. 'Their evidence will be of little use. We need hard facts and I expected you to get far more of them at the hospital.'

'So did I, sir, but it was not to be. As for the cleaners,' said Marmion, 'it's unfair to sneer at them. They have both seen inside that house, which is far more than any of the neighbours have done. When he was not on duty, Dr Tindall appears to have been something of a recluse.'

'With luck, his parents will be more sociable.'

'I'll leave you to get in touch with the police in Aberdeen, sir.'

'Remember what I said,' warned Chatfield. 'The commissioner will be watching this investigation closely. If you fail to make visible progress, you'll have Sir Edward barking at your heels.'

'That makes two of you,' said Marmion. 'You'll be able to bark in unison.'

Pounding the streets had become much easier for them with no rain beating down. Alice Marmion and Iris Goodliffe kept their eyes peeled for incidents that might require some intervention on their part. Iris kept pressing for details of her friend's wedding plans but Alice tried to steer the conversation in another direction. She and Keedy had not finalised the list of those who would attend their wedding. Eager to keep the numbers down, they had yet to include Iris's name on the list.

They were coming around a corner when they saw a woman approaching them. The newcomer stared at Alice before letting out a cry of pleasure.

'Alice!' she exclaimed. 'It is you, isn't it?'

'Yes, Gwenda, it is,' said the other, recognising her.

'I'd heard that you were a policewoman.'

'Somebody has to be,' said Alice.

She introduced Iris to Gwenda Powell and explained that they had worked together as teachers. Her friend was a stout, middle-aged woman with a warm smile and a pleasant manner.

'Why aren't you at school this afternoon?' asked Alice.

'We have a half-day off,' explained the other.

'We have a whole day off tomorrow,' Iris told her, 'and we're going shopping in the West End.'

'I wish that I could have done that, Iris, but I had to visit my parents instead. They're in their seventies now and both are in poor health. They keep wondering if this war will ever be over.'

'We all ask that question,' sighed Alice. 'But how are things at school?'

'There have been some changes since you left. The big one, I suppose, is that Mrs Latimer has finally retired.'

'Ah, so you've got a new headmistress.'

'Actually,' said the other, 'I've replaced her.'

'Congratulations, Gwenda!' said Alice, embracing her. 'You should have been promoted years ago.'

51

'Thank you. I got there in the end. How are you enjoying your new life?'

'I love it – don't I, Iris?'

'We both enjoy it,' agreed Iris, 'most of the time, anyway.'

'That's a pity,' said Gwenda. 'It means that I can't lure Alice back to teaching. We could really do with you. The children are a handful at times, and you always had the knack of controlling them.'

'I'll stay where I am,' said Alice.

'You obviously enjoy your new job but it's only voluntary. If you policed children instead, you'd get paid as well.'

'We can't spare her,' said Iris, laughing as she put a possessive arm around Alice. 'She belongs to us now.'

'But she always loved teaching,' said Gwenda, 'and the children loved her. They still ask after Miss Marmion.'

'I'm sure they do. It's nice to be wanted like that, Alice.'

'Yes, it is,' agreed her colleague.

'Think about it,' urged Gwenda. 'We'd love to have Miss Marmion back.'

'That will soon be impossible,' said Iris with a grin. 'Miss Marmion is going to become Mrs Keedy in the new year. Alice is marrying a detective sergeant, so she'll be handcuffed to the police for life.'

When they reached the house, they saw that it was a small, neglected, end-of-terrace dwelling with faded paintwork and missing slates. The detectives knocked on the door and waited. They could hear a distant door opening and the sound of a walking stick tapping on the tiled passageway. The front door finally opened to reveal Kathleen Paget, a heavy woman in her late fifties with thick lenses in her spectacles that enlarged her eyes dramatically. She regarded the visitors with suspicion.

'Mrs Paget?' asked Marmion.

'Yes,' she replied. 'That's me.'

'I'm Detective Inspector Marmion from the Metropolitan Police Force and this is Detective Sergeant Keedy.'

'We've done nothing wrong, have we?' she asked, fearfully.

'No, Mrs Paget. We've come to talk to you about a gentleman whose house you used to clean.'

'Which one? There were lots over the years.'

'Dr Tindall.'

'Why? Has something happened?'

'Perhaps we'd better come in,' suggested Marmion.

'Well, yes, if you must, but you'll have to excuse the mess. I can't look after the place the way I used to, and Alf is in no position to help. He's my husband.'

She stood back so that they could step inside, then she closed the door behind them. Moving with difficulty, she led them down the passageway and into the living room. It was cold, gloomy and noisome, smelling of a compound of stale food, pipe tobacco and the dog sprawled on the mat in front of the tiny fire. After giving them a welcoming yap, the animal went back to sleep.

'It's all right,' said Kathleen. 'He doesn't bite.'

'That's good to hear,' said Keedy.

'Sit down.'

She moved her knitting off a mottled sofa and they lowered themselves onto it. As they glanced around, they noticed for the first time that there was someone else there. Alfred Paget was sunk deep in an armchair in the corner, sucking a pipe that no longer housed any tobacco. He gazed at them with a mixture of resentment and apprehension.

'These gentlemen are from the police,' said his wife, raising her voice

53

and talking very slowly. 'You just sit there and be quiet, Alf. I can handle them.' She looked at the visitors. 'My husband doesn't remember things any more. And he has other problems. Take no notice of him.'

Marmion and Keedy found themselves unable to obey her. Looking at Paget, they saw that he was a skeletal man in a collarless grey shirt, baggy trousers and gravy-stained waistcoat. His head kept nodding and his body made involuntary lurches from side to side.

'Now, then,' she continued, 'what's this all about?'

'We have sad news, Mrs Paget,' said Marmion, quietly.

'Oh?'

'I'm afraid that Dr Tindall ... died earlier today.'

'Are you sure?' she asked, eyes widening in alarm. 'This can't be true. I mean Dr Tindall was in good health. People like him don't die.'

'Someone killed him.'

'Never!' she exclaimed, hand to her heart. 'Not our dear Dr Tindall, surely.'

'Some time in the night, intruders got in.'

'Your sister, Mrs Hobbes, discovered him,' said Keedy. 'There was a telephone in the house, so she called the police.'

'Yes, I know there's a telephone. In fact, I showed Ada how it worked before she took over the cleaning. She'd never held one before, you see.' She suddenly buried her face in her hands for a couple of minutes before making a partial recovery and staring at them through misted spectacles. 'I'm so sorry but ... it was a pleasure to work for Dr Tindall. He was kind to me, and Ada told me he treated her just the same.' She removed the spectacles to dab at her eyes with a handkerchief. 'I kept that house gleaming,' she said, proudly, 'and I kept my own home the same until my arthritis got the better of me. It turns my hands into claws some days.'

'We're sorry to hear that,' said Marmion, 'and we're sorry about your husband's problems.' He cleared his throat. 'Before we discuss what happened last night, we must warn you not to talk to any reporters about the murder. We want to protect you from them.'

'I won't tell them a thing, Inspector.'

'With luck, they may not even find you.'

'What about Ada?'

'We've given her the same advice.'

'How is she?'

'Mrs Hobbes is bearing up,' said Keedy. 'I had her taken home in a car. She's had a very nasty experience, as you can imagine.'

'I must go to her. She needs me.'

'Before you do that, there are some questions we'd like to ask.'

'Yes,' said Marmion, taking over. 'Without realising it, you may have information that could be helpful to us.'

'I'll tell you whatever you want,' she said, handkerchief still at the ready.

Marmion nodded to Keedy who took out his notebook and pencil.

'How long did you work for Dr Tindall?' asked the inspector.

'It must be ... oh, almost two years,' she replied. 'With Alf being like he is, I was ready to take on all the work I could get. Well, we had to survive somehow. I don't often have any luck, but I got it that time. I couldn't have found a better person to work for. Dr Tindall was wonderful ...'

Patricia Redwood had left the sewing circle so Ellen felt able to go there that afternoon. She was still jangled by her earlier confrontation with the other woman but, the moment she stepped into the room, her discomfort vanished. She was among friends, dedicated women who got together on a regular basis to make gloves, socks, scarves and anything that soldiers might need at the front in the freezing days of December. Ellen loved to work with such a companionable group and enjoy a gossip while she did so. Since they all knew about the disappearance of her son, none of the others ever mentioned Paul. In any case, many of them had their own sorrows to bear. Some had lost sons in the mud of France and Belgium. Others had seen them invalided out of the army and trying to adjust to a new life after their ordeal. Their individual tragedies had helped the women to bond.

Fear of rationing was the main topic of conversation. Ellen was able to pass on what Geoffrey Biddle had told her. They envied her for being able to buy extra sugar.

'I couldn't do that,' admitted one of them. 'My husband wouldn't let me. He checks the order before I leave the house. Money is scarce and every penny counts. That's what he keeps saying. If I'd bought anything extra like Ellen did, he'd make me pay for it myself.'

'Them German submarines are going to win this war,' said another, gloomily. 'Most of the food from abroad is at the bottom of the sea.'

'We'll manage somehow,' said Ellen.

'How do you do it?' asked the woman.

'Do what?'

'Well, you always keep your spirits up somehow. Even when things go wrong, you never complain whereas the rest of us would be screaming our heads off. What's your secret?'

Ellen shrugged. 'I don't know that I have one, Marge.'

'Something keeps you afloat.'

'Yes, it's a cup of tea whenever I want and a good old gossip with friends.'

'There's more to it than that, Ellen.'

'I suppose there is,' said the other, thoughtfully. 'Whenever I have bad things in my life, I try to think of the good things as well. They take my attention off something nasty and give me a boost. Today, for example,' Ellen went on, 'I had a row with a woman who likes to bait me. I couldn't get away quick enough. It troubled me. Then I stepped in here and forgot all about her – because I was among friends. Something good drove out something bad.'

'I wish that worked for me,' said Margery.

'You should try it.'

'In my case, the bad always drives out the good.'

'Then try to fix your mind on something special,' advised Ellen. 'It's what I've been doing for days. My daughter is going to spend tonight at home for a change. Ever since Alice moved into that flat of hers, I've missed her dreadfully – but not tonight. We're going to spend the whole evening catching up on each other's news and just enjoying each other's company.' She beamed. 'Just thinking about that has put a smile on my face for days.'

Listening to Kathleen Paget had been a revelation. In the twenty minutes or so that they were there, the detectives learnt far more about George Tindall than they had from any other source. In view of her arthritis, it was amazing that she had kept cleaning the house until she did. Other women would have given up earlier, but she hated the idea of letting her employer down.

'Dr Tindall was special,' she said. 'That's why I struggled on until he was the only person I used to work for.'

'You speak of him as if he was a friend,' observed Marmion.

'That's exactly what he was, Inspector. He didn't look down his nose the way that most of the others did. He treated me with respect. When

I told him about Alf, he gave me some advice about how to make life a little easier for him. It's what the nurses do at the hospital, see. They think of special ways to help each of their patients. They really care. So do I.' She glanced across at her husband. 'Alf knows that. I'm nursing him. I'm doing what Dr Tindall suggested.'

'Why do you think he lived alone?'

'But he didn't, Inspector. He shared it with the ghost of his wife.'

'What was Mrs Tindall's first name?'

'Eleanor.'

'Was she from Scotland as well?'

'Oh, no, Inspector. She was from somewhere in Devon. He told me that he was born near Aberdeen, but the funny thing was that he didn't sound Scottish. He was … well, posh.'

'He probably had an expensive education,' said Keedy. 'If you go to the right school, they train you to speak with that toffee-nosed accent.'

'Did he ever have guests to stay at the house?' asked Marmion.

'None that I knew of,' she said. 'I'd have seen the signs. Mind you,' she added with a smile, 'I did fancy that he might have had a lady staying there one night. There was this smell of perfume in the bathroom. When I mentioned it to him, the doctor said that it was his wife's favourite. Every so often, he liked to sprinkle a little of it in memory of her.'

'That's an odd thing to do.'

She was philosophical. 'People remember loved ones in different ways. For the doctor, it was Mrs Tindall's perfume. When Alf goes,' she said, 'I'll always remember the smell of his pipe.'

'Why were some of the rooms never used?'

'I've no idea, Inspector.'

'What about his wife's clothes?' asked Keedy. 'We know she never lived there but we expected to find some of her things hanging in the wardrobe.'

'He got rid of them for some reason.'

'Do you have any idea what that reason might be?'

'No,' said Kathleen. 'I was there to clean, not to ask questions.' She gave a shudder. 'Oh, I do feel so sorry for Ada. She always has such bad luck. Finding him like that must have frightened her to death. Wish it had been me. I don't scare so easy.'

'What do you mean?' asked Marmion.

'It's the other job I had, see. We have a lot of old people around here. When one of them passes away, I'm often called in to lay them out proper. They need to be cleaned and made decent, like. I enjoyed the work. It never upset me.'

'You provided a valuable service,' said Keedy. 'I used to work for the family undertaking business and we sometimes found cadavers in a shocking condition. I wish that everyone had someone like you to call upon.'

'Let's go back to Mrs Hobbes,' said Marmion. 'You told us that she always had bad luck.'

'It was more like a curse, Inspector,' she explained. 'Her first baby was stillborn, then her second died of diphtheria before he reached his fourth birthday. They never had another child. Then Bert died when he was only thirty-nine. He was a sweep, you see, and he'd always had a weak chest. If my husband had gone at that age,' she admitted, 'I'd have been grieving for years. Do you know what Ada did?'

'Please tell us.'

'She took over his round. Yes,' she went on as they both looked surprised, 'she carried on where Bert left off and came home filthy at the end of the day. She's not the only woman who's become a sweep, you know. The work did get too much for her in the end, so she let someone pay her to take over her customers. After that, she went cleaning full time. Ada's a fighter,' she told them, 'but I don't think she'll have much fight left in her just now.'

Ada Hobbes had volunteered to clean the local church once a week. Although she had been there two days earlier, she went back and gave it a supplementary clean, working away with her usual vigour. Anybody coming into the church would have assumed that she was simply there to do a job but that was not the case at all. As she got on her knees to brush under a pew, she was praying for the image of Dr Tindall's corpse to be taken out of her mind, but the plea evoked no response from above.

Chatting with her beat partner made Iris Goodliffe's job much easier. She was therefore surprised and disappointed when Alice fell silent for five minutes and failed to hear her companion's voice. Iris resorted to a nudge.

'Oh,' said Alice, coming out of her reverie. 'What's happened?'

'Nothing has happened and that's the point. You went off into a daydream and didn't hear what I said.'

'I'm sorry, Iris.'

'You're entitled to think about Joe. I would, in your place.'

'I wasn't thinking about him. It was what Gwenda told me about the school.'

'You don't want to go back there, do you?' asked Iris, worriedly.

'In a way, I do.'

'You can't leave the Women's Police Force. You were made for it.'

'I used to be made for teaching,' recalled Alice. 'But don't worry. I'm not thinking of resigning. I just wondered if I might go back to give the children a talk about something.'

'Such as?'

'Well, the importance of obeying the law and why we now have women in police uniform as well as men. I'd never have considered offering to do that if Mrs Latimer was still headmistress.'

'Why not?'

'She was a real dragon. When I went to the school as a child, I was terrified of her and it was no different when I taught there. Mrs Latimer never let any of us forget that she was in charge.'

'What about the friend we met earlier?'

'Oh, Gwenda Powell was the opposite. She was warm, kind and ready to help me in any way. I missed her when I left the school. I'm so glad that she's the headmistress now. Mrs Latimer was a tyrant.'

'I can't even remember the teachers at my infant school,' confessed Iris, 'and I'd never dream of going back to give a talk there. I'm hopeless at speaking in public. I get so flustered. How would you remember what to say?'

'I'd write it down beforehand, then learn it.'

'You must have a good memory then. Mine is like a sieve.'

'Public speaking is easy when you've had some practice.'

'It's all right for you, Alice. Being a teacher gave you confidence. All I ever did before I joined the WPF was to serve behind the counter in a pharmacy.'

'You must've talked to dozens of different people every day and I've seen how good you are with complete strangers who ask us for help.'

'That's not the same as giving a talk.'

'I've got an idea,' said Alice, turning to her. 'Why don't you come with me? We could give the talk together. Before the war, there was no

Women's Police Force. If we explain how and why it came into being, we might give some of the girls the ambition to do what we did.'

'But there may not be a WPF after the war.'

'Oh, yes, there will be.'

'How do you know?'

'We've proved that we can do a valuable job during a crisis,' said Alice, proudly. 'There's no turning back now. We're here to stay.'

As they got back into their car, the detectives were able to discuss their visit.

'What did you make of her, Joe?' asked Marmion.

'She's different from her sister. Mrs Paget looks as if she eats too much, and Mrs Hobbes looks as if she eats too little. The other thing is that Mrs Paget has much more to say for herself than her sister. When the two of them get together, I bet that only one of them does the talking.'

'How many pages of your notebook did you fill?'

'Too many.'

They shared a laugh. 'I'm glad we met her,' said Marmion. 'Her version of Dr Tindall differs a lot from the one that I got from Major Palmer-Loach. He talked about him as a surgeon. Mrs Paget talked about him as a human being.'

'According to her, he spoke as if he had a plum in his mouth.'

'Yes, that was a surprise. Scots tend to keep their native accent.'

'Maybe he had a good reason to change it.'

'What did you make of Mrs Paget's story about the perfume?'

'It made me think how weird Dr Tindall must have been. What sort of man sprays perfume to remind him of his late wife?'

'I think he's the sort who tells barefaced lies to his cleaner.'

Keedy was surprised. 'Didn't you believe what he told her?'

'Frankly, I didn't.'

'Why not?'

'It's because I reckon that Mrs Paget made the right assumption. A woman had stayed at the house one night. That could be an important discovery. We've found a human weakness in him, after all,' said Marmion with a smile. 'Dr Tindall may not be as spotless as we've been led to believe that he was.'

CHAPTER SIX

Superintendent Claude Chatfield was accustomed to using the telephone to issue orders or to demand information. His rank ensured that officers obeyed him at once. That, at least, was what happened in England and – to a lesser extent, perhaps – in Wales. Both countries seemed to play by the same rules. Scotland, he had now learnt, was a foreign country that operated on a system he could neither understand nor admire. Ringing the Aberdeen City Police was an essay in frustration. It took him an age to make what he thought was a simple request. He wanted someone to track down Mr and Mrs Bruce Tindall of Kilbride Avenue, Dyce and give them some distressing news about their son. The parents would be asked to get in touch with Scotland Yard for more detail. By the time he lowered the receiver, Chatfield's arm was aching, and his temper frayed.

It was over an hour when he finally got news about his request.

Someone spoke to him in an impenetrable accent that meant he only understood one in ten of the words that were fired at him like so many bullets. When he asked the caller to talk in English, he got an indignant reply. The man went on to speak to him as if he were a child, putting great emphasis on each word. Chatfield eventually understood much of what he was being told.

'Thank you, Inspector,' he said, mastering his irritation.

'It's nae trouble.'

'You've been . . . helpful.'

'Aye, I know.'

Replacing the receiver, Chatfield sat back in his chair and breathed a sigh of relief. Next time he rang anyone in Aberdeen, he promised himself, he would have an interpreter standing beside him.

It was only when she left the church that Ada Hobbes remembered how early she had had to get up. Every bone in her body seemed to be crying out in protest. On the walk back home, she acknowledged greetings from some of her neighbours but made sure that she did not stop to talk to them. She simply wanted to get back to the safety of her own four walls. When the house came into view, however, she was dismayed to see someone standing outside the front door. Her first instinct was to dodge down a side street and hide there until her visitor had left. Then she realised who the woman was. Breaking into a trot, she waved her arms in greeting.

'Kathy!' she cried. 'Thank goodness you've come.'

'I felt that I had to, Ada. Oh, come here,' she said, spreading her arms to embrace her sister and plant a kiss on her cheek. 'Let's go inside and have a cup of tea. Then we can talk.'

'But we can't, I'm afraid.'

'Why not?'

'The police told me I was to speak to nobody. I gave them my word. They'll be very cross with me if I break my promise.'

'It's different now, Ada.'

'Is it?'

'Yes. When I told them I'd come here, they didn't try to stop me. I think they wanted me to comfort you.'

Ada was taken aback. 'You've seen them?'

'I've seen them and had a long talk with them. They asked me all sorts of questions about Dr Tindall. As soon as they left, I came straight here. Now, get your key out and let us in.'

'Oh, I'm so relieved to see you, Kathy.'

'Hurry up, woman. I want my blooming tea.'

Ada smiled and hugged her.

Before they went back to Scotland Yard, they returned to the hospital. Marmion was keen to make a second visit because Major Palmer-Loach had promised to search for as many photographs of George Tindall as he could find.

'It will make a big difference if we can release a photo of him to the press,' said Marmion. 'It's bound to jog memories.'

'Why were there no photos of him at his home?' asked Keedy.

'I suspect that they were deliberately stolen, Joe. The killers removed lots of things that might have been of use to us.'

'That's worrying.'

'It's annoying, I grant you that.'

'It tells us something about those two men. They were cold, brutal and well-organised. They've obviously gone out of their way to make our job more difficult. We're up against professionals, Harv.'

'Then we must rise to the challenge.'

When the car stopped outside the main building at the hospital, Marmion got out and went inside. Keedy decided to take a walk around the complex. He had read a great deal about military hospitals but had never been inside one before. As he strolled off, another building soon came into view and he was able to identify it at once as the nurses' home. He stopped to admire the nurses going into or coming out of the building. Marmion had been right. There was something about their crisp, white uniforms that gave the women a special lustre. Even the older ones looked attractive. He stood there gazing at the nurses as they flitted to and fro.

His surveillance was interrupted by a firm tap on the shoulder.

'Excuse me, sir,' said a voice.

Keedy turned to see a uniformed soldier glaring at him.

'Do you have a legitimate reason to be on the premises,' continued the man, 'or did you just come here to ogle the nurses?'

'I resent that question,' said Keedy, taking out his warrant card. 'I'm Detective Sergeant Keedy of the Metropolitan Police Force and I'm investigating the murder of one your surgeons.' He showed his card. 'Are you satisfied now?'

'Yes, sir. I'm sorry. I was only doing my job.'

'Do it better next time.'

'We don't allow intruders on the site.'

'Do I really look like an intruder?'

'To be honest – yes, you do.'

Keedy grinned. 'Fair enough,' he said, putting his card away.

'Which surgeon was it?'

'Dr Tindall – George Tindall.'

The soldier recoiled. 'No – I don't believe it.'

'I'm afraid that it's true.'

'Someone killed him? Why ever would they do that? I don't know the names of all the surgeons here, but I know his. Dr Tindall stood out from the others. He was so popular.'

'That's what we've been told. His patients will be shocked.'

'Not only his patients,' said the soldier with a sly wink. 'Think of those nurses. Some of them worshipped him – lucky devil. If he'd wanted to, he could have had his pick of them.'

During the time that Marmion had been away, the major had been busy. By raiding his files and scouring the hospital, he had gathered a whole dossier of photographs. Most of them were taken of groups of patients and staff, carefully arranged by the photographer. Everyone looked happy in front of the camera. Once the doctor had been pointed out to him, Marmion found it easy to pick out George Tindall in every group. He was a tall, slim man in his early forties with a dignified air.

'The patients in this one,' said Palmer-Loach, handing him a photograph with over fifty people on display, 'were all due to be released. It's a farewell photo. That's why they've got those broad grins. They were the lucky ones,' he added. 'Many of their friends left in a hearse.'

'They must have arrived here in a bad state,' observed Marmion.

'Some came straight from the battlefield with their mud-covered uniforms still clinging to them. They had to be cut off.'

'These photos are fascinating, Major, but they're not really suitable for our purposes, I'm afraid.'

'That's why I brought some others.'

The major showed him some photographs taken of three surgeons, holding their masks as they stood outside the operating theatre. Tindall was among them. Of the new batch, the best photograph showed him standing beside a colleague in the open air. He looked weary but managed a smile.

'This is the one for me,' said Marmion, 'but, if I may, I'll borrow a couple of the others as well.'

'We would like them back, Inspector. They're a precious record of how this hospital works. Take great care of them. I'm only sorry that we don't have one with Dr Tindall entirely on his own.'

'Don't worry. We have a man at Scotland Yard who is a genius at cropping photographs. And if we still fail to get a satisfactory result,' said Marmion, 'we have an artist who can produce a good likeness of Dr Tindall.'

The major put the selected photographs in a large brown envelope and handed it over to his visitor. Marmion thanked him once again.

'You've made a significant contribution to the investigation, sir,' he said.

Since they had started their shift early, Alice and Iris had finished by mid afternoon. When they returned to their headquarters, the redoubtable Inspector Thelma Gale was waiting for them. Even though relatively short, she had an imposing presence. She ran a critical eye over their respective uniforms to see that they were clean and being worn properly.

'Anything to report?' she asked.

'Not really,' said Alice. 'All in all, it was a rather quiet day.'

'It's true,' added Iris. 'The most exciting thing that happened was the chat that Alice had with an old friend.'

The inspector bristled. 'You are there to keep the peace,' she snarled, 'not to talk to a passing acquaintance.'

'Oh, she was more than an acquaintance, Inspector. Alice used to work at the same school with her. Mrs Powell was rather naughty,' she went on with a giggle. 'She tried to poach Alice from the WPF.'

'I don't like the sound of that.'

'It was not serious, Inspector,' explained Alice. 'Gwenda – Mrs Powell – is now the headmistress at the school. They have some unruly children there now, apparently. She remembered that I was good at keeping discipline.'

'You're far more use to us than you'd be in a classroom,' said the other with a peremptory snort. 'Put the idea out of your head.'

'Yes, Inspector.'

'You hold a responsible position. Never forget that. Women are making an important difference in the war effort. We've proved ourselves in every way.'

'Alice knows that,' said Iris, unguardedly. 'She'd never desert us. But there's no reason why she shouldn't help the school when she's off duty, is there?'

'There's every reason,' hissed the inspector, turning to glare at Alice. 'Have you made this friend of yours some sort of promise?'

'Not really,' said Alice. 'I was just thinking, that's all.'

'Thinking about what, may I ask?'

Iris blurted it out. 'She thought it might be a good idea to give a talk to the pupils. Alice was a born teacher. They'd listen to her.'

'And what sort of talk did you have in mind?' demanded the inspector.

'It was just an idea,' said Alice, wishing that the subject had never come up. 'I can see now that it was a mistake. For a start, I simply don't have the time.'

'You could make time,' suggested Iris.

'I'd rather forget the whole thing.'

'But the children keep asking after you. In fact—'

'That's enough,' said Alice, cutting her off. 'The matter's closed.'

'It certainly is,' agreed the inspector. 'When you joined the WPF, you made certain commitments. I expect you to honour them and not get distracted by the prospect of working in a school again. You operate in the adult world now.' She drew herself up to her full height. 'Do you understand what I'm saying?'

'Yes, Inspector.'

'Don't forget it.' She turned on Iris. 'The same goes for you.'

'Yes, Inspector,' said Iris, meekly.

'The Women's Police Force must always come first!'

Having delivered her final warning, Inspector Gale gave each of them a withering look before stalking off to her office. Alice was dazed by the confrontation and angry with Iris for mentioning the conversation about the school. There were times when her beat partner's loose tongue maddened her, and this was one of them. Iris sensed that she had done the wrong thing.

'We're still going to the West End tomorrow, aren't we?' she whispered.

The first pot of tea steadied them and gave them the strength to cope with the shock they had both had. By the time that Ada Hobbes had brewed a second pot, they felt restored. Kathleen Paget rolled her eyes.

'Dr Tindall was my best client,' she said. 'I'd do anything for him.'

'So would I, Kathy,' said her sister.

'Apart from anything else, he paid me more than the others.'

'I didn't do his cleaning for the money. It was just a pleasure to be on my own in such a lovely, big house. I was able to set my pace without having someone standing over me. I just wish Bert had still been alive for me to tell him all about Dr Tindall.' She became reflective. 'He was funny, though.'

71

'Who – Bert or the doctor?'

'The doctor, of course,' said Ada. 'When I first saw all those photos of his wife, I thought it was wonderful of him to remember her that way. I'm not so sure now. I mean, it's not something I did when my husband died. If I put a photo of Bert in every room, it would unsettle me. Wherever I went, he'd be watching me.'

'I'd feel the same about Alf.'

'Does that mean we're bad people?'

'It means that we grieve in our own ways, Ada.'

They drank their tea and lapsed into a companionable silence. It was minutes before Ada remembered something.

'Thank you, Kathy.'

'I should be thanking you. It's a lovely cup of tea.'

'I'm so grateful that you recommended me to Dr Tindall.'

'What's the point of family if we can't help each other?'

'That's true.'

'And you deserved something good for once. You've had so many blows in your life, Ada, and you never felt sorry for yourself.'

'Yes, I did,' recalled her sister. 'When I took over Bert's round, I felt very sorry for myself. Sweeping chimneys almost crippled me. The soot got everywhere. And I hated being laughed at by children in the street.'

'Those days have gone now.' Kathy sipped her tea. 'I've got to do some thinking,' she said, putting the cup back in the saucer. 'The police told me that, if I remembered anything about Dr Tindall I thought might be useful, I was to get in touch with them at once. But my brain just won't work properly.'

'Mine's the same, Kathy. It's the shock.'

'That'll wear off, I hope. When it does, I'll remember things he said or did. Think of that, Ada. What I tell them about the doctor might help them to catch whoever killed him.' She tapped her head. 'I might have some important information locked away inside here.'

On the drive back to Scotland Yard, they studied the photographs. Keedy was fascinated by the way that Tindall caught the eye immediately.

'Even when he's wearing a white coat,' he said, 'he somehow manages to look smart. The two doctors with him in this photo just disappear.'

'Think of those suits in his wardrobe, Joe.'

'I'm still green with envy.'

'He really cared about his appearance.'

'Yes, and he was a good-looking devil. No wonder he made so many hearts flutter in the nurses' home. It makes you wonder, doesn't it?'

'What do you mean?'

'Well,' said Keedy, 'both the neighbours and those two cleaners told us that Dr Tindall was obsessed with his late wife. Yet that smile on his face and those expensive suits of his suggest he might – just might – be a ladies' man.'

'Then there was the smell of perfume in his bathroom.'

'I hadn't forgotten that.'

'Let's not jump to conclusions,' warned Marmion. 'Mr and Mrs Crowe knew him much better than us and so did Mrs Hobbes and Mrs Paget. Then there was Major Palmer-Loach, of course. He gave me the impression that Dr Tindall was on duty at the hospital almost every single day. In fact, he stayed the night there sometimes. That's real devotion to duty.'

Keedy studied the last of the photographs, then handed it back. Marmion slipped it into the envelope. He remembered something.

'The major has been extremely helpful,' he said, 'but, on my first visit there, we did have a difference of opinion.'

'What about?'

'Endell Street Hospital.'

'Ah, yes,' recalled Keedy. 'You went there with Alice, didn't you?'

'I was intrigued to find out if a hospital with an entirely female staff could function properly. Endell Street gave me the answer. It could match any other military hospital. I thought it was remarkable.'

'What was the major's opinion?'

'He called it "the Suffragettes Hospital" as if that were something obscene. I told him how impressed I was, but he'll never change his mind. He prefers hospitals where men make all the decisions.'

'You'll have to set Alice on to him.'

'It would be a waste of time. The major has a closed mind.' Marmion patted the envelope. 'We got what we came for, that's the main thing. A photo is better than a thousand words. If we can get Dr Tindall's face in tomorrow's papers, we're going to reach people nationwide.'

'My guess is that we'll have a big response,' said Keedy.

'It's what I'm hoping for, Joe. Before we can solve this murder, we need to find out a hell of a lot more about the victim.'

It was weeks since Ellen Marmion had seen her daughter and she was filled with nervous excitement. She had baked some cakes for the occasion and cleaned Alice's room in readiness. Uncertain of what time she would arrive, Ellen was torn between going to meet the bus and waiting at the house. In the event, the decision was taken for her. Before she could put on her coat to go out, she heard a key being inserted in the front door. When her daughter suddenly appeared, her mother flung her arms around her.

'You're earlier than I expected,' said Ellen.

'Is that a complaint, Mummy?'

'Of course not. This is a wonderful surprise.'

After an exchange of greetings, Alice took off her coat and hat and followed her mother into the kitchen. She saw the plate of cakes on the table.

'Oh, that's just what I need!'

'You look exhausted. Have you had a tiring day?'

'Not really,' said Alice. 'It was just ... irritating.'

'Sit down and tell me all about it. I'll put the kettle on.'

'Can I have one of those cakes first?'

Ellen laughed. 'Have as many as you like.'

The two of them were soon sitting opposite each other at the table. Alice was able to relax for the first time that day. Being back home was a tonic for her.

'Now, then,' said her mother. 'What made the day so irritating?'

'Iris.'

'I thought the pair of you got on so well together.'

'We do as a rule,' said Alice. 'In fact, I was enjoying her company so much, I suggested that the pair of us should go to the West End tomorrow on our day off.'

'She'd have been thrilled at that.'

'Iris couldn't stop talking about it. Then we bumped into a friend of mine ...'

Alice told her about the chat with Gwenda Powell and about the latter's attempt to get her back to school again. Ellen was interested to hear that Gwenda was now headmistress.

'I thought that Mrs Latimer would never retire,' she said. 'You used to be so frightened of that woman.'

'I still am.'

'But she's left the school altogether.'

'Yes,' said Alice, 'and she's turned up under another name. Inspector Gale is Mrs Latimer in disguise – just as strict and twice as nasty. And what does Iris do?'

'Tell me.'

'When we get to the end of our shift, Gale Force is waiting for us. Iris tells her that Gwenda Powell was trying to lure me back into teaching, so I get told off good and proper. Oh,' she cried through gritted teeth, 'I could kill Iris sometimes. The worst of it is that I've got to spend most of the day with her tomorrow.' She held up an apologetic hand. 'I'm sorry, Mummy. I shouldn't go on about it. And I have got something lined up for tomorrow. It will wipe away all memory of Iris Goodliffe. Joe is taking me out.'

'Ah,' said Ellen, 'I'm glad you mentioned Joe.'

'We haven't spent time together for weeks.'

'You may have to wait a little longer, I'm afraid.'

'Why?'

'Joe rang me from Scotland Yard about an hour ago. He sends his love and says how sorry he is, but something has come up – a murder in Edmonton. He and your father will be working on it around the clock.'

Alice sagged. The next day began to look bleak.

They were still examining the body when Marmion came into the morgue. Harrison broke away and took him into his office where the smell was less pungent.

'There's still a long way to go, Harvey,' explained the pathologist. 'I tell you the same thing every time. You can't rush a post-mortem.'

'Just bring me up to date, Tom.'

'Time of death is what I told you earlier.'

'It fits in with what Joe discovered.'

'Oh?'

'He did a stint at door-knocking. At a house on the corner, he found an old man who was in his bathroom when he heard two motorbikes drawing up and stopping. We think that whoever had been riding them walked up to Dr Tindall's house and somehow got in. The result is out there on your table.'

'How do you know that the motorcyclists committed the murder?'

'They came as quietly as possible,' said Marmion, 'and left as fast as they could. Everybody in the next street heard them roar away.'

'I see.'

'What can you tell me about the nature of the injuries?'

'Do you really want to know?' Marmion nodded. 'They made sure he died slowly and in great pain. He was tortured. They cut lumps off him as they went along. His stomach was cut open and his testicles sliced off. I could go on and on.'

'That's enough, Tom. I'd prefer to see it all in a report.'

'There's one thing you might care to know.'

'Is there?'

'Something bigger than a knife was used to inflict some of those wounds. If you asked me for a guess, I'd say it was a bayonet.'

Marmion gulped. 'A bayonet?'

'Now where would they get hold of that?'

As soon as they had reached Scotland Yard, Keedy had gone off to pursue a line of enquiry on his own. He kept thinking about the suits hanging in the wardrobe in Dr Tindall's house. A surgeon would be paid far more than a detective sergeant but not enough, he believed, to be a regular client in Savile Row. A large amount of money had been lavished on the suits and other items of menswear they'd found.

There had also been three pairs of gold cufflinks. The array of hats alone would have been well beyond the reach of Keedy's modest income.

When he was dropped off by the police car in Savile Row, he remembered a case that had taken him and Marmion to nearby Jermyn Street. It had concerned the murder of a Jewish tailor, the rape of his daughter and the burning down of his premises. Keedy hoped that the current investigation would be less complex and bewildering. Before he went into the shop, he looked in the window of Boyle and Stoddard, Bespoke Tailors. To someone as interested in the latest styles as he was, the suits on display were minor works of art. He enjoyed a momentary fantasy of wearing one of them as he took Alice to dinner at The Ritz.

Keedy entered the shop to be given a practised smile by an immaculately dressed man in his thirties with carefully barbered hair and moustache.

'Good afternoon, sir,' he said. 'How may we help you?'

'I've come in search of information about a client of yours.'

'I'm sorry, sir, but such information is strictly confidential.' Keedy produced his warrant card and held it in front of his face. 'Ah,' said the man, reading the name and changing his tone, 'that's different.'

'Good.'

'In which of our clients are you interested?'

'Dr Tindall.'

'May I ask why?'

'We are investigating his murder.'

After his visit to the pathologist, Marmion went off to report to Claude Chatfield. The superintendent was as peppery as ever and was only partly mollified by the sight of the photographs from the hospital. He sifted through them before picking out the one with only two figures in it. 'Let's see what we can do with this,' he said. 'Now, what else have you found out? Were he here – as he was, a mere twenty minutes ago – the commissioner would be asking you the same question.'

'Then my answer is this, sir …'

Marmion gave him an abbreviated account of the visits to Kathleen Paget and the hospital, then mentioned that Keedy had gone off to Savile Row. The superintendent was not encouraged by the news.

'What the devil is he doing there?' he howled.

'Well, he hasn't gone to be measured for a new suit,' said Marmion, drily. 'The sergeant felt that he might get another piece of the jigsaw named George Tindall. Slowly and surely, we'll build up a complete picture of the man.'

'You won't do that if you rely on the word of two cleaners and a tailor.'

'You missed out Major Palmer-Loach.'

'He at least seems to have been helpful to us.'

'You also overlooked the people living next door to Dr Tindall.'

'They admitted quite frankly that they never really got to know him. And please don't tell me that a tailor is going to supply us with a fund of insights.'

'Be patient, sir. In the past, tailors have provided vital information and I am not simply referring to the case that took us to Jermyn Street. Tailor and client have a close relationship. They get to know each other well.'

'Does that mean Sergeant Keedy will come back here with the doctor's chest measurement?' said Chatfield, scornfully. 'Or has he gone there in search of details regarding his inside leg?'

'You may be pleasantly surprised, Superintendent.'

'I doubt it.'

'Let's wait and see,' said Marmion. 'Meanwhile, I'm dying to ask if you got anywhere with your call to Aberdeen. If you sent them off to speak to the doctor's parents, we may soon get several new pieces of the jigsaw.'

'That's a forlorn hope, Inspector.'

'Why?'

'I'll draw a veil over my protracted attempts to get the Aberdeen City Police to speak in a language compatible with English,' said Chatfield. 'Eventually, they managed to understand my request and were, to be fair to them, quite efficient. They went in search of Dr Tindall's parents in Kilbride Road.'

'And?'

'It does not exist.'

'Are they sure?'

'Yes, Inspector. They also went through a list of residents in Dyce. Bruce Tindall and his wife were not among them – nor were they living anywhere else in the area. The police were thorough. We've been misled.'

'Major Palmer-Loach gave me that address in good faith.'

'I'm not blaming him. The finger points at Tindall himself. He deliberately gave false information.' Picking up a photograph, he studied the doctor's face. 'He looks so honest and trustworthy, doesn't he?'

'The major vouched for his reliability.'

'Then he was mistaken,' said Chatfield. 'Dr Tindall lied about his parents' whereabouts. How many more lies has he told? I'm sorry, Inspector,' he went on. 'You've just lost most of the pieces in your jigsaw. I suggest that you start this investigation all over again.'

CHAPTER SEVEN

Though she was bitterly disappointed, Alice Marmion adapted quickly to the news that she would not, after all, be spending the following evening with her fiancé. When Keedy was involved in a major investigation, it took precedence over everything and she accepted that. Besides, there was something that she did not tell her mother. Even if he were forced to cancel an arrangement with her, Keedy often went out of his way to make amends. On the last occasion when it happened, he had turned up at the house where she lived and woken her up by throwing pebbles at her window. Instead of the meal she had been promised, Alice had enjoyed a romantic walk with him in the moonlight.

'It's something I had to get used to,' said her mother.

'I know. Marry a policeman and you must take the rough with the smooth.'

'Work always comes first.'

'I've no quarrel with that, Mummy,' said Alice. 'Having been involved in police work myself, I know how the job can take over your life.'

'Perhaps you should have stayed in teaching.'

'I've wondered about that. Maybe I'll go back to it after the war.'

'If it ever ends, that is.'

They were seated together on the sofa in the living room. Darkness was falling so the curtains had been drawn. Alice felt warm, cosy and relaxed.

'It's strange, isn't it?' she said. 'I'm less upset about Joe's phone call than I am about the prospect of a day out with Iris. It's an awful thing to admit, but I find myself wishing that she was the person who rang to say that she had to pull out.'

'You'll enjoy it once you get there, Alice.'

'I'd enjoy it even more if you were with me.'

Ellen was interested. 'Would you like me to come along as well?'

'I'd love you to come, Mummy, but that would be unfair on Iris. I sort of promised that it would just be the two of us, off duty and on the loose. It means so much to her.'

'Then you'll be doing her a favour.'

'It's embarrassing sometimes. I'm fond of Iris but I do wish that she'd stop trying to be like me. She has to make her own decisions, not get me to make them for her.'

'Tell her that she has to find her own Joe Keedy.'

Alice laughed. 'There's only one and he's mine,' she said. 'I'm counting the days until I can walk down the aisle on his arm.'

'It won't be all that long now.'

'Iris reminds me of it every day.'

'What will you be looking for tomorrow in the West End?'

'The moment when I can say goodbye to her and go back to my

flat. 'No,' she went on, apologetically, 'that sounds spiteful and I don't mean it in that way. It's just that I can only cope with so much of Iris's enthusiasm.'

'Is she looking for anything in particular?'

'That's my job, Mummy. What she wants is a new dress, but she won't actually choose it herself. I'll have to choose it for her – after she's tried on just about everything in her size.'

Ellen rolled her eyes. 'I'm relieved that I'm not coming with you.'

'Iris is Iris, I'm afraid.'

'Have you and Joe decided if she'll be invited to the wedding?'

'He's against the idea,' said Alice. 'I'm in favour.'

'Who is going to win that argument?'

'You'll have to wait and see.'

After making the call, Marmion lowered the receiver. He had just spoken to Major Palmer-Loach at the hospital, telling him that Dr Tindall had told a deliberate lie about the whereabouts of his family. There were no parents living near Aberdeen or anywhere else in the region. The major had been angry and embarrassed, furious at Tindall and red-faced at having been so easily deceived. Left on his own, Marmion looked through his notebook to see how much of the information he had gathered about Tindall must be considered as suspect. Identifying the killers was going to be difficult enough as it was. Before he and Keedy could do that, however, they now had the problem of finding out much more about the murder victim.

Marmion was still reviewing the case when the sergeant knocked and came into the office. He was beaming.

'You won't believe this,' he began.

Marmion silenced him with a raised hand. 'Let me have my turn first, Joe.'

'But this is interesting.'

'Everything has to be revalued in the light of what Chat has discovered. We've all been led up the garden path, Joe.'

Keedy blinked. 'Have we?'

'Yes – you, me, the superintendent, Mrs Hobbes, Mrs Paget, Mr and Mrs Crowe and, most of all, Major Palmer-Loach.'

'You've lost me, I'm afraid.'

'We've all been assuming that Dr Tindall has been telling the truth. He told the major that his family home was in Scotland. I passed on the parents' address to Chat. When he contacted the police in Aberdeen, he asked them to track down Mr and Mrs Tindall. They tried and failed.'

'Why?'

'It was a false address, Joe. If they're still alive – and I'm beginning to doubt even that now – they're not in Scotland.'

'Then where exactly are they?'

'God knows!'

'But I thought the major got the details from his official records.'

'They'll have to be amended.'

'How did Chat take the news?'

'He said that it was like being slapped in the face by a wet cod. I suppose that's appropriate for a fishing port like Aberdeen.'

'Wow!' said Keedy, dazed. 'You've taken the wind out of my sails.'

'Have I?'

'Yes, I thought I had big news to pass on, but it feels small now. If Tindall lied about his parents, he's obviously told a string of other lies as well.'

'What's your big news?'

'It's hardly worth telling.'

'You were grinning from ear to ear when you came in.'

'I can't even manage a smile now,' admitted Keedy. 'For what it's worth, here's what I found out. I went to Boyle and Stoddard, looked at the suits on display and realised I was in the wrong profession. Even as a superintendent, I could never afford the prices they charge.'

'Go on.'

'I went into the shop and was greeted by a man named Hugh Lucifer.'

Marmion gaped. 'Who?'

'Hugh Lucifer. Believe it or not, that was his name, and, in a strange way, it suited him. When I asked about Dr Tindall, he told me what a nice man he was and how he was regarded as a privileged customer.'

'That means he's spent a lot of money there.'

'When war broke out, Tindall stopped coming. Lucifer picked up a rumour that he'd gone to France to work in a hospital there. Then one day last year, he walked in out of the blue and bought a new hat.'

'As news goes, Joe, this doesn't really qualify as "big".'

'I'm coming to the best bit.'

'Then let me hear it before I go to sleep out of boredom.'

'Tindall was living in that house in Edmonton, yet he gave an address on the south coast. Hugh Lucifer told me that that had been his permanent address for years. He assumed that Tindall was still based there.'

'Forgive my cynicism,' said Marmion. 'You did well to find that out. I believe that it could be significant news. The major told me that Tindall used to work at a hospital in Brighton.'

'He can't have two houses, can he?'

'I'm learning that anything is possible with him.'

'I've got the address but, unfortunately, not the telephone number. Tindall refused to give that.' Taking out his notebook, he flipped to a page, then showed it to Marmion. 'Hipwell Manor – sounds grand, doesn't it?'

'We'll have to find out,' said the other, getting to his feet.

Keedy was surprised. 'We're going there now?'

'Why not?'

'Don't you have to speak to Chat first?'

'No, he'll be too busy holding a press conference. He's hoping to give out copies of Dr Tindall's photograph so that it can appear in tomorrow's newspapers. It's time for us to show initiative.' He reached for his coat and hat. 'Come on, Joe. Let's be on our way.'

'But it's evening.'

Marmion grinned. 'Since when were you afraid of the dark?'

Ada Hobbes was in her kitchen, trying to cook herself a frugal meal. She felt rather queasy but told herself that she needed food inside her. While her sister's visit had cheered her up, Kathleen's departure had the opposite effect. Ada felt lonely and troubled. Though she had only known Dr Tindall for a short time, she had warmed to him. He had been so kind and considerate. To find his dead body in such a terrible state that morning had rocked her. As she recalled the horror, she closed her eyes tight. When she opened them again, she realised that the gas had gone out. Turning off the stove, she went across to the cupboard where she kept a supply of small change. After taking a shilling from the pot, she went into the front room and crouched down to put the coin into the meter. Gas began to flow again.

Ada then remembered something.

'That was a such a nasty thing to say,' protested Alice. 'She used to be a friend.'

'Paul put a stop to that friendship,' said Ellen.

'Mrs Redwood had no right to gloat.'

'It was upsetting, I must admit.'

'If I'd been there, I'd have given her a piece of my mind.'

Ellen gave a hollow laugh. 'Then I'm glad you weren't,' she said, 'or she'd have two reasons to get back at me – you and your brother.'

'Why did you bother to talk to her?'

'I had no choice. She just descended on me.'

Ellen had told her daughter about the bruising encounter with Patricia Redwood. Enraged by the woman's behaviour, Alice had leapt to her mother's defence. She had an urge to go in search of Mrs Redwood.

'There's nothing you can do,' said Ellen. 'Besides, I can fight my own battles.'

'I felt sorry for Sally Redwood when we were at school together. She was so shy. The other girls teased her about her freckles and the boys called her rude names.'

'But none of them went to the lengths that Paul did. He not only drew a disgusting picture of her, he pinned it up on his dartboard and threw darts at it. I was ashamed of him.'

'Blame the war,' said Alice. 'It warped his mind.'

'It gave him a vicious streak, I know that. Sally was a nice enough girl and she had never done Paul any harm. Yet when she got that job at the jeweller's shop in the high street, he leered at her through the window. It gave her a real fright,' said Ellen. 'Her mother told me that Sally had difficulty sleeping.'

'It was wrong of Paul to stalk her. I accept that, Mummy. But it was also wrong of Sally's mother to crow over you.'

'Forget it. I have.'

'Then why did you mention it?' asked Alice. 'It's obviously preying on your mind. Mrs Redwood intended to hurt you and she did. I'm glad that Sally has found herself a boyfriend at last, but that doesn't give her mother the right to goad you about Paul. It's cruel.'

'It's also understandable.'

Alice was incensed. 'Whose side are you on – hers or Paul's?'

'Don't shout.'

'Then don't give me a reason,' said Alice. She took a few deep breaths before speaking. 'Let's get off the subject, shall we? As soon as I hear Mrs Redwood's name, I just want to—'

'That's enough,' said Ellen, interrupting firmly. 'I was hoping to enjoy some time alone with you. I've got so much more to tell you and I'm sure there are things you want to tell me. Promise me that you won't even mention Patricia Redwood again.' Alice glared mutinously. 'That's settled then.'

They burst out laughing and hugged each other.

Because they were anxious to get to Brighton, they got on the first train about to leave even though it was reserved for troops. Their status as detectives earned them a place in the middle of a mass of khaki uniforms. Marmion spoke to the soldiers packed into their compartment.

'Where are you going, lads?' he asked.

'We're orff to Paris to 'ave some fun,' replied a soldier with a cigarette in the corner of his mouth. 'Stand by, girls – we're on our way!'

'Don't listen to him,' said another. 'We're sailin' to Boulogne.'

'Where do you go from there?' said Keedy.

'They 'aven't told us but it'll be somewhere crawlin' with bleedin' Huns.'

'Watch out for mustard gas. That's what they're using now.'

'We know. We been practisin' with gas masks.'

'Where are you from?'

'Lambeth.'

'You don't look old enough to join the army,' said Marmion.

'Eighteen's old enough for anythin',' boasted the soldier. 'This time next year, I'll be sittin' back in Blighty, polishin' my medals. Before that, next summer, I'm gettin' married.'

'Don't bank on it, lad,' advised Marmion.

'I give Lil my word. Come 'ell or 'igh water, it'll 'appen some'ow.'

'I hope it does.'

Marmion spoke with more confidence than he felt. British casualties were still dauntingly high. Many of the soldiers on the train might add to the numbers of dead and wounded. Someone told a joke and there was ribald laughter. In the short time they had spent together in the army, they had obviously developed a sense of camaraderie. Marmion was reminded of Paul, going off with the same spirit and determination as the young men all round him.

For his part, Keedy had felt a pang at the mention of marriage. His own wedding would certainly go ahead in the new year, but he doubted very much if the youth seated opposite him would marry in the following summer. He was more likely to be killed, maimed or simply brutalised by the experience of warfare. Whatever happened, the cheeky grin would be wiped off his face.

'Why are you two goin' to Brighton, then?' asked someone.

'We plan to walk down to the beach,' replied Keedy, 'and dip our toes into the water. Then we split up and search for mermaids.'

The soldiers roared with laughter.

After addressing the press conference, Claude Chatfield went back to his office with a spring in his step. He felt that he had handled the various questions adroitly. The important thing was that he had been able to issue a copy of Tindall's photograph to each of the reporters.

Before he could wallow in self-congratulation, he was joined by the commissioner.

'Good evening, Sir Edward,' he said.

'I just wanted a word, Superintendent.'

'Have as many as you wish.'

'I'm told that the press conference went well.'

'Did you have someone watching?'

'Yes,' said the other. 'I like to keep abreast of the latest developments. I'm glad that you were able to issue a photograph of the victim.'

'We need to thank our photographers for that, Sir Edward. They worked wonders. Because I impressed upon them how urgent it was, they managed to provide copies just in time. When I went to see how they were getting on, they also showed me the photos taken at the scene of the crime.'

'I made a point of looking at them myself. They were horrific. I also went out of my way to talk to the fingerprint expert who went to that house in Edmonton.'

'I thought you might, Sir Edward,' said Chatfield with a knowing smile. 'Fingerprints are your speciality.'

'They've proved their value time and again – but not in this case, I fear.'

'Why is that?'

'The killers were careful not to leave any. That means they had the sense to wear gloves. The fingerprints there belonged almost exclusively to Dr Tindall. They were able to take a set from him before he was cut open in the path lab.'

'I'm still waiting for the post-mortem report, Sir Edward.'

'The cause of death is all too apparent, alas,' said the other. 'Have you made any headway regarding the parents?'

Chatfield heaved a sigh. 'I'm afraid not.'

'Is there a problem?'

'Yes, there is – and it's a big one.'

He told the commissioner about his telephone call to the Aberdeen City Police and how they had established that Tindall's parents had not lived at the address given by their son. Indeed, they had no link whatsoever with the area.

Sir Edward was shocked. 'Can this be true?'

'The Aberdeen police were thorough.'

'But that means Dr Tindall deliberately misled everyone. What was the purpose of doing that?'

'The honest answer is that we don't know.'

'I have to say that the doctor's behaviour beggars belief. What was he hiding?'

'Whatever it is, Sir Edward, we'll find out.'

'Does the inspector have any theories?'

'He's usually prone to have too many of them,' said Chatfield, grimacing. 'In this instance, he's stumped.'

'Oh dear!'

'Wait until that photograph appears in the newspapers tomorrow. It is bound to be seen by one or more of Tindall's relatives.'

'Let's hope so,' said the commissioner. 'What is Marmion doing meanwhile?'

'I was just about to find out, Sir Edward, but you came into my office before I could do so.' He crossed to his desk. 'If he leaves Scotland Yard, he always tells me exactly where he's going. Here we are,' he said, picking up an envelope. 'I recognise his handwriting.'

Opening the envelope, Chatfield took out a sheet of paper. When he read the short message, he blenched.

'What's the trouble?' asked the commissioner.

'Inspector Marmion and Sergeant Keedy have gone to Brighton.'

'Did you authorise that?'

'I most certainly did not.'

'They must have a good reason for doing so.'

'It's a pity they didn't tell me what it was,' said Chatfield, ruefully.

'Let me know what they find, Superintendent. The inspector always comes back with some new evidence. He has an uncanny gift for sniffing it out.'

Since they could not discuss the case in a crowded compartment, the detectives sat back and listened to the soldiers who, at one point, broke into a toneless rendition of 'It's a Long Way to Tipperary'. What it lacked in harmony, however, it made up for in sheer gusto. Marmion had heard it sung by Irish soldiers who had brought out the full pathos in the lyrics. It had a defiant note here, sung by young men to keep up their spirits and conceal their fears. Listening to their companions helped the detectives to defeat time. They seemed to reach their destination far sooner than they expected.

When they arrived at Brighton railway station, they let the soldiers get out first and line up with the other members of their regiment. Only then did Marmion and Keedy step out onto the platform.

'We came too late, Joe,' said the inspector.

'I thought we were too early,' said Keedy. 'I've never known a train journey go so quick.'

'I was not talking about that. I was thinking about the early days of the war when a train or a convoy of lorries brought soldiers to Brighton. They would have been given a rousing welcome by a big crowd. The chief constable would have been here with the mayor and the local worthies. There might even have been a brass band. They were greeted as heroes.'

'They weren't greeted as heroes on the battlefield,' said Keedy, pursing his lips. 'I remember what Paul told me. It was a living hell over there.'

'We need a taxi.'

'Where do we go first – hospital or Hipwell Manor?'

'We'll go to the house first. That's where Dr Tindall used to live.'

'Do you want to bet on that?' teased Keedy.

Marmion grinned. 'I'm not that stupid, Joe.'

After picking their way past the soldiers, they found the taxi rank and climbed into a waiting car. The driver told them that their destination was over ten miles away. On their way there, he felt obliged to give them a potted history of life in Brighton since the war had begun. Keedy pulled a face and stopped listening to him, but Marmion was fascinated by what the man was saying.

Situated on the south coast, Brighton was not a regular target from the air or from the sea. If the Germans did try to invade, it was felt, they were more likely to approach the east of the country. Along with London, that was the major target for bombing raids. Since it had a marked degree of safety, Brighton was still a popular seaside resort during warmer months. Thousands of people, the driver boasted, poured in for Easter and summer holidays. While it was certainly not a case of life as usual, the town was still able to operate as a magnet for pleasure-seekers.

'Our beach is the best in Britain,' claimed the man. 'You can go bathing, fishing or boating there. There's tennis for the younger visitors and bowls for the older ones. Our shops are as good as any in Oxford Street, and we have theatres and such like what do a roaring trade. This is the place to be, gents.'

His monologue took them all the way to Hipwell Manor. Marmion asked the taxi driver to wait for them. It was dark now and there was no light showing from the house because of the blackout. All they could see was a fuzzy outline of a Tudor farmhouse.

'Are you sure we've got the right place?' asked Keedy, doubtfully.

'Let's find out.'

Marmion went to the front door and pulled the bell rope. A curtain was tugged back, allowing a shaft of light to cut across them. It disappeared almost immediately. Moments later, the door opened to reveal a manservant. In the subdued light, they could hardly see his face, but his voice suggested age and gravitas.

'Yes?' he asked.

Marmion introduced them and asked if a George Tindall had lived there.

'I'm afraid not, Inspector.'

'He's an orthopaedic surgeon.'

'The house is owned by Captain Langford. He's away at sea at the moment but his wife and daughter are here. Would you like to speak to Mrs Langford?'

'We certainly would.'

The servant stood back so that they could enter the dimly lit hall. They were able to see that he was a short, round-shouldered man in his sixties with a quiet dignity about him. As he closed the front door, the one to the lounge opened and a woman popped her head out.

'Who is it, Pearson?' she asked.

'These gentlemen are detectives from London, Mrs Langford,' he told her.

She was irritated. 'Why have they come here? We're scrupulously careful about maintaining a blackout.'

Marmion introduced himself and Keedy, then asked if they could have a private word with her. She conducted them into the lounge, a large, characterful, half-timbered room with a low ceiling that warned them to duck under the beams. A log fire was crackling in the grate. There was a piano in one corner. After sizing them up, she waved them to a seat. Hats in hands, they sat together on the sofa.

'What is this all about?' she asked, taking an armchair opposite.

Caroline Langford was a tall, shapely woman in her late thirties with a sense of breeding about her. While Marmion admired her cheekbones, Keedy was struck by the quality of the jewellery she was wearing. She was patently annoyed at the intrusion and spoke with a slight edge to her voice.

'Well?' she prompted.

'The sergeant and I are leading a murder investigation,' explained Marmion.

She was taken aback. 'Really?'

'The victim was a George Tindall – Doctor George Tindall.'

'What has that got to do with me, may I ask?'

'We understood that he had some connection with this house.'

'Then I'm sorry but you've been misinformed. Who gave you this address?'

'It was a tailor in Savile Row,' replied Keedy. 'Dr Tindall had his suits made there. We knew that he once worked at a hospital in Brighton and wondered if he'd perhaps kept this house and rented it out.'

'I beg your pardon!' she said, clearly offended. 'Hipwell Manor has belonged to my family for generations. We would never rent it out to strangers, Sergeant.'

'I understand that your husband is in the navy,' said Marmion.

'That is correct. Michael is in command of a destroyer.'

'Where exactly is he at this moment, Mrs Langford?'

'Really, Inspector,' she replied. 'Shame on you for asking such a question. For obvious reasons, deployment of our navy is a matter of secrecy. I have no idea where my husband is and, even if I did, I would never tell you.'

'How long have you and Captain Langford been married?'

'What relevance can that possibly have to your investigation?'

'None at all,' he conceded.

'Then I need detain you no longer,' she said, rising to her feet. 'You have clearly made a ghastly mistake in coming here.'

'I blame Hugh Lucifer for that,' said Keedy under his breath.

'We are sorry to have disturbed you unnecessarily,' said Marmion, getting up from the sofa. 'Before we go, however, might I ask a favour?'

'What is it?' she asked, warily.

'Might we see a photograph of your husband?'

She bridled. 'Why on earth should you want to do that?'

'I'd be interested, that's all.'

'So would I,' added Keedy, standing up.

'Well,' she said, haughtily, 'I take exception to that request. Are you in the habit of invading people's privacy and asking to see family photographs? This really is intolerable. May I ask the name of your superior?'

'It's Superintendent Chatfield,' said Marmion.

'I'll need the address,' she said, crossing to a bureau and taking a notepad and pencil out of the top drawer. 'I'm ready, Inspector.'

Feeling chastened, Marmion gave her the full address. If she complained about their behaviour, there would be repercussions at Scotland Yard. He was already fearing the superintendent's reaction to the fact that they had returned empty-handed from Brighton. A letter from Mrs Langford would give Chatfield even more reason to berate them.

Once she had the details she requested, her manner softened slightly.

'I refuse to show you any photographs of myself and my husband,' she said, 'because they are private. But, if you must see what he looks like, I'll show you this one.' She took a framed photograph from the top of the piano. 'This appeared in one of the local newspapers.' She handed it to Marmion. 'My husband is the one in the captain's uniform.'

They looked at the photograph. It showed a group of men on the deck of a ship. Marmion picked out Captain Langford at once. He was a big, broad-shouldered man with a full beard. His upright stance gave him an air of authority.

'Are you satisfied now?' she asked, extending a hand.

'Yes, we are, Mrs Langford,' said Marmion, returning the photograph. 'I apologise for our mistake in coming here. We'll trespass on you no longer.'

After mumbling their goodbyes, he and Keedy left the house. As they got into the back of the waiting taxi, Marmion held up repentant hands.

'Yes, I know,' he said. 'It was my idea to come here.'

'Does that mean you'll take all the punishment from Chat?'

'No, it doesn't because I'm hoping we'll have more luck at the hospital. We know for certain that Tindall lived and worked down here in Sussex. He's bound to have left large footprints. Let's find them.'

CHAPTER EIGHT

Evenings were short for Ada Hobbes. Instead of being able to linger beside the fire and do some more knitting, she had to be in bed early so that she had a decent night's sleep before leaving the house at four the next morning. Her sister, Kathleen, had advised her to take a day off but Ada felt duty-bound to keep to her routine. In any case, if she failed to turn up, offices would not be cleaned and those who worked there would be justifiably livid. She winced at the thought that her name would be taken in vain. Her job was at stake and, since she relied on the money, she simply had to abide by her contract. Finding similar work elsewhere would be difficult for her. There was a great deal of competition, especially from younger women who would have more appeal to employers because they appeared stronger.

The fire had dwindled to a few glowing ashes, but she nevertheless put the fireguard in place. Ada slowly got herself ready for bed, shivering in the cold as she took off her clothes and put on her nightdress. Climbing into bed, she huddled under the sheets. At the end of a tiring day, she usually fell asleep quickly but there was no hope of her doing that now. The memory of what she had seen in Dr Tindall's house was still too fresh and painful. Ada believed that it would stay at the forefront of her mind until the police caught whoever was responsible for the crime.

She recalled the moment when she had fed a shilling in the gas meter. It had triggered a memory of something that might – just might, she prayed – be of some use to the police. Did she dare pass it on? Ada was unsure if she had the courage to do so. It was such a trivial incident that it should perhaps be best forgotten. The last thing she wanted to do was to invite Sergeant Keedy's scorn. He had been good to her, treating her gently and sending her home in the police car. If she bothered him with useless information, he might be less tolerant. The impulse she had felt beside the gas stove had to be suppressed and forgotten. Ada decided that she would need all her strength to fight off her demons in the night.

The reporters who swooped on Edmonton Military Hospital found little to fill their columns. Major Palmer-Loach gave them short shrift. He treated them with brisk politeness but refused to speculate on the possible motives behind the murder of one of his surgeons. When they tried to apply pressure on him, he strolled across to the door and held it open.

'A war is on,' he told them. 'Look in any of my wards and you'll see the results of it. Those wounded soldiers out there are my primary concern. If you have any more questions about Dr Tindall, please address them to Inspector Marmion.' He raised his voice. 'Good day to you, gentlemen.'

They trooped out resentfully. Neil Irvine watched them go. When the door had been closed behind them, he turned to Palmer-Loach.

'That was masterly, Howard.'

'Thank you.'

'You gave absolutely nothing away.'

'Inspector Marmion warned me to be economical with the facts.'

'You followed his advice to the letter.'

Irvine was a senior doctor in the hospital's medical team. He was a thin, dark, gangly man in his forties with a Scots accent. He was also Palmer-Loach's best friend. When alone together, they were completely at ease with each other.

'Out with it,' said Irvine, jocularly.

'Out with what?'

'Come on, Howard. I've known you long enough to be able to read the expression on your face. You hid something important from those reporters. Are you proposing to hide it from me as well?'

'No, of course not – I can trust you.'

'I'm all ears.'

The major told him about Marmion's telephone call regarding the futile search for Tindall's parents. They were not, after all, living at the address provided and they had never done so. Palmer-Loach was fuming.

'He had the gall to mislead us,' he said.

'Perhaps he had a good reason to do so,' suggested the other. 'Some of us are ashamed of our parents or have fallen out with them. I was guilty of both. When I decided to live and work in England, they accused me of betraying my country. In fact, I just wanted to put distance between me and them.'

'The inspector wonders if Tindall was a true Scot.'

'Oh, there's no doubt about that.'

'Why do you say that?'

'Because we once had a row about football,' said Irvine. 'I'm a Glaswegian and my loyalty is to Rangers. Tindall was a diehard Celtic fan. He was born within a mile of their ground.'

'If you're both from the same city, why don't you have the same accent?'

'I fancy that snobbery comes into it somehow, Howard. When I moved to England, I emphasised my accent – George did his best to lose his. He wanted to fit in. I chose a Scots wife, and he married an Englishwoman.' His eyes twinkled. 'That's when the rot set in.'

'I'll ignore that jibe,' said the major, good-naturedly. 'I'm just annoyed with myself for trusting the man.'

'What you trusted were his surgical skills and they were real. It's why you took him on in the first place, Howard.'

'True. He was exactly what we needed at the time.'

'Remember that,' said Irvine. 'Let these detectives explore his private life. You have other priorities.'

'I do, Neil,' said the other, seriously. 'To start with, I've got the job of replacing him with someone of equivalent ability. That's one heck of a challenge.'

When he was told which hospital they wanted, the taxi driver seized the opportunity to acquaint them with the various options available to them.

'Are you sure it's the Royal Sussex?' he asked.

'Yes,' said Marmion.

'The Kitchener Indian Hospital is more interesting. They have over two thousand beds in there. When the first load of wounded soldiers from the

Indian regiments were shipped back to Brighton, there were big crowds at the dock to give them a welcome. Sir William Gentle was there in person.'

'Who is he?'

'He's the chief constable.'

'Do we need to be told all this?' complained Keedy.

'You're detectives, aren't you?' retorted the driver. 'Gathering facts is what you do, sir. It's the reason I'm giving them to you. Brighton is a town of hospitals, you see. The Royal Pavilion, the Dome and the Corn Exchange have all been turned into hospitals and so have other places. Then, of course, there's the French Convalescent Home. Don't forget that.'

The driver rambled on, unaware of the fact that neither of his passengers was listening. When they reached their hospital of choice, Marmion paid the fare and the two of them got out of the vehicle. The Royal Sussex County Hospital had been founded almost ninety years earlier and grown steadily ever since, becoming an accretion of buildings of varying shapes and sizes. Seen in silhouette against a dark sky, it looked rather forbidding. Marmion and Keedy headed for the main entrance.

'I'm beginning to wish we hadn't come here,' said Keedy.

'Don't be such a pessimist, Joe.'

'Why did Tindall give everyone a fake address in Brighton?'

'It wasn't fake,' said Marmion. 'It was all too real. Unfortunately, Dr Tindall never actually lived there. So why pretend that he had? It's near the top of the list of questions for which I want answers.'

'We're groping in the dark.'

'No, we're not.' When they reached the main door, Marmion opened it and light flooded out. 'There you are,' he said with a chuckle. 'Things are starting to brighten up already.'

* * *

Ellen Marmion had been relishing her daughter's visit so much that she had allowed something important to slip her mind. When she finally remembered what it was, she sat up guiltily on the sofa.

'Oh,' she said, 'I forgot something. Mrs Halliday is ready for you.'

'There's no great hurry, Mummy. We have weeks and weeks yet.'

'Making a wedding dress takes time, Alice. She must take measurements. Then you must choose the material. After that, there'll be a series of fittings.'

'I'll see Mrs Halliday next time I'm here.'

'And when will that be?'

'I don't know,' said Alice.

'You can't muck Minnie Halliday about,' warned her mother. 'You're not the only one on her list, remember. There will be quite a few weddings coming up in the new year. You need to see her soon. On the other hand,' she added with a grin, 'perhaps you want to order your dress from somewhere in the West End.'

Alice spluttered. 'How on earth would I pay for it?'

'You wouldn't. That's why we asked Minnie Halliday to make it.'

'Don't keep on at me. I know that I've been dragging my feet and I'm sorry. What about one day next week?' she said, mentally consulting her diary. 'I finish early on Thursday.'

Ellen was content. 'Let's settle for that, then. I'll tell her.' Her face clouded. 'There's still the thorny problem of Paul to consider.'

'He won't turn up, Mummy.'

'He might.'

'But he has no idea of the date of the wedding,' said Alice, 'and even if he did, he'd never dream of coming.'

'Just in case he does . . .'

'No, I won't even think about it.'

'I'm simply looking ahead, Alice.'

'Well, please don't bother.'

'It was your father's idea. He wants to cover every possibility.'

'Paul ignored our birthdays and didn't even bother to send a Christmas card. What else does he have to do to prove that he's left for good?'

Ellen bit her lip. 'You never know …'

'I do know, Mummy, and so do you in your heart. We should accept the truth. You no longer have a son, and I don't have a brother. In fact, I'm doing my best to pretend that he never existed.'

Wells was a cathedral city in the heart of Somerset. Reputedly the smallest city in England, it had a plethora of historic buildings, a bewitching charm and an air of tranquillity. During the day, it functioned in the same unhurried way it had done for centuries. Once engulfed by evening shadows, however, it obeyed the rules, dousing its lights and closing its curtains. Most people stayed in their houses or cottages, but a group of regulars could always be found at the City Arms in the high street. Seated around a blazing log fire, the men would talk endlessly about the progress of the war, breaking off from time to time to complain once more that their beer and cider had been watered by government decree.

That evening, it was different. There was a stranger in the bar. He was a stocky young man with a face half-hidden behind a ragged beard. Arriving in Wells on foot, he had come into the pub, dropped his haversack on to a settle and ordered a pint of cider. He had ignored the muttered welcomes of the regulars and sat down with his tankard held firm. In less than ten minutes, he had emptied it and put it on the table with a thud. Shortly after that, he had fallen asleep. Complaints soon surfaced. The newcomer had brought a stink into the pub. Dressed in tattered clothes, he looked like a tramp who had only come in to get warm. Worst of all, he was an interloper, disturbing the usual flow of conversation.

At length, the landlord was forced to act. He shook the young man's shoulder.

'Wake up, sir,' he said.

'Eh?' grunted the other, stirring. 'What's up?'

'If you've finished drinking, sir, it's time to go.'

'Piss off!'

'I'm asking you nicely,' said the landlord, injecting a note of warning. 'If you want to sleep, you'll have to pay for a room.'

But the words went unheard. The stranger had nodded off again. There was a barrage of protests from the regulars. The landlord waved them into silence.

'Leave him be,' he said. 'This is a job for the police.'

Their visit to the Royal Sussex County Hospital was productive. Its administrator was Cecil Wetherbridge, a stringy man of middle years with a straight back and close-cropped fair hair. His voice had a military authority to it. When he heard why the detectives had come, he was anxious to help. He pulled a file out of the cabinet and handed it over. As a result, Marmion and Keedy discovered that George Douglas Tindall had been born in Glasgow then educated privately in Edinburgh before going on to study medicine at St Thomas's Hospital in London. He had then moved on to a hospital in Kent and, when he had gained enough experience as a doctor, had set his sights on becoming a surgeon.

'His progress was quick and well deserved,' said Wetherbridge. 'By the time he came here, he'd worked at three other hospitals. Before the war broke out, he had become an orthopaedic surgeon but, as soon as wounded soldiers poured in here in large numbers, he had to turn his hand to anything.'

'How well did you know him?' asked Marmion.

'Not very well at all,' replied the other. 'I came here early in 1915 and he left a few months after that.' He grinned. 'I like to think that the two events were unrelated. In fact, we got on extremely well and I was sorry to lose him. But he had this urge to work in a hospital at the front and deal with casualties in need of immediate surgery.'

'He came back after six months or so, didn't he?'

'Yes, Inspector.'

'Why was that?'

'Personal reasons,' said Wetherbridge. 'His wife had been ailing for some time and began to go downhill rather fast. Dr Tindall took time off to nurse her.'

'Did you ever meet her?' asked Keedy.

'No, I didn't. When you work flat out during a crisis, you have little time for a social life. I have enough trouble meeting my own wife, let alone someone else's.'

'When he did work here, where did he live?'

'Didn't you see an address in the file?'

'Yes, but it's a flat here in the town.'

'We thought that he had a house closer to Worthing,' said Marmion.

'That's news to me, Inspector,' said Wetherbridge.

'When we called there earlier, we were told that they had never heard of Dr Tindall. Why should he provide false information like that?'

'It's uncharacteristic of him.'

'What about the flat?' asked Keedy. 'Are you sure that he lived there?'

'Oh, yes. I went there once. It was not all that far away and very comfortable. Dr Tindall had high standards.'

'We know. We saw his house in Edmonton.'

'It's odd,' said Marmion, leafing through the file. 'There's no mention of a house in this area. Where was his wife living at that time?'

'He mentioned a property in Kent on one occasion,' recalled Wetherbridge, 'but I fancy that it might have belonged to his wife's parents. They looked after her while he was away.'

'It would be useful to have that address. There are far too many loose ends in this case,' Marmion told him, handing back the file.

'We need to speak to a family member of some description,' added Keedy. 'At the moment, it seems, we're chasing shadows.'

Though she had seen it many times, Alice was always pleased to study the wedding photographs in the family album. Her parents looked impossibly young as they stood in the church porch. The bridegroom wore his best suit while the bride was in her wedding dress. Seated beside her mother, Alice picked out a detail.

'Your hair was much darker then, Mummy.'

'It was the same colour as yours.'

'I just wish that Daddy could have looked a bit smarter.'

'He wasn't your father at that point,' Ellen pointed out, 'and I loved him for his kindness and his crinkly eyes, not for the way he wore his clothes. Whenever he puts on a suit, it always manages to look crumpled somehow.'

'Why were there so few people at the service?'

'It was all we could afford, Alice. Times were hard for people like us. My father had scrimped and saved to pay for everything.'

'Well, that's not something Daddy will have to do on his own. Joe and I are insisting on making our contribution, whatever he may say.'

'You may have a job getting your father to accept it.'

'We've made up our minds.'

'So has he.'

Alice flipped over the pages until she came to a sequence of photographs of herself and her brother as toddlers. She stopped to scrutinise a snap of the two of them, standing on a sandy beach and wearing sun hats.

'Did we really look like that?' she wondered.

'Yes, you were angelic at that age.'

Alice laughed. 'Nobody would say that about me now.'

'You were such a biddable child.'

'What about Paul?'

'He behaved himself most of the time. In fact, he could be quite placid. He's a picture of innocence in this photo,' said Ellen, studying it. 'You'd never think that he'd turn out the way that he did.'

It took three of them to overpower him. In response to the landlord's summons, Constable Pellew, a brawny man in his thirties, was sent to the City Arms. Grabbing the shoulder of the sleeping customer, he shook him rudely awake.

'Wake up, sir,' he shouted. 'Time to go.'

'Get off me!' yelled the other, rising to his feet and pushing him away. 'I'm not going anywhere.'

'Oh, yes, you are,' said Pellew, grabbing him by the collar.

'Let go!'

'You're coming with me. sir.'

'Take your hands off me, you fat bastard!'

'I'm placing you under arrest.'

The young man picked up the glass tankard and swung it at him.

Pellew moved his head quickly out of the way, but he still had to take a glancing blow on his cheek that ripped the skin away. It made him release his hold immediately.

'Who's next?' challenged the stranger, brandishing the tankard.

'Put it down,' ordered the landlord, waving a fist.

'Make me.'

Blood was trickling down the side of Pellew's cheek, but he did not back off. Instead, he got behind the young man and put an arm around his neck. It was the signal for the landlord to move in, grab the tankard and twist it out of the customer's hand. In return, he was given a sharp kick in the leg. The young man went berserk, pummelling the policeman with his elbows to get free, then swinging punches at random. There was uproar. Pellew and the landlord got hold of him again, then a third man joined in. Their quarry was held but by no means subdued. The moment that the policeman tried to reach for his handcuffs, the stranger fought like mad, kicking over a table and sending half-full tankards crashing to the floor. He was cursing at the top of his voice and spitting at anyone who came within range.

Constable Pellew had had enough. Taking out his truncheon, he felled him with one blow to the head. As the troublemaker slumped to the ground, the policeman turned to the landlord.

'When I've locked this maniac up,' he said, 'I'll be back for a free pint.'

Neither Marmion nor Keedy could stop yawning. The train to London stopped at almost every station on the way. The one benefit was that they had an empty compartment in which to discuss what they would tell the superintendent.

'He'll crucify us,' said Keedy.

'Chat is not that vindictive.'

'We've wasted time and money on a jaunt to the seaside.'

'I see it differently,' said Marmion, trying to raise his own spirits as well as those of his companion. 'It was a valuable fact-finding mission. We learnt things about Dr Tindall that we'd never have got from anywhere else.'

'All we learnt is that he was a compulsive liar who gave people the addresses of houses where he didn't actually live.'

'He lived in the flat in Brighton. We verified that. When we called there, the people who now own it said they bought it from him. Tindall was capable of honesty sometimes.'

'What did you think of it?'

'I was rather envious, Joe.'

'So was I,' said Keedy. 'It's the sort of place Alice and I would love to move into. There was so much space. Why did Tindall need a place of that size?'

'I can't answer that.'

'What puzzles me is the information in that file. Why didn't you get the same details at the hospital in Edmonton?'

'When the major searched for an orthopaedic surgeon, he got an application from Tindall, complete with wonderful references from two hospitals. The major took him on trust and never regretted it.'

'He's regretting it now.'

'Like us, he's learning about Tindall's defects.'

'He didn't just tell lies, he told whoppers.'

'Somehow he got away with it.'

'And what made him claim he owned Hipwell Manor?'

'It's too late to ask him.'

The train slowed, then came to a sudden halt, jerking them both forward.

'We should have come by car,' said Keedy.

'We'd have missed the fun of being with those soldiers on the way there. They were brave lads.'

'Yes, but only because they don't know what they'll find over there.'

'It'll change their lives for ever.'

'That's what it did for Paul.'

'Keep him out of this, Joe,' said Marmion, seriously. 'There are times when I can't bear thinking about him. Concentrate on the pleasure of our return to Scotland Yard. I bet that Chat is pacing up and down his office right now, wondering where his favourite detectives have gone.'

Badgered by the commissioner, Claude Chatfield was, in fact, standing behind his desk, trying to persuade his superior that headway had been made. Sir Edward Henry was not convinced. He needed hard evidence to appease the War Office. Dr Tindall had been an asset to the army. He had saved many lives and made many others more bearable thanks to his surgical expertise. Whoever had killed him had to be called to account.

'What did they find out in Brighton?' asked the commissioner.

'They have yet to return, Sir Edward.'

'They might have telephoned you.'

'They might indeed,' said Chatfield with a low growl. 'I intend to ask them why it never crossed their minds.'

'I'll be here until late.'

'So will I.'

'Then I expect to hear from you in due course.'

'Once I have their report, I'll come straight to your office.'

The commissioner took his leave and Chatfield was alone at last. He hated being put under pressure. Though he felt unfairly criticised, he had things to do. Instead of fretting about the murder investigation, he addressed his mind to the mass of paperwork on his desk. Since he had responsibility for other cases, there was a great deal to process. He was soon beavering away.

Constable Pellew did not stand on ceremony. With the help of the landlord, he dragged the semi-conscious stranger to the police station. Still in handcuffs, the prisoner was thrown into a cell. Sergeant Dear, the duty officer, looked at his colleague.

'You've got a bruise on your cheek,' he noted, 'and a spot of blood.'

'He caught me with a beer tankard,' said Pellew.

'It was my fault,' volunteered the landlord. 'I should have refused to serve him. I could see that he might cause trouble.'

'He fought like a demon. I had to use my staff in the end. When he wakes up, he'll have a lovely big lump on the back of his head.'

'Who is he?' asked Dear.

'You'll have to look in here, Sarge.'

Pellew handed over the prisoner's haversack and Dear began to take out the meagre belongings inside it. Among a motley collection of items was a long knife.

'You were lucky, Dave,' he said. 'He might have pulled this on you.'

'We'll have a lot to charge him with,' said Pellew. 'And if he turns out to be a deserter from the army, he'll be sentenced to death.'

The landlord nodded. 'It's no more than he deserves.'

'He was arrested in the right place,' observed Dear. 'The City Arms used to be the gaol in the old days. Pity you don't still have cells there.'

When he listened to their report, the superintendent's expression changed from one of exasperation to one of sheer incredulity. By the

112

time that Marmion had finished his account, Chatfield was agog.

'Is that all you achieved?' he asked.

'We believe that we uncovered new and valuable intelligence, sir.'

'I agree,' said Keedy. 'Going to Brighton was a wise decision.'

'Let me deal with your mistake first, Sergeant' said Chatfield. 'You charged off – without asking my permission – simply because you'd picked up some bogus information from a tailor in Savile Row.'

'It didn't sound bogus, sir.'

'Let me finish, Sergeant.'

'That was the address Dr Tindall had given them.'

'Did it never occur to you that there was a much easier means of finding out the correct address? All you had to do was to ask the tailor for the name of the doctor's bank. It would have been simple for him to tell you from which bank the cheques were drawn. Even someone as slippery as Tindall,' he argued, 'would have to be honest with his bank manager.'

'I did ask for his bank details,' said Keedy, 'but he always paid in cash.'

Chatfield looked glum. 'Oh, I see.'

'The sergeant did well,' said Marmion, 'and our visit to Brighton did yield results. The background information we found about the murder victim was far more comprehensive than anything the Edmonton Military Hospital could supply. In fact,' he went on, 'we learnt something that may prove to be highly relevant.'

'What was it, Inspector?'

'He had private wealth, sir. He could indulge his taste in expensive clothing and in other things. That confirms what Major Palmer-Loach told me about him. Tindall was fully committed as a doctor. Most people as well off as him would be tempted to seek a more pampered and independent life.'

'We're dealing with a very unusual man,' said Keedy.

'I had the commissioner in here earlier,' Chatfield told them. 'He thinks you should spend less time on the doctor and much more on the people who killed him. So far you have yet to uncover a motive for his murder.'

'The inspector just gave you one, sir. Dr Tindall was a wealthy man.'

'That's right,' said Marmion. 'His safe had been emptied.'

'You told me earlier in the day that the theft was incidental,' Chatfield reminded him. 'Their primary purpose was a vicious murder.'

'I was only speculating.'

'Then perhaps you'd omit any further speculation and concentrate on the search for those villains. Thieves would have watched and waited, choosing a time to break into the house when it was unoccupied. These men came for blood.'

'We had reached the same conclusion,' said Marmion.

'Then let us forget about wasteful visits to Brighton, shall we?' said Chatfield. 'Or to any other addresses that may lead you astray.' He checked his watch. 'It's almost midnight. That means the pair of you have been involved in this investigation for somewhere in the region of sixteen hours.'

'Don't worry,' said Keedy. 'We'll apply for overtime.'

'Spare me your flippancy, Sergeant.'

'What I meant was that time is immaterial on a case like this. The inspector and I will work until the cows come home.'

'I'd prefer you to work until you get positive results.'

'We will, Inspector,' said Marmion. 'This case intrigues us.'

'Well, it's proving to be a flaming nuisance to me,' said Chatfield. 'I've got the combined weight of the commissioner and the War Office on my back – and I don't like it! Get them off!'

CHAPTER NINE

Though Alice Marmion woke early the next day, she was too late to catch sight of her father. He had been up over an hour before her and left the house the moment he had finished his breakfast. Marmion had asked Ellen to pass on his apologies to his daughter for not being able to spend time with her.

'When did Daddy come home?' asked Alice.

'It was past midnight. That's all I know.'

'Joe was right. It's a case that will take up all their time.'

'It pushes everything else aside,' said Ellen.

'Did you never have qualms about marrying a policeman?'

'Yes, but they were never about him working long hours. I was afraid that he might get seriously hurt. His own father was killed while on duty, remember. Anyone who tries to police a city like this is putting himself in danger. When he was in uniform, I was terrified that your father would be injured.'

'Daddy can look after himself. Besides, he was never on patrol alone.'

'That didn't stop me worrying, Alice.'

'The irony is that the streets are much safer now. Thanks to the war, many of the worst criminals in London joined the army and went abroad. Unfortunately,' she added, 'so did a lot of young police officers. I'm glad Joe was not among them.'

'He and your father went to Brighton yesterday.'

'Why?'

'He didn't have time to tell me. Anyway,' said Ellen, 'let's forget about them and think about your trip to the West End.'

Alice shuddered. 'I'm dreading it.'

'Once you're there, I'm sure you'll enjoy it.'

'Oh, I'll enjoy being part of a crowd and looking in shop windows. I always love that part. But I'd love it even more if I was not saddled with Iris.'

'It was your idea, Alice.'

'Yes, I know and I'm still glad that the invitation gave her so much pleasure. It's just that she will be expecting to get far too much out of today.'

'And you're expecting to get too little.'

'I'm afraid so.' Alice looked at the clock on the mantelpiece. 'Oh, I must be off,' she said, rising from her chair.

'I'll come with you to the bus stop,' said Ellen, getting up.

'In that case, we can take the long way there.'

'Why should we do that?'

'Because we'll go right past Mrs Redwood's house,' said Alice, thrusting out her chin. 'If we bump into her, I'll have a few choice words to say.'

116

'Don't be ridiculous.'

'I'm not having her upsetting you, Mummy.'

'It was nothing.'

'Oh, yes it was. I know when you've been wounded.'

'I've got over it now.'

'Mrs Redwood needled you about Paul.'

'So what?'

'It must have hurt you, Mummy.'

'It did – and it didn't.'

'I don't understand.'

'Then you've obviously forgotten what you told me yesterday,' said Ellen. 'You don't have a brother named Paul any more, and I don't have a son of the same name. He vanished into thin air. No matter what Mrs Redwood says about him, it will not hurt me. Come on,' she said, giving Alice a hug. 'We'll go the shorter way to the bus stop.'

When he arrived at the police station in Wells, Constable Pellew found that Sergeant Dear was already there. The latter looked up from the pile of papers on his desk and they exchanged greetings. The sergeant noticed the purple bruise on the newcomer's face and the sticking plaster over part of it. Pellew nodded towards the cells.

'How did he behave last night?'

'He didn't. I'm told that he yelled his head off.'

'Who was on duty?'

'Constable Myler.'

'Frank Myler wouldn't stand for any nonsense.'

'You're right,' said Dear. 'He tried being reasonable but that didn't work so he threatened him. The prisoner gave him a real mouthful. Frank was not standing for that. He gave him another tap and knocked him out. That shut his gob.'

'What's the prisoner doing now?'

'He's fast asleep on his bed. I'm just checking through these lists,' said the sergeant, indicating the papers in front of him. 'I'm starting with army deserters. If he's not on any of these – and my guess is that he will be – then I'll have a go at the list of missing persons.'

'Why bother, Sarge?'

'It's my job.'

'You've seen the way he behaves,' said Pellew. 'He's wild and dangerous. Who would want someone like him back in their family? They'd be glad that the maniac had left home.'

After reporting to the superintendent, Marmion and Keedy were driven to the house once more. They were pleased to see a uniformed policeman on duty outside the front door. Letting themselves in with the key, they went slowly from room to room, searching for clues they might have missed on the previous day.

'Someone ought to clear up that mess in the room off the kitchen,' said Keedy. 'It will never sell if it's left in that state.'

'Does that mean you're interested in buying it, Joe?'

Keedy laughed mirthlessly. 'Oh, yes, I'll put in an offer tomorrow.'

'Then you must be on a better rate of pay than me.'

'What me and Alice want is a terraced house with a small garden at the back. The trouble is that we never have a chance to search for it together.'

'Look in the windows of estate agents.'

'They only shove the prices up so that they can get a good commission. We'd prefer a private sale. That means looking at adverts in the paper. That way we'd be dealing with the owner of a property and not a pushy estate agent.'

'Take Alice with you. She's good at haggling.'

'Chance would be a fine thing, Harv.'

'Then let's try to put this case to bed as quickly as we can,' said Marmion. 'The pair of you can then go house-hunting properly.'

They went upstairs and into the master bedroom. Keedy was thoughtful.

'He must have been asleep in here when they got into the house,' he said.

'How? The doors were securely locked.'

'Your guess is as good as mine.'

'Then let me try this idea,' suggested Marmion. 'Suppose that they didn't break in at all.'

'How else could they have got in?'

'There's one obvious way.'

'What is it?'

'Dr Tindall may have invited them in.'

'That's a barmy idea,' said Keedy.

'Is it? The major told me that Tindall sometimes worked at night. Suppose that there was an emergency and they needed him. What would they do?'

'Well, I daresay that they'd ring him up.'

'How would he get to the hospital?'

'How did he get there when he was still alive?'

'They must have sent transport.'

'A taxi, do you mean?'

'Well, they'd hardly send an ambulance, would they?' said Marmion. 'You must have noticed the motorbikes at the hospital. They came in and out all the time.'

'Yes,' said Keedy, 'but they were driven by soldiers.'

'All you need is a khaki uniform, and you'd look just like a soldier.'

'I suppose that's true.'

'A motorbike can carry two people. Perhaps that was how Tindall expected to get to the hospital.'

'Wait a moment,' said Keedy. 'Neither of the motorbikes came into this avenue. They were parked around the corner.'

'The killers didn't want to rouse the neighbours.'

'Wouldn't the doctor have been listening out for the sound?'

'All he knew – if I'm right – was that someone was coming to pick him up. When he heard a knock on the door, he opened it. Before he could protest, he was overpowered.'

Keedy pondered. Unlikely as the theory had seemed at first, it now had the ring of possibility. He was about to accept it when he spotted a problem.

'Are you saying that they rang the house first to alert him?'

'Yes, Joe. That's what they must have done.'

'How did they get hold of his number?'

'Ah,' said Marmion, sobered. 'I didn't think of that.'

Attending to the fire was an effort for Kathleen Paget. As she struggled to get up off her knees, she winced at the pain.

'My arthritis is worse than ever this morning, Alf.'

Her husband gave a grunt and shifted his pipe to the other side of his mouth. As soon as she moved out of the way, the dog resumed its position on the hearth. She headed for the kitchen.

'I'll put the kettle on.'

She was getting the cups off their hooks when there was a knock on the door.

'That sounds like the milkman,' she muttered to herself.

Kathleen went slowly along the passageway and opened the door. She was surprised to find her sister standing outside, looking anxious.

'I didn't expect to see you today, Ada,' she said.

'I felt I had to come.'

'Did you go to work?'

'Yes,' said Ada, 'I've not long finished. It's been preying on my mind.'

'What has?'

'I had to tell someone, Kathy.'

Her sister stood aside. They went into the kitchen where the kettle was beginning to sing. Kathleen was concerned.

'You don't look well, Ada. I told you to take a day off for once.'

'I couldn't do that. I had to keep my mind occupied.'

'Why?'

'It was something that happened at the doctor's house, you see.'

Forgetting about the tea, Kathleen sat opposite her at the table. Her sister had weathered many setbacks in her life and shown remarkable courage. Yet she was now pale and dithering. Something was amiss.

'Take a deep breath,' advised Kathleen, 'then tell me what's happened.'

'I put a shilling in the gas meter yesterday.'

'That's never upset you before, Ada.'

'Listen to me,' pleaded her sister. 'I need your help. It made me think of something that happened earlier in the week – only it wasn't my gas meter then.'

'You've lost me.'

'It was in the doctor's house. I was cleaning the kitchen when a man came to read the gas meter. He was dressed like the one who comes to read mine, so I let him in and thought no more of it.'

'The doctor's meter is under the stairs, isn't it?'

'Yes, it is.'

'What did you do while he was there?'

'I got on with my work.'

'Then what happened?'

'After a couple of minutes – maybe more – he called to say he was leaving. I heard the front door open and shut.'

'And that's it?'

'Yes, it is. Did I do the right thing, Kathy?'

'I'd have done the same as you,' said the other, 'except that I'd have stayed to keep an eye on him. It doesn't take long to read a meter, does it? When someone comes to read ours, he's in and out in less than a minute.'

'I hardly slept last night, thinking about it.'

'You must tell the police.'

'I'm afraid that I might be wasting their time.'

'Think what might happen if you don't mention it. It could be evidence, Ada.' She got up from the table. 'Let's forget about the tea.'

'Why?'

'Because we're going to the police station. Let me put my coat on.'

'I'll be too nervous to say a word.'

'No, you won't,' said her sister. 'You were the one who rang the police yesterday and they were glad that you did. That man who read the meter could be quite innocent, of course, but I have my suspicions. Let's go, Ada.'

Because they wanted to make an early start, the two friends had arranged to meet outside Swan and Edgar at ten o'clock. Alice Marmion was late but there was no complaint from Iris Goodliffe. Standing on the corner, she was enjoying the sight of a busy Piccadilly Circus and Regent Street. More to the point, she was wearing her best clothes and had no duties

122

to perform in the policewoman's uniform she hated.

'Alice!' she cried, waving to her friend. 'Over here!'

Fighting her way through the crowd, Alice arrived and greeted her with a hug.

When she saw the beatific smile on Iris's face, she forgot her reservations about the outing. She was simply pleased to be able to give her friend so much joy.

'How long have you been here, Iris?' she asked.

'Oh, I don't know – twenty minutes, maybe?'

'I'm sorry to have kept you.'

'I don't mind. Watching people go past has been fascinating. Three soldiers came earlier,' said Iris, beaming. 'One of them whistled at me.'

'Were they British or American?'

'British, of course. I'd have looked the other way if they'd been American.'

'They're our allies, Iris.'

'I know, but they act as if London belongs to them.'

'It belongs to us today,' said Alice.

'Then we must savour every single moment of it,' said Iris, giggling. 'Now then, where do we start?'

'Right here in Swan and Edgar, I think. We can have endless fun looking at things we could never afford. After that, we'll work our way up Regent Street then visit all the big stores in Oxford Street.'

'I must buy something as a souvenir – and a new dress, of course.'

'I'm in search of Christmas presents.'

'What have you got in mind for Joe?'

Alice grinned. 'That's between me and him.'

* * *

When Pellew took him his breakfast, he thought that the prisoner was asleep. The latter was curled up under a blanket on the wooden board that acted as his bed. After unlocking the door, Pellew went into the cell with a tray in his hands.

'Wake up,' he called. 'I've brought you some grub.'

The prisoner suddenly came to life, throwing off the blanket and leaping up to knock the tray out of the constable's arms. Pushing him aside, he ran through the open door and along a short corridor until he reached another door. He flung that open and found his escape route blocked. Sergeant Dear stood there with his arms folded and an eyebrow arched.

'Where d'you think you're going, lad?' he asked.

Before the prisoner could work out what to do, he was seized from behind, lifted off his feet and hurled back to his cell. The door was locked behind him. On the floor, now empty, lay the tin teacup. Beside it was the sandwich that Pellew had deliberately stamped on. He glared at the prisoner.

'That's the last food you'll get all day,' he warned.

He ignored the howls of rage that came through the bars at him.

Moments after he had answered the telephone in Tindall's house, Marmion's face lit up. He was soon writing something down. Keedy wondered why the inspector had become so animated. Eventually, Marmion put the receiver down.

'Let me guess,' said Keedy. 'It was Chat, offering us a pay rise.'

'You're wide of the mark, Joe.'

'Who was on the other end of the line?'

'It was someone from the local constabulary,' said Marmion. 'Mrs Hobbes told them she might have some useful information to give us.

They, in turn, contacted Chat who gave them this number.'

'What is this useful information?'

'That's what you're going to find out. She's over at her sister's. Get the driver to take you to Mrs Paget's house and bring Mrs Hobbes back here as quickly as you can.'

'You sound optimistic.'

'Let's just say that I'm … more than hopeful.'

Keedy let himself out and gave orders to the driver. The car pulled away. In little over ten minutes, it was back again. Marmion watched the sergeant helping Ada Hobbes out of the vehicle. The inspector held the door open for them to walk straight into the house. The three of them adjourned to the lounge. While the detectives sank into the sofa, Ada was perched on the edge of an armchair, looking around as if she feared being caught trespassing.

'What is it that you want to tell us, Mrs Hobbes?' asked Marmion.

'I could be mistaken,' she said, nervously.

'We're grateful to you for coming forward.'

'It was Kathy's doing.'

'I don't know the full details,' said Keedy. 'I thought we should hear them together. Right, Mrs Hobbes,' he continued. 'Tell your story.'

'Well,' she said, 'it was when I put a shilling in my gas meter …'

They listened patiently as she recounted the visit to the house of a man claiming that he had come to read the gas meter. Nothing about him aroused any suspicion at the time. In retrospect, however, she wondered if she should have been more watchful. While she spoke, Keedy took notes.

The moment she had finished, Marmion took over.

'Did you mention this man to Dr Tindall?'

'Yes, I did, Inspector. He said that I did the right thing.'

'We can soon find out if he was an employee of the Gas Board.'

'How?' she asked in surprise.

'If he was on his rounds,' said Marmion, 'he'd have called at each house in turn.' He looked at Keedy. 'Sergeant, will you please speak to Mr and Mrs Crowe next door to see if they had a visit from him that day?'

Keedy was on his feet at once. 'Just to make sure,' he said, 'I'll check the neighbours on the other side of the house as well.'

'Good idea.'

As soon as the sergeant had gone, Marmion tried to bolster Ada's confidence.

'Thank you so much for getting in touch with us, Mrs Hobbes.'

'It was my sister's idea, really.'

'You were the one who remembered the incident and had the sense to tell Mrs Paget about it. I wanted to speak to you here because you can show us exactly what you were doing while this man was on the premises.'

'Kathy thinks he was here far too long.'

'If that's the case, he came with an ulterior motive.'

Her face went blank. 'What's that?'

'He wanted to see the house from the inside.'

'Oh, I do feel guilty, Inspector,' she said. 'I shouldn't have let him in.'

'Can you describe him?'

'Well, let me think. He was a nice, good-looking man with a beard.'

'How old was he?'

'Oh, in his fifties, I'd say.'

'What else can you tell me about him, Mrs Hobbes?'

Ada struggled hard to chisel a few details out of her memory.

When he returned, Keedy came back into the house with a quiet smile.

'Well?' said Marmion.

'Nobody called to read the meter at the houses on either side. According to Mr Crowe, the man usually calls near the end of the month. Well done, Mrs Hobbes,' he said, turning to her. 'You've given us an important clue.'

'Have I?' she said.

'Yes,' said Marmion. 'Earlier on, the sergeant and I were wondering how the killers might have got hold of the telephone number here. Now we know. One of them tricked his way into the house. Thanks to you, we know the disguise he used. How long was he here? Earlier on, you said that it must have been almost a few minutes.'

'I couldn't be sure, Inspector. I was busy cleaning the kitchen. It could have been much longer, I suppose.'

Marmion got to his feet. 'If you'll excuse us,' he said, 'the sergeant and I will conduct a little experiment.'

They went into the hall and compared the time on their watches. Marmion then pretended to let Keedy into the house before opening the door under the stairs and switching on the light for him. While Keedy knelt beside the meter, Marmion walked to the kitchen and closed the door behind him. The sergeant came out at once and examined the rooms on the ground floor at speed. He then dashed upstairs to continue his search, starting with the master bedroom and looking in the wardrobe. He pretended to search and find the safe. That left three more bedrooms and a bathroom to inspect. By the time he had finished his reconnaissance, he still had time in hand. While he waited, he made a note of the telephone number. A minute later, Marmion emerged from the kitchen.

'How did you get on, Joe?'

'I cased the whole house.'

'Well, I didn't hear a thing,' said Marmion, 'and neither did Mrs Hobbes when that man was here. I no longer believe they needed to wake the doctor up that night by claiming there was an emergency at the hospital. The man Mrs Hobbes let in here came in search of a means of getting into the house when it was locked.'

Claude Chatfield was disappointed. Seated behind his desk, he pored over a collection of the morning's newspapers. Only one of them had managed to put a photograph of Dr Tindall on the front page. As ever, the latest news about the war edged out events on the Home Front. The capture of Jerusalem took pride of place and General Allenby was lauded for his stunning achievement. The fall of the iconic city marked the climax of a brilliant offensive against the Turks that had begun over a year earlier. Understandably, most editors had wanted to trumpet good news about the war on their front pages. The fate of an orthopaedic surgeon at a military hospital could not compete with that. Reports of the murder were consigned to the inside pages and, in one case, reduced to a mere six lines. What irked Chatfield most was that his original statement to the press had been either truncated or mangled. He threw aside the last of the newspapers with something close to despair.

When he looked up, he saw that Sir Edward Henry was standing in front of his desk. The commissioner personified disappointment.

'You've obviously seen the papers, Sir Edward,' said Chatfield.

'Unfortunately, I have.'

'Don't they understand the importance of the murder?'

'The capture of Jerusalem has elbowed out everything else.'

'Why couldn't they print what I told them,' wailed the superintendent. 'I answered questions from reporters for almost an hour, yet little of what I said has been given any prominence.'

'Well,' said the other, philosophically, 'give Allenby his due. His success is a real shot in the arm for the British Army. I hope that it will serve to deflect the War Office away from us. What we really need is news of some startling progress in the murder investigation, but it's far too early to expect that. One thing is crystal clear,' he added, striking a pose. 'Letting your detectives slope off to Brighton was a bad mistake.'

'Inspector Marmion was responsible for making it.'

'You should have stopped him.'

'How could I? He sneaked off when my back was turned.'

'You failed to impose your authority, Superintendent. That's unlike you.'

Without another word, the commissioner turned on his heel and left the office. Chatfield was left yet again with the feeling that he was being blamed unjustly. He was blazing with suppressed fury.

'Damn you, Marmion!' he cursed. 'Do your job properly for once.'

The surge of pleasure that Alice experienced when she first met up with Iris Goodliffe had been steadily eroded. As she had feared, her friend's indecision was a huge problem. Even when trying to buy something as simple as a scarf, Iris kept changing her mind time and again. Constantly seeking Alice's advice, she would accept it, question it, reject it, accept it again, then decide she might be able to get more of a bargain at another store. By the time they stopped to have a cup of tea, Alice's patience was in tatters.

'I have an idea,' she said.

'So have I,' decided Iris. 'You were right about that scarf. I bought the wrong one. It's not my colour at all.'

'It's too late to worry about that now, Iris.'

'No, it isn't. We can go back and change it.'

'That would mean walking hundreds of yards. In any case, when you try on that red scarf again, you will probably want a second look at all the others as well. We've only got limited time.'

Iris was hurt. 'I thought we were here all day.'

'I promised my mother that I'd be back by mid-afternoon.'

'What a shame! I'm having such a wonderful time.'

'There's no reason why you can't stay here until the shops shut.'

'Yes, there is. I won't have you to advise me.'

Alice was sorry that she had invented an excuse to curtail the shopping spree, but it had turned out to be worse than she had feared. She felt less like a friend of Iris than a substitute mother, advising, cossetting, humouring and being at the mercy of her whims. Her irritation had evanesced into a sense of mild panic. Alice sought a means of escape.

'I have an idea, Iris.'

'What is it?'

'When we get to John Lewis's,' said Alice, 'why don't we split up?'

Her friend was shocked. 'I thought we were together.'

'We are. It's just that you were talking about a pair of slippers and I need to go to the menswear department to buy Joe a tie. We can arrange to meet somewhere in the store, then go our separate ways.'

'But I'd need your opinion about the slippers.'

'Buy the pair that feel most comfortable.'

'I could tell you which tie I think would suit Joe.'

'Oh, no,' said Alice, firmly. 'When it comes to my presents, I don't need a second opinion, thank you. Joe is very particular about every item he wears. That's why he always looks so smart.'

'What about that scarf I should have bought?'

'If it's that important,' said Alice, 'go back and change the one you bought by mistake. We can meet in the restaurant in John Lewis's. Will that suit you?'

'No,' replied Iris. 'I'll stay with you while I can. I feel safer that way.'

After hours with a colleague on their usual beat, Constable Pellew came back to the police station. Sergeant Dear looked up from his desk.

'Trouble?'

'It's as calm as a duck pond out there, Sarge,' said the other, 'but that wasn't the case last night. Before he got to the City Arms, our favourite prisoner was making enemies left, right and centre.'

'I'm not surprised.'

'He was turned away from the first pub he tried to get into, so he broke a window in the outhouse just to get even. Other landlords turned him away as well. They could see at a glance that he was bad news.'

Pellew went on to list other petty crimes that the young man had committed before going into the City Arms. Sergeant Dear made a note of each one, then looked up at the constable through doleful eyes.

'He's the last kind of visitor we need in Wells,' he said. 'His charge sheet gets longer and longer. Wherever he goes, he seems to enjoy causing havoc. Look what he did at the City Arms – assault, causing an affray, damage to property, possession of a dangerous weapon, foul language in a public place. Then there is his unruly behaviour since he got here and his attempted escape. Frank Myler said he was roaring like a bloody animal.'

'Has he calmed down a bit now?'

'Oh, no, he's complaining that we're trying to starve him.'

'He doesn't deserve food, Sarge.'

'What he really deserves is a good hiding. Unfortunately, I'm forbidden by law to give it to him. Why can't he be like everyone else?'

131

asked Dear. 'If any of the local lads get drunk and start throwing punches, they go out like a light when we lock them up. Next morning, they have a pounding headache and are full of apologies. When the time comes, they pay the fine straight away. Not this one,' he continued, jerking a thumb towards the cells. 'He's been yelling his head off and stinking the place out. If we have any more of it, I'll turn a hose on him.'

'He won't be staying, Sarge. You found out he was a missing person.'

'Somebody had better reclaim him pretty soon,' threatened Dear, 'or off he goes. I'm not having that skunk polluting one of my cells.'

CHAPTER TEN

Using the telephone at Dr Tindall's house, Marmion rang the Gas Board. As soon as his suspicions were confirmed, he put down the receiver and turned to Ada Hobbes.

'You were right,' he told her. 'That man was an impostor.'

'But he looked so real, Inspector.'

'He chose a time when he knew you'd be here alone. He must have watched this house for some time to see who came and went.'

'That makes me shiver,' admitted Ada.

'Thank you again, anyway. There is no need for you to stay a moment longer. Since you've been so helpful, the least we can do is to send you home in a car again.'

'There's no need.'

'We can't let you walk all the way back home.'

'I'm not going to my house,' she said. 'It was my sister who made me get in touch with you. If I can have a lift, I'd like to be taken to Kathy's house, please. She'll want to know what happened.'

'Then you can tell her we think you're a real heroine.'

Ada tittered then let Marmion take her out to the police car and help her into it. After waving the vehicle off, he went back inside the house. Keedy was waiting for him with a triumphant grin on his face.

'I think I've found it,' he said.

'Found what?'

'The way they got in.'

Marmion's interest quickened. 'Show me.'

Keedy took him into the dining room, a large well-appointed room with an oval table that could accommodate six or more people if necessary. Marmion was envious. In his house, meals were eaten around the kitchen table. Once again, he wondered why Dr Tindall had bought a property full of rooms he never used. He thought of the flat where the surgeon had lived in Brighton. That, too, was an extravagance for someone living alone.

'Over here,' said Keedy, leading him to a window. 'What do you see?'

'The side of the house next door.'

'Look again, Harv.'

'I see a sash window, that's all.'

'You see a sash window with a dodgy catch.' He flicked a finger and the catch swung inwards. 'Hey, presto!'

'It wasn't locked properly.'

'Look at my finger,' said Keedy, holding it out. 'That's not moisture on the tip, it's oil. When he came to read the meter, that man made time to come in here, loosen the catch with a screwdriver, and oil it.'

'That would have taken no time at all.'

134

'My theory is that he left it almost in the closed position but ...'

Using his knuckles, he tapped both sides of the frame at the same time and the catch slowly moved inwards until the window was unlocked. It would have been easy for someone to climb through it in the dark. Marmion was impressed.

'You should have been a detective, Joe,' he said.

'I've got the mentality of a crook – that's why I found it.'

They traded a laugh then moved to the table, sitting either side of it and luxuriating briefly in the fantasy that they were waiting for a maid to bring in a delicious meal prepared by their cook. Marmion opened his notebook.

'This is how Mrs Hobbes described the meter reader. He was clearly fit enough to get in through that window. His partner would have been equally lithe, I fancy. What else do we know about them?'

'They rode on motorbikes.'

'And?'

'They took no chances. Their preparation was meticulous.'

'How did they leave the house – window or front door?'

'Front door,' said Keedy, 'but only after they had pushed the window catch into its closed position. That's why we didn't spot the lubrication earlier.'

'Let's think about the safe,' suggested Marmion. 'There was no sign of it being jemmied open. How did they get hold of the key?'

'Intimidation, probably.'

'Tom Harrison told me they might have used a bayonet. If they had waved that in his face, I think Tindall would have given them the key. He probably hoped they would empty the safe and vanish.'

'Once they had the key,' said Keedy, 'I reckon they took him downstairs to kill him.'

'Why were they so considerate?'

Keedy was shocked. 'I don't call hacking a man to pieces an act of consideration. It was sadistic.'

'Yet it took place in the room off the kitchen. If they murdered him in his bedroom, imagine the unholy mess they would have made. That beautiful carpet would have been stained red. Until we found that open safe,' Marmion reminded him, 'the bedroom looked undisturbed.'

'That's true.'

'There's another possible reason why they chose the room downstairs.'

'Is there?'

'They knew that it would be the first place the cleaner would go to when she got here. If someone had kept watch, he would have seen Mrs Hobbes come and go. They wanted their crime discovered as soon as she arrived yesterday morning.'

'I don't agree,' said Keedy, 'and I can't see how they kept the house under surveillance. Neighbours would have noticed strangers hanging about all day.'

'They didn't need to do that, Joe. Their first task would have been to find out if anybody else was living in the house and that was easily done.'

'How?'

'By knocking on the front door during the day,' guessed Marmion. 'Once they knew that Dr Tindall had no servants, they established when the cleaner came and chose the night before one of her visits.'

'I find that baffling. Most killers would delay the discovery of what they had done. You claim that these two did the opposite.'

'Don't ask me why.'

'Someone must have seen a stranger lurking outside for long periods.'

'He didn't need to lurk, Joe. He went past in disguise.'

'Dressed as an employee of the Gas Board, you mean?'

'No,' said Marmion, 'he'd have been in army uniform, I fancy. And he would have driven past the house from time to time on his motorbike. Nobody would have given him a second glance. Soldiers on motorbikes are a common sight.'

'They're also trained to use a bayonet.'

'Neither of these men were real soldiers, Joe.'

'How do you know?'

'You've forgotten what their victim did for a living. He worked in a military hospital. Dr Tindall saved the lives of soldiers. He'd be revered by anyone in the army. One thing is certain,' Marmion concluded. 'The killers were not soldiers.'

Seated in the living room of her sister's house, Ada Hobbes sipped her tea and looked at her brother-in-law with a mingled pity and curiosity.

'How is Alf?' she asked.

'Much the same,' said Kathleen.

'When I came in here the first time, he looked at me as if he'd never seen me before. The second time, I did at least get a nod from him.'

'His memory comes and goes. Mostly, it goes. He can still do some things, mind you. Alf lights the fire every morning and does odd jobs, but that's about all.' She gave a weary smile. 'He's not the man he used to be. If it wasn't so cold, I'd take him to the shops with me. Alf would like that.' She pursed her lips. 'We're in the same boat, Ada.'

'Are we?'

'Yes, we've both outlasted our husbands.'

'Alf is still alive.'

'Well – if you can call it that.'

'I miss Bert so much,' said Ada, sadly. 'I'd love to have seen his face if I'd come home in a police car like I did yesterday.'

'And you had a second ride in it today.'

'That was your doing. If you hadn't egged me on, I'd never have gone to the police. Inspector Marmion was so grateful to you.'

'Does that mean I get a lift in a police car as well?'

Their laughter brought Alf out of his reverie and he nodded his head.

'That was wrong of us, Ada,' said her sister, guiltily. 'A nice man like Dr Tindall gets murdered and we're laughing. We should be ashamed. We ought to be wondering if there's anything else we can remember that might help the police.'

'I still can't believe that he's dead, Kathy.'

'Why choose him of all people? Unless the killers made a mistake.'

'There was no mistake,' said Ada. 'The inspector was certain about that. He said it was all carefully planned. The doctor was the man they were after.'

Days were usually quiet at the police station in Wells, but their latest prisoner had changed all that. When he was not complaining, he was kicking the bars of his cell repeatedly or singing filthy songs as loud as he could. Pulsating with anger, Sergeant Dear went off to the cells.

'Shut up!' he yelled.

'Hello, Sarge,' said the prisoner. 'Any chance of some grub?'

'No, there isn't, but there's a good chance of a punch on the nose if you keep bellyaching. I know your game, lad. You're cold, hungry and your money's run out. You want to cause as much trouble as possible so that the magistrate will send you to prison for three or four months. That way, you have a roof over your head, regular meals and a warm cell.'

'That sounds good to me, Sarge.'

'Don't push me, lad. Your charge sheet is already long enough to get you a custodial sentence, so you can shut your trap. If you bother me again,' warned Dear, jabbing a finger by way of emphasis, 'we'll kick seven barrels of the smelly stuff out of you and leave you half-dead in the middle of it. Understand?'

The prisoner at last fell silent.

Iris Goodliffe was so afraid of losing sight of Alice that she clung to her like a limpet. Over lunch in John Lewis's, she apologised profusely.

'I know,' she admitted. 'It's all my fault. I just can't make up my mind. I can see how maddening that is from your point of view, Alice. I've been behaving like a child and not like a grown woman who's old enough to know what she likes.'

'We all like a second opinion about something we're about to buy.'

'You must have wanted to strangle me.'

'No, I haven't,' said Alice, trying to sound convincing. 'We're just not used to shopping when it's so crowded. It takes all the fun out of it.'

'But I was having great fun until I realised how unhappy you were.'

'I'd just like a little breathing space, Iris.'

'Yes, of course.'

'I don't blame you for getting overexcited.'

'Well, I blame myself,' said the other. 'From now on, we'll concentrate on buying your Christmas presents instead of mine. Agreed?'

'Agreed,' said Alice before dipping the spoon in her soup.

She was touched by Iris's apology and angry with herself for trying to get rid of her sooner than she had planned. When they had first walked the beat together, she had been the more experienced officer and acted as her friend's mentor. Iris had learnt quickly and no longer depended on Alice so much. Meeting up with her friend outside Swan and Edgar, however, the old Iris had been reborn – needy, indecisive, highly emotional and putting herself first. Now that she had recognised her faults, she would be a different person. Alice softened towards her.

'I tell you what,' she said. 'Let's look for your slippers together.'

'We're going up to the menswear department,' said Iris. 'It's time you took first place for once.'

'Thank you.'

'What sort of tie are you going to buy Joe?'

'Something I can actually afford,' said Alice. 'Most of the prices here are well beyond the scope of my purse.'

'I just love looking at all these Christmas decorations,' said Iris, gazing up at them. 'They lift my spirits.'

She grinned broadly and Alice's guilt stirred again. Because she had been so frustrated with her friend, she had cut hours out of their day together. Alice tried to offer something by way of compensation.

'I tell you what,' she said. 'I'll go an hour or so later than I planned. Mummy will understand. Is that okay?'

'It's wonderful!'

'That will give us plenty of time to buy your slippers and Joe's present.'

'There's something else we can fit in as well.'

'What is it?'

'We can go back to that shop and change my scarf.'

Alice sighed inwardly.

Claude Chatfield was in a less waspish mood than usual. Editors of two newspapers had rung him to apologise for being unable to give more prominence to the statement he had issued at the press conference the previous day. The report that Marmion had just given sweetened him

140

even more. Signalling progress, it was useful ammunition to use against the commissioner.

'I think that all of your assumptions are sound,' he said.

'But they still are only assumptions, sir,' Marmion pointed out.

'Mrs Hobbes's account is based on fact. Someone pretending to be from the Gas Board did indeed come to the house and – as you found out – stayed long enough to find a means of getting into it at night.'

'Sergeant Keedy deserves credit for that discovery, sir.'

'Where is he, by the way?'

'He's using the telephone in my office. I asked him to ring all the places that advertise costume hire. We think that the killers acquired two army uniforms and one that seemed to have come from the Gas Board.'

'Good thinking.'

'We do get it right sometimes, Superintendent.'

'I always give praise where praise is due.'

Though the claim was far from the truth, Marmion did not challenge him. Chatfield went off into a brooding silence for a while, then blinked as if waking up.

'There's a cruel irony here,' he said.

'Is there, sir?'

'Yes. A man who spends most of his time slicing bodies open is himself the victim of surgery – albeit of a more grotesque kind. It is almost as if his death is a kind of parody. Do you get that impression?'

'I can't say that I do, sir,' said Marmion. 'You're introducing subtleties that don't exist, in my view. We believe the two men responsible were cold-hearted killers acting on orders from someone else.'

'Are you sure a third person was involved?'

'We're fairly certain.'

'Yet you're unable to provide a motive for him.'

'I can provide one now, sir.'

'What is it?'

'Punishment.'

'Why do you think that?'

'Look at the nature of the murder, Superintendent. Tom Harrison said that it must have been excruciating for Dr Tindall. It was almost medieval. They kept the victim alive to prolong the agony. I read the post-mortem report when I got back here earlier on and it was—'

'Yes, yes,' said Chatfield, cutting him short. 'I know. I read it myself. We're dealing with monsters here.'

'With two of them,' corrected Marmion.

'There may be no third person, Inspector.'

'Yes, there is, sir. I feel it in my bones.'

'Let's deal with the killers first,' suggested Chatfield. 'We know that they exist. Catch the pair. If we have clear evidence they were obeying orders from someone else, we can then go after him.'

'In my view,' said Marmion, 'we need to make three arrests. If we do that, newspaper editors will not be able to hide the murder behind the capture of Jerusalem. It will be front page news everywhere in this country.'

Keedy was unable to concentrate. Sitting in Marmion's office, he had been given an important job to do yet his mind kept straying to Alice. The promise of a whole evening alone with her had disappeared before his eyes. It was an all too frequent setback in their romance. Even when they were married, he knew, they would continue to be separated by the demands of Scotland Yard. But at least he would be able to go home at the end of the day to a loving wife in a warm bed. The thought revived him.

He dialled another number. Keedy was soon talking to a woman in charge of a costume hire shop. Like so many of the places he had contacted, she was unable to help him. He put the receiver down and crossed off the last name on his list. Marmion then came in.

'Any joy?' he asked.

'Yes and no,' said Keedy.

'What does that mean?'

'I'll explain in a moment. First, I need to pass on a message. I took a call from that Major Somebody at the Edmonton Military Hospital. He wants you to ring him.'

'Did he say why?'

'No, he didn't.'

'I'll get in touch with him after I've heard your news.'

'Most of the places I contacted had neither of the costumes I asked for, but there was one that's promising.'

'Where is it?'

'It's just off Shaftesbury Avenue and deals mainly with professional theatres. They've never been asked to supply a uniform like the one that employees of the Gas Board might wear.'

'What about army uniforms?'

'They had a fair number in stock,' said Keedy, 'because they are in demand. Companies have been putting on plays about the war to lift the morale of people on the Home Front.'

'We can all do with a boost to our morale, Joe.'

'There was an amateur company in Camden Town that hired two army uniforms from them. They were due to be returned but they never came back. Do you know why?'

'The company doesn't exist.'

'Oh, it exists but it denies hiring any army uniforms. For a start, they can't afford to do so. They always make their own costumes. I think I should get over to the place off Shaftesbury Avenue right away and ask for a description of the person who hired the uniforms.'

'When you've done that,' advised Marmion, 'track down this amateur theatre in Camden Town. Nobody would simply pluck their name out of the air. The man who hired those uniforms may have had some connection with the company in the past. Off you go, then.'

Keedy was on his feet at once. 'Where will you be?'

'I suspect that I may have to go to Edmonton again. Major Palmer-Loach would only want to speak to me if he had important news to pass on.'

Running a military hospital on such a large scale was a demanding assignment. It was not surprising therefore that Major Palmer-Loach rarely had time for chit-chat with members of his staff. They, too, were working hard. When he wanted a few words with Neil Irvine, he had to walk along a corridor beside him as Irvine was on his way to an operating theatre. Dressed in his surgeon's garb, he spoke to the major through his mask.

'You pick the weirdest times for a conversation, Howard,' he said.

'It's one we should have had years ago.'

'Why?'

'Well, I didn't know that you actually got any details out of George Tindall about his background. All he ever talked about with me were medical matters.'

'I had an advantage over you. Like George, I'm a fellow Scot.'

'Except that you're very unlike him in every way. While you are open and approachable, he was secretive. Inspector Marmion has discovered more about him in two days than I learnt in over two years.'

'I'd like to meet the inspector.'

'When the operation is over, you'll get your chance.'

Irvine was mystified. 'Will I?'

'Yes,' said the other. 'I've not long come off the telephone to Scotland Yard. He is anxious to question you. When I told him that you had to operate first, he said that he'd be waiting when you came out of theatre.'

'I can't shake hands with surgical gloves on, Howard.'

'He'll give you time to change, I'm sure.'

'It's not just a question of getting out of these clothes' said Irvine. 'Surgery demands total concentration. When I come out of theatre, I'll be locked in another world. The inspector will have to wait until my mind adjusts to reality again. I hope that he is a patient man.'

The major smiled. 'I got the feeling that patience is his watchword.'

It took Keedy some time to find the premises. He went down a street off Shaftesbury Avenue, turned into a lane and walked the length of it without seeing a sign for Pegasus Costumes Ltd. It was only after retracing his steps that he realised he had walked past a mews so narrow that he had never noticed it. The company was in a jumble of Victorian properties redolent of one of Dickens's darker novels. From the outside, the building looked too small to house a large collection but, once inside it, he saw that it opened out substantially at the rear. It also ran to four storeys.

A middle-aged woman was seated behind a desk, leafing through old theatre programmes. Plump, flame-haired and ostentatiously dressed, she reminded him of a madame he had once arrested in a brothel. She produced an open-mouthed smile for his benefit.

'Can I help you, sir?' she asked.

'My name is Sergeant Keedy,' he said. 'I rang earlier.'

'Ah, yes. You were asking about army uniforms.'

'That's right. Do you happen to remember who came to pick them up?'

'I remember him very well, Sergeant.'

'Did he give a name?'

'John Morris.'

'How would you describe him?'

'He was about your age,' she replied, 'but shorter than you and nowhere near as handsome. He was slim, dark and walked with a limp. Oh, and he had an ugly face. On the other hand,' she went on, 'he was offering me money and we never turn that away even if it is from a small amateur company.'

'Did he try on an army uniform?'

'He tried on two or three until he found one that fitted him. Then he picked out a second one that was bigger. To be fair to him, he'd brought the measurements to make sure he got the right size.'

'What were the uniforms supposed to be for?'

'It was a play called *Soldiers of the Cross*,' she said. 'I'd never heard of it and, after thirty-eight years of working in the business, I've heard of most plays. This one sounded a bit too serious for my taste.'

'Was the theatre in Camden Town putting on a play of that name?'

'No, it wasn't. When I spoke to the man who runs the company, he'd never heard of it either.'

'Did he know anyone by the name of John Morris?'

She shook her head. 'I think it was a false name,' she admitted. 'He paid the fee and a deposit then walked off with two of our costumes. I was tricked, Sergeant, and that doesn't often happen. I can usually size up a man at a glance.'

'You said that he was ugly.'

'His face was but that didn't mean he was a wrong 'un. He had a

Midland accent and a strange sort of charm. I liked him. That was before I realised what he'd done. Why are you trying to track him down, anyway?'

'This is a murder inquiry.'

'Goodness!' she cried. 'Do you mean that two of our costumes were involved? That's frightening. If they got covered in blood, they'd be ruined.'

'Let's just say that I don't think you'll be seeing the costumes again.'

'Thank goodness for that. We get all sorts in here, Sergeant, but, as far as I know, we've never had a killer before.'

'Did he tell you much about that play, *Soldiers of the Cross*?'

'All he said was that it was inspiring, and his eyes lit up. Do you know what I think?'

'What?'

'I fancy that he wrote it.'

Marmion did not complain about being kept waiting. He was able to update the major on the progress of the investigation, careful to release only some of the intelligence so far gathered.

'You and the sergeant have done splendid work,' said Palmer-Loach. 'I never thought that you'd find out so much so soon.'

'We're simply following routine, Major.'

'I'm impressed.'

They were eventually interrupted by Neil Irvine, who apologised for the delay. The major slipped out of the office so that the two men could talk alone.

'I suppose that we could have had this conversation over the telephone,' said Marmion, 'but it would not have been the same. How is it that you know so much about Dr Tindall while the major knows so little?'

'George and I were fellow surgeons, Inspector. We understand each other. Howard – Major Palmer-Loach, that is – is an administrator so he has different pressures to deal with. The honest answer to your question,' he continued, 'is that George Tindall was a closed book to me until he confided one day that it was his birthday. A true Scotsman like me could not let an event like that go uncelebrated. We were here overnight so we kept ourselves awake with a bottle of malt whisky that I happened to have hidden in my desk.'

'Did that open the closed book for you?'

'It allowed me a glimpse of a few chapters, that's all.'

Marmion took out his notebook. 'Carry on, please.'

He listened with fascination as Irvine recalled his conversation with Tindall. The murder victim slowly began to appear in a completely different light. In his younger days, he had been a fine all-round athlete and had won cups for his achievements as a tennis player. He had met his wife, Eleanor, at their tennis club and the first thing they did at the house they bought in Kent was to instal a lawn court in their garden.

'I'd never have dared to play tennis,' confessed Irvine.

'Why not?' asked Marmion.

'I was too afraid that I'd damage my hands or sprain my wrists. Surgeons live by the skill of their hands, Inspector. I took no chances. George was confident that he would never injure himself and he never did.'

Marmion remembered that Tindall's hands had been sliced off by his killers. It was a detail he kept from Irvine along with other grim discoveries contained in the post-mortem report.

'Why did Dr Tindall and his wife lead such a private life?' he asked.

'That was only the case when he worked in Brighton,' said Irvine.

'Oh?'

'In Kent, he told me, they had an active social life. Eleanor was a wonderful cook, apparently.'

'Did you never meet her?'

'No, she had died before I got to know George. However,' he went on, 'he did show me a photograph of her that he carried with him in his wallet. She was beautiful.'

Marmion knew that no wallet had been found in the house. The treasured photograph of Eleanor Tindall had vanished along with all the photographs of her. It was as if she had never existed.

'There's one thing I must ask you, Dr Irvine.'

'What is it?'

'I was told that Dr Tindall was a rich man.'

'It's true. He never boasted about it, but he was far wealthier than any surgeon can hope to be. It's the reason he was able to own a number of properties.'

'We know about the house in Edmonton and the flat in Brighton. And there was mention of a property in Kent.'

'There were at least two others. His favourite was the one in the south of France. He called it his escape hatch.'

'He won't have seen much of that during the war.'

'The closest he got to it was when he worked in a field hospital somewhere in north-east France. His command of the language came in useful there. He dealt with British casualties from the Battle of Loos.'

It was clear that Irvine had managed to get closer to Tindall than anybody else but there was a point beyond which even he was unable to get. Marmion asked him the question burrowing into his brain.

'Where did all his money come from?'

'Ah, well,' said Irvine, 'that's an interesting story. George's father was strict and a teetotaller into the bargain. Ironically, he inherited the family whisky distillery in Galashiels and promptly sold it. Instead of using the money to buy a bigger house, he left it in the bank. George hated having to live in such a modest house and be dragged to the kirk every Sunday. He promised himself that, if he ever got his hands on all that money, he would live in style. When his parents both died in a flu epidemic one winter, George became a rich man and spread his wings. He'd waited so long for that moment. Frankly,' added Irvine with a twinkle in his eye, 'I'd have preferred to keep the distillery.'

The latest developments in the case had pleased Sir Edward Henry. When he heard Superintendent Chatfield's account, he nodded in approval and congratulated him on having the sense to assign Marmion and Keedy to the case.

'They respond well to a challenge,' said the commissioner.

'As long as I keep cracking the whip, Sir Edward.'

'It's a complex investigation full of twists and turns. I daresay that there'll be a lot of surprises yet to come.'

'Incidentally,' said Chatfield, 'I had grovelling apologies from the editors of two national newspapers. They will give the murder of Dr Tindall better coverage tomorrow and be sure to include his photograph.'

'That's essential. A photograph of the victim may well jog memories.'

'Is it too early to think of offering a reward?'

'Let us see what happens in the next couple of days first.'

'I suppose that it's no use asking the War Office to provide the money?'

'No use at all,' said the commissioner. 'Every penny is already spoken for. The army's coffers have been drained to the limit and the same goes for the navy. War is ruinously expensive.'

'We have to pull out all the stops to win, Sir Edward.'

'I'm trying to remain optimistic but the news from Russia is ominous. Why the devil did they decide to have a revolution at a time like this?'

'It's an act of madness.'

'Because they made the insane decision to drop out of the war, we lost one of our major allies and are now struggling to survive. The Bolsheviks have a lot to answer for. However,' he continued, 'we must not be led astray. We are fighting our own war on the Home Front and it needs all the resources we can muster.'

'It's something I remind myself of every day.'

'Carry on the good work, Superintendent.'

'I will, Sir Edward.'

'And congratulate Marmion on the advances he's already made.'

'I'll be sure to do so,' said Chatfield, manufacturing a smile devoid of either warmth or sincerity. 'Encouragement from you is always heartening.'

'Then do something else to deserve it.'

The commissioner let himself out of the office and closed the door behind him. Chatfield sat down with a mixture of relief and envy, grateful to have survived a meeting with Sir Edward Henry without being criticised, yet wounded by the latter's appreciation of Marmion and Keedy. Not for the first time, the superintendent wondered what he had to do to receive the kind of praise that routinely went to detectives of a lower rank.

Before he could squirm at the injustice of it all, the telephone rang. He snatched it up as if he were trying to rescue it from a blazing fire.

'Superintendent Chatfield here,' he snapped.

As he listened to the voice at the other end of the line, he began to reel from the news he was given. It left him speechless. Reaching for a notepad, he wrote down all the details. When he put the receiver down, he tried to think of a way to conceal the information from the commissioner.

'Damnation!' he exclaimed. 'Why did that have to happen?'

CHAPTER ELEVEN

After a hectic day in the West End, Alice Marmion and Iris Goodliffe paused to compare their takings. While Alice had bought presents for Keedy and for her parents, her friend had bought a dress, gloves, scarf and slippers for herself. Before they parted, Iris embraced Alice and kissed her on both cheeks.

'What was that for, Iris?'

'It was my way of thanking you for putting up with me. This has been the best day of the year for me. I'm so grateful. It's been a struggle in the crowds but who cares about that?'

'We came through it,' said Alice.

'You'd better go. Your mother will be waiting.'

'Yes, she will, won't she?'

'Please give her my regards.'

'Of course.'

Iris gave her a long, affectionate stare. It was as if she had realised that Alice had been lying about her appointment and understood why her friend had deceived her. There was no malice in Iris's eyes. It was simply an unspoken acknowledgement that her behaviour had forced Alice to look for an early escape.

After taking their leave of each other, they headed off to their respective bus stops. The most she could hope for that evening was a chat with her fellow tenants or, at best, a game of cards with them. The prospect paled beside the pleasure of an evening with Joe Keedy.

Reviewing her day, Alice realised that everything she had done had been earmarked for somebody else. Though she had been tempted by many items on sale, she never yielded to it. At the time, it hadn't worried her. Buying for someone she loved was a treat. On the long bus ride to her digs, however, she began to feel lonely and neglected. The Christmas jollity in the West End had given way to boredom and resentment. One question dominated her mind.

'Where are you, Joe Keedy?'

The Camden Town Arts Theatre was in a backstreet, looking sad and down-at-heel. As soon as Keedy got there, the door opened and he was greeted by Roland Mandeville, a silver-haired man in his sixties with a full beard and a tendency to gesticulate. He was wearing a cloak and wide-brimmed hat.

'You must be Sergeant Keedy,' he said, offering his hand.

Keedy accepted the handshake. 'It's good of you to see me at short notice, Mr Mandeville. I got your telephone number from the lady at Pegasus Costumes.'

'Ah, Pegasus! They have an excellent stock of costumes, but they are far too expensive for us to hire. Anyway,' he went on, 'come on in, come on in. Enter the world of the Camden Town Arts Theatre.'

Keedy followed him into the foyer, then the auditorium, and saw that the inside of the building was a vast improvement on its shabby exterior. The place was clean and well appointed. Rows of chairs had been set out. Along the walls were framed photographs of former productions. The proscenium arch looked as if it had been recently painted and the drawn curtains were of good quality.

'This is my domain,' said Mandeville with a sweeping gesture. 'That's why I've invested so much of my hard-earned money in it.'

'How many people can you seat in here?'

'At a pinch, we can get a hundred and sixty patrons for each performance.'

'What sort of plays do you put on?'

'It's an eclectic mixture, Sergeant. We have staged everything from Ibsen to Music Hall. I shone in the title role of *The Master Builder* only last month.'

'Is that a play about a bricklayer?'

Mandeville laughed. 'I can see that you are no thespian,' he said. '*The Master Builder* is a dramatic gem by Henrik Ibsen. I think that Music Hall might be more to your liking – or even Shaw, perhaps. His plays are popular with our audiences. They usually have plenty of laughs in them.'

'The lady at Pegasus Costumes said you had never heard of a play called *Soldiers of the Cross*.'

'Even if I had, I'd never put in on here.'

'Why is that?'

'Because it sounds as if it's about the Crusades. Think of the cost of all that fake armour. It would be way beyond our budget.'

'I don't think it's anything to do with the Crusades,' argued Keedy.

'It's more likely to be about the Salvation Army, isn't it?'

It was an organisation that he knew a great deal about because Marmion's brother, Raymond, was a member of it. They had once investigated a murder at the hostel run by Raymond Marmion and his wife.

Mandeville was brusque. 'Then we'd certainly never have put it on.'

'Why not?'

'Let me show you.'

He led Keedy across to a framed photograph on the wall. It showed a young actress in the uniform of the Salvation Army, standing between a sizeable, dignified woman in her late fifties and an imposing man. Keedy recognised that the man was, in fact, Mandeville.

'We did *Major Barbara* last April because it is Bernard Shaw at his best. The heroine is in the Salvation Army. My dear wife – God bless her – took the role of Lady Britomart, Barbara's mother, and I was her father, Andrew Undershaft.'

'I see.'

'It was a case of art imitating life because the title role was played by our own daughter, Philomena.'

'There is a likeness between her and your wife,' observed Keedy.

'The point is that nobody needs two plays about the Salvation Army,' explained Mandeville, 'so we'd reject the one you mentioned. Our production was well received by the critics and my performance as Andrew Undershaft was singled out for its excellence.' He struck an attitude. 'I can still remember those famous speeches word for word. Listen to this one—'

'I'd rather not,' said Keedy, forcefully. 'I'm sorry to interrupt but you obviously don't understand the seriousness of the crime that brought me here.'

'Stealing a couple of army uniforms is only a minor infringement of the law.'

'The man who stole them took part in a gruesome murder.'

'Good gracious!'

'So, if you don't mind, sir, I'll hear your memoirs another time. Right now, all my attention is fixed on a hideous crime.'

'Quite so.'

'The lady at Pegasus Costumes mentioned a name to you.'

'I remember it well – John Morris. I know nobody of that name.'

'It could be false,' said Keedy, 'but he did mention this theatre and that is what brought me here. He was described as around my age but a little shorter. She told me that he was an ugly man who had a limp. He spoke with a Midland accent and had a certain charm.'

'I still can't pick him out,' said Mandeville. 'As it happens, we do have someone in our ranks who fits your description, having both an unprepossessing face and a pronounced limp – but she happens to be a woman.'

'Thank you for your help, sir.'

'I wish I could have been more use.'

'If, however, you do remember meeting someone who looked like the man I described, please ring Scotland Yard.'

'I most certainly will, Sergeant. You know,' he said, warming to the idea, 'it's rather exciting, being involved in a murder case, if only tangentially. I wish you good luck in your search.'

'We'll need it,' said Keedy under his breath.

Marmion was buoyant. On his return to Scotland Yard, he headed straight for the superintendent's office, eager to impart what he felt was enlightening information about the murder victim. When he came face to face with Chatfield, however, he was not even given a chance to speak. The superintendent indicated a chair.

'Sit down, Harvey,' he said, solemnly.

Marmion was worried. In all the years they had known each other, he could count on one hand the number of times that Chatfield had addressed him by his Christian name. He lowered himself onto a chair.

Chatfield took a deep breath. 'I have some news for you, I'm afraid.'

'What sort of news?'

'The serious kind.'

'You're not going to take me off this case, are you?' said Marmion in alarm.

'I'm hoping to do exactly the opposite.'

'What do you mean, sir?'

'I had a phone call from a police station in Wells, Somerset. A Sergeant Dear had been trawling through a list of Missing Persons. He recognised a name.'

Marmion felt his stomach tighten. His son had been found and that set off a whirl of emotions. As he wondered if Paul was alive or dead, he braced himself.

'Your son is in custody, I'm afraid,' said the superintendent.

'On what charges?'

'There's quite a list of them and they include being in possession of an offensive weapon.' Marmion gulped. 'Perhaps you'd like a moment to adjust to the news. I know you'd accepted that you might never hear of him again.'

Marmion gave a nod and considered the implications. It was painful for him to hear that Paul – the son of a detective inspector – was in trouble with the police. How had he lived until he had come to Somerset?

What had he done in Wells to merit arrest? Were the police certain of his identity?

Chatfield read his mind. 'Yes,' he said, 'it definitely is him. He fits the description issued and has documents with his name on them. He admits to being Paul Marmion. It is your son.'

It was difficult for Marmion to adjust to the news, and he knew that his wife and daughter would have the same problem. As a family, they believed that Paul had deliberately walked out on them, never to return. Out of the blue, he had now surfaced in disgrace. Marmion made one decision immediately.

'I want to carry on leading this investigation, sir,' he declared.

'Are you absolutely sure?'

'Yes, I am.'

'I could easily draft in Inspector Gallimore.'

Marmion was emphatic. 'This case is mine.'

'I was hoping you'd say that.'

'All I need is time to contact my wife and daughter,' said Marmion. 'It's not the kind of thing I want to do over the telephone.'

'I understand. Do what needs to be done.'

Marmion rose to his feet. 'Thank you, sir.'

'I'll tell Sergeant Keedy that you're temporarily unavailable. He has a personal interest, of course. Your son will soon become his brother-in-law.'

Too dazed to reply, Marmion walked slowly out of the office.

Alice Marmion was angry with herself. Rather than inventing an excuse to part with Iris Goodliffe, she could have stayed in the West End until the shops had started to close. Instead of that, she was sitting at the window of her first-floor flat, gazing out at traffic rolling past in the fading light. A dull evening beckoned. Her only hope was that Joe Keedy would somehow contrive to see her at the end of the day, if only for a brief time. Realistically, she knew that it was a doomed fantasy, but it was the one possibility that gave her any sense of pleasure.

Forcing herself away from the window, she took out the Christmas wrapping paper she had bought and found the presents. She was soon on her knees with a pair of scissors. It was a task that occupied her mind and stopped her brooding. Before she could finish it, however, she heard a car arriving outside the house. When she looked out of the window, she saw her father getting out of the rear of the vehicle. Alice reeled. Only an emergency would bring him to her flat and it would almost certainly involve Keedy. Trembling with fear, she raced downstairs. She flung open the door and saw the grim look on her father's face.

'What's happened, Daddy?' she asked.

'Thank heaven you're here!' said Marmion.

'Is it Joe?'

'No, Alice, it isn't.'

The relief she felt suddenly turned to a mixture of shock and foreboding.

'It's Paul, isn't it?'

'Yes.'

'Has he been found alive?'

'Oh, he's very much alive.'

'What do you mean?'

'Jump into the car,' he said, 'and I'll tell you. We need to discuss this at home with your mother. The superintendent has given me time off to do so.'

'Where is Paul?'

'He's in trouble.'

* * *

159

Claude Chatfield delayed passing on the news. He was anxious to listen to Keedy's report of his trips to Pegasus Costumes Ltd and to the Camden Town Arts Centre. Once he had heard the full details, he told the sergeant about the reappearance of Paul Marmion. Keedy was astounded.

'I thought he'd gone for good,' he said.

'So did the inspector.'

'How did he take the news, sir?'

'It shook him up badly,' said Chatfield. 'In a sense, it's like someone coming back from the dead. As a father myself, I sympathise with him. I know how strong the bond is between parent and child.'

'Where is the inspector now?'

'I gave him time off to speak to his wife and daughter.'

'That was kind of you, Superintendent.'

'It wasn't kindness that prompted me. It was practicality. I need him to stay in charge of this investigation. That is why I made allowances. He'll be back as soon as he's discussed the situation with Mrs Marmion and their daughter.'

'It's a conversation that I would have liked to be involved in.'

'Your place is here, Sergeant.'

'It could make such a big change to their lives.'

'That's not necessarily true,' said Chatfield. 'When the police in Wells realised that he was on the list of Missing Persons, he begged them not to get in touch with his parents. Fortunately, they knew where their duty lay.'

'Is he still being held at the police station?'

'No, he was too disruptive. He was taken before a magistrate and remanded to Shepton Mallet prison. Imagine how the inspector felt on hearing that his son is a criminal.'

Keedy was more interested in Alice's reaction than in that of her father. He had to master an urge to go to her at once and offer support, but that was impossible. There was a murder to solve, and his energies had to be focused on that.

'So,' said Chatfield, 'our killers got their army uniforms from a costume hire company, did they? What about their motorbikes?'

'That's the next thing I need to find out.'

'I'm sorry you had slim pickings at that theatre.'

'It was an education for me, sir,' said Keedy. 'I learnt that *The Master Builder* is a play by someone called Ibsen. And I had the pleasure of meeting a man who had actually played the character onstage.'

Roland Mandeville arrived back home to a cordial welcome from his wife. They lived in one of the better areas of Camden Town. Over a glass of gin and tonic, they were able to chat. Cassandra Mandeville had the remains of an almost dazzling beauty. However, she still retained the effervescence and love of the theatre that had first attracted her husband to her.

'How did you get on, Roland?' she asked.

'I was shaken rigid.'

'Why?'

'I thought I was meeting Sergeant Keedy to talk about the theft of two army uniforms. It turns out that those costumes were worn by men who committed a murder. The uniforms were part of the killers' disguise.'

'What a chilling thought!'

'He asked me if I knew a man named John Morris.'

'It's not a name that I remember,' she said, frowning.

'It's one that was given at Pegasus Costumes.'

Mandeville went on to give her the description of the man being sought. His wife pursed her lips and shook her head. Like her husband, she could think of nobody who came close to fitting the description.

'While you were out,' she told him, 'Desmond called.'

'What did he want?' asked her husband, grimacing.

'Can't you guess?'

'I'm afraid that I can. Desmond is demanding to know what the final play in next year's spring season will be.'

'That's right.'

'We haven't decided yet, Cassie.'

'What you mean is that you have, but it has to be ratified by the committee.'

'No, I'm still hovering, to be honest. Desmond only wants to know our choice in the hope that there is a part in it for him. I made sure that there is not. Desmond Cooper can single-handedly ruin any production. That's why I try to keep him off the stage and serving drinks in the intervals.'

'Is it still a choice between *Charley's Aunt* or Pinero's *The Magistrate*?'

'Yes – which would you choose, Cassie?'

'Whichever one has a delicious role for a tubby old woman,' she said with a giggle. 'If Desmond is going to push himself forward, then so am I. It's months since I had a starring role and I'm a born actress.'

'You don't need to tell me that, my love,' he said, fondly. 'You belong on the boards. I tell you what,' he joked. 'Why don't we put on Shakespeare's *Antony and Cleopatra* and play the lead roles? We could both show our mettle in that.'

'Show our mettle?' she repeated. 'I'd be too busy hiding my fat bottom.'

She went off into peals of laughter. When she finally stopped, Cassandra took a sip of her drink and became thoughtful.

'I'd rather forgotten him.'

'Who are you talking about?'

'John Morris,' she said.

'But that's not his real name.'

'I know. It's just that I'm wondering if I might have come across him, after all. Give me that description of the man again.'

Ellen Marmion was just about to draw the curtains in the living room when she saw the police car arrive outside the house. She was at first pleased that her husband had somehow found the time to slip back home, then she watched her daughter getting out of the vehicle as well. Concern made her rush to the front door. Opening it wide, she embraced Alice then looked enquiringly at Marmion.

'I'll tell you inside,' he said.

The three of them adjourned to the living room. Before he spoke, Marmion made sure that his wife was sitting down. Alice sat beside her on the sofa.

'Paul has been found alive,' he said.

'Oh, my God!' exclaimed Ellen, bringing both hands to her face.

Alice put an arm around her shoulders. 'It's bad news, Mummy.'

'Yes,' said Marmion. 'He's in custody.'

'Where?' demanded Ellen. 'And what has he done? It's not something really serious, is it? Paul hasn't ...?'

'It's serious enough, Ellen. He was arrested in Somerset.'

'What was he doing there?'

'If you let me speak, I'll tell you all I know.'

'It's ironic, isn't it?' said Alice, bitterly. 'Only yesterday, Mummy and I agreed that Paul had disappeared for ever and that we had to accept the fact. No sooner do we do that, than he pops up again.'

* * *

Any pleasure the commissioner gained from the apparent progress in the investigation was overshadowed by the news about Paul Marmion. He was sympathetic.

'It's every policeman's nightmare,' he said. 'Having a son in trouble with the law is more than an embarrassment.'

'It might be even more painful if it was a daughter, Sir Henry.'

'Ah, yes, I suppose it would. As the father of daughters, you would feel ashamed if it happened to you. Not that it ever would, of course, because you've brought your children up to respect the law.'

'Inspector Marmion did the same with his children.'

'What went wrong?'

'His son was a victim of the war.'

'Yes, I remember that he was wounded at the Battle of the Somme.'

'The major damage appears to have been psychological.'

'Then we're bound to feel sorry for the lad.'

'He's more than a lad, Sir Edward. Paul is a fully grown man now. He has somehow managed to keep himself alive all this time. The sergeant who contacted me from Wells said that he looked and smelled like tramp.'

'Oh dear!'

'To his credit,' said Chatfield, 'the inspector is not insisting on being allowed to dash off to Somerset. He's putting his duty first and continuing to lead the case.'

'I call that a blessed relief.'

'We just have to hope that this business doesn't affect his concentration.'

'He's the most committed officer we have,' said the other. 'You and he are on a par in that regard. The difference is that you operate solely from here whereas Marmion goes out and faces recurring dangers. I'm not sure that even you could do that with the same record of success.'

Chatfield looked bilious.

Making the use of the telephone in Marmion's office, Keedy was ringing garages in the London area that sold motorcycles. He was less interested in those that had been sold than in two that might have been stolen together. When he put the receiver down, he ticked another name off his list. Before he could move on to the next one, the telephone rang.

'Sergeant Keedy,' he said, picking up the receiver.

'Ah, wonderful,' said Roland Mandeville, 'they've put me through to the right person. Mandeville here – we met earlier today.'

'I recognised your voice immediately, sir.'

'I take that as a compliment.'

'How may I help you?'

'Well, I'm hoping it's a case of my helping you or – to be more exact – of my wife helping you. When I got home earlier, I gave her the description of one of the men you're after.'

'John Morris.'

'At first, my wife had no memory of someone who looked like the false Mr Morris. After a while, however, she changed her mind.'

'You have a name?' asked Keedy, hopefully.

'I'll let Cassie talk to you herself,' said Mandeville.

Keedy heard some whispering at the end of the line then a woman spoke up.

'Sergeant Keedy?'

'Good evening to you.'

'I'm Cassandra Mandeville and I help my husband to run the theatre you visited earlier. What he omitted to tell you is that we are dedicated to the arts in general, not simply to the theatre. Musicians, singers and dancers perform regularly onstage and artists are not neglected.'

Keedy was intrigued by her voice. It was deep, fruity and vibrant, each word enunciated with resounding clarity. He could well imagine her playing a member of the nobility in a play by Bernard Shaw.

'I organise the art exhibitions in the foyer,' she explained. 'Talent is not confined to those whose paintings are hung at the Royal Academy. It abounds everywhere. We display work with artistic merit that not only interests the visiting public, it sometimes induces them to buy a painting.'

'Excuse me interrupting,' said Keedy, 'but I don't see what this has to do with a suspect in a murder case.'

'Our last exhibition was over two weeks ago. I believe I might have met John Morris there.'

'What makes you think that?'

'It was a very casual contact,' she told him. 'He was a man in his thirties with an unbecoming face and a limp. The moment I talked to him he dispelled my misgivings about him.'

'How?' asked Keedy.

'He was so complimentary about the exhibition.'

'What did he say to you?'

'How much is this?' she replied.

'I'm sorry, Mrs Mandeville, you've lost me.'

'I was on duty there. I knew the prices of everything.'

'Did he want to buy the painting?'

'He was thinking about it. When I told him how much it was, he went in search of the artist to see if he would lower the price.'

'Can you remember what the painting was like?'

'Of course, Sergeant – once seen, nobody could forget it.'

'Was it so striking?'

'To be candid, it was rather nauseating.'

'Why was that?'

It was a depiction of Christ on the cross,' she replied, 'standing amid the carnage of the Battle of the Somme.'

For a couple of minutes, Ellen Marmion was too stunned to reply. Face pale and body frozen, she tried to cope with the enormity of what her husband had told her. Having written her son out of her life, she found that he had just written himself back into it. While his abrupt departure had left her feeling she had failed as a mother, the threat of his return awoke deep fears rather than maternal tenderness. Paul had reportedly become an itinerant criminal, living rough, working his way from county to county and stealing what he could not get by begging.

Marmion exchanged a glance with his daughter. Both had experienced the same reaction. It was one of shock, if not disgust, tempered by the fact that, whatever he had done, Paul was still part of the family. There had to be pity as well as regret. At such a low ebb in his life, he needed them more than ever.

Taking out a handkerchief, Ellen dabbed at her tears.

'How can they be certain that it is him?' she asked.

'He had Paul's papers,' replied Marmion.

'He might have stolen them.'

'The prisoner matches the description we gave of our son.'

'I'm still not convinced, Harvey.'

'Then there's only one thing for it,' he suggested. 'I'm too entangled in this case to go to Somerset myself but you can go in my place.'

'I'll go with you, Mummy,' Alice volunteered.

'Would you be able to get permission from Inspector Gale?'

'I can ask her. If she refuses, you can get Superintendent Chatfield to speak to her. It may not come to that. Gale Force let me go last time and I'm in her good books for once.' She turned to her mother. 'We'll go together, Mummy.'

Ellen was uncertain. 'I'm not sure that I want to.'

'Why not?'

'I suppose … I suppose that I'm afraid of what I might find.'

'One look is all you need to see if it's Paul,' said Marmion.

'Yes, but what sort of look will he give me in return?'

'You stay here, Mummy,' said Alice. 'I'll go on my own.'

'That's unfair on you,' said Ellen.

'Well, someone has to find out the truth.'

'He may not even agree to see us, Alice.'

'I think I see the trouble here,' said Marmion, gently. 'In your heart, you're almost afraid to learn the truth. When there was a sighting of Paul before, the pair of you went with high hopes. Both of you believed that Paul was working on the farm just outside Coventry.'

'Well, he definitely had been, Daddy,' said Alice.

'Yes, I know, and he might still have been there now if he'd behaved himself. But he stepped out of line and became interested in the farmer's daughter. There was no way he could stay after that,' he continued. 'Do you see my point? We all felt that Paul was still part of the family then. Now, we're not so sure.'

'We can't pretend he doesn't exist,' said Ellen.

Alice gave a wan smile. 'That's what we agreed to do yesterday.'

'I know and it was wrong of us.'

'Does that mean you'll come to Somerset with me?'

'I need time to think it over.'

'If you prefer, I can delay the visit by a day or so.'

'You heard your mother, Alice,' said Marmion. 'Give her time to take it all in. The news has knocked me for six, and I don't mind admitting it. Ideally, I'd be on a train to Somerset right now, but I can't just abandon this investigation.'

'We know that,' said his wife. 'It was kind of the superintendent to let you come home. If you had simply rung me from work with this news, I'd have been in a terrible state.' She squeezed Alice's hand. 'Having you both here with me has … well, I was going to say that it softened the blow but it's still painful enough.'

'Take time to think it over, love.'

'I'll stay, if you want me to,' offered Alice.

'I do,' said Ellen, tightening her grip on her daughter's hand.

Marmion glanced at his watch. 'I'll have to go, I'm afraid.'

'Yes, of course. Please ring us if there's … any other information.'

'I will.'

After kissing his wife and his daughter, Marmion let himself out of the house and climbed into the car. Ellen and Alice were left to discuss the latest news.

'What do you think, Mummy?' asked Alice.

'I'm not sure.'

'That makes two of us. Daddy was right. It's not as easy as last time, is it? When we went to the farm near Coventry, we were dying to see Paul again. That feeling is no longer there, somehow.'

'I don't have feelings of any kind, Alice. I'm just numb.'

'We have to ask ourselves a simple question.'

'What is it?

'Would we rather that it was Paul – or that it wasn't?'

Ellen shrugged. 'I wish I knew,' she said.

CHAPTER TWELVE

Keedy had spent so much time on the telephone in Marmion's office that his ear was buzzing. He was glad to be interrupted by the inspector's return and was on his feet at once.

'How did Alice take the news?' he asked. 'Did she send a message for me? What did the police in Wells say about Paul? Is it true that you told Chat that this case took priority? Did he put pressure on you? Is Alice thinking about going to Somerset with her mother? What exactly is happening?'

'Let me get my breath back, Joe,' said Marmion. 'The last couple of hours have been rather hectic for me.'

'Then come and sit down.'

Keedy vacated the seat behind the desk so that Marmion, weary and careworn, could take his seat. The inspector needed a few minutes to regain his concentration.

'I'm his father, Joe,' he said, eventually. 'I want him back home where we can look after him. But I must be realistic. It may never happen. Paul has rejected us as a family. We can hardly force him to come back to us.'

'And even if you could,' said Keedy, 'there'd be endless difficulties. If Paul has been living rough, he will not fit back easily into normal life.'

'There's no such thing as normal life for Paul. He must be one of many rudderless soldiers invalided out of the army and sent home with damage we can never understand, let alone try to heal.' He slapped the desk. 'Right, that's enough about family problems. Let's get back to the job we are paid to do.' He glanced down. 'I see that you've got a list of garages here. Most of them are ticked off.'

'That means I've contacted them,' said Keedy, 'but to no avail.'

'What else have you been doing?'

Keedy told him about the visits he had made, then moved on quickly to an account of his telephone conversation with Cassandra Mandeville. He was hoping that she might accidentally have met one of their suspects. Marmion was curious.

'It's a long shot, Joe,' he said, 'but we've been lucky with those in the past.'

'If it is the man we want, he must live in or near to Camden Town.'

'Why?'

'The Arts Theatre is well known in the area but less so outside it. They have limited funds so are unable to advertise widely. In other words, the people who go to their exhibitions tend to be local.'

'What interests me is this painting of the Battle of the Somme.'

'It sounds weird to me,' said Keedy, pulling a face. 'Paul actually fought in that battle and he never mentioned seeing Christ on a cross there.'

'Was that painting actually sold?'

'No, it wasn't.'

'Why not?'

'Mrs Mandeville said that most people were rather horrified by it. When a vicar came in, he called it obscene and wanted it taken down. He had an argument with the artist about it.'

'Who won the argument?'

'Mrs Mandeville did. Having accepted the painting for display, she defended her decision fiercely. I've only spoken to her on the phone but I'd think twice about having a row with her. She's the sort of woman who always gets her way.'

'I've got a daughter like that,' said Marmion, grinning. 'Be warned.'

'There was another reason why the painting didn't sell. The artist was asking far too much, apparently.'

'What was his name?'

'Colin Voisey.'

'Any idea where he lives?'

Keedy opened his notepad. 'I made a point of getting his address.'

After a long discussion with her daughter, Ellen Marmion finally reached a decision.

'I'm simply not ready to go there tomorrow, Alice.'

'Then I will have to visit the prison instead of you.'

'I'd rather you didn't.'

'One of us has to go, Mummy.'

'It's a trip that we must make together. I feel that it's my duty to go,' said Ellen, 'but I need a full day to get up the courage.'

'You don't need courage to visit your own son,' said Alice.

'In this case, I do.' She shuddered. 'Isn't that a terrible thing to admit?'

'Given what's happened, it's … understandable. I've had a few tremors myself. Let's think about the day after tomorrow, shall we? If it's possible, that is.'

'I don't follow.'

'Well, we can't just turn up at the doors of Shepton Mallet prison and ask to be let in. We'll need permission in advance. Daddy will have to organise that.'

'What if Paul refuses to see us?'

'He's within his rights to do that, Mummy.'

'We'd have had a wasted journey.'

'It's a risk I'm ready to take,' said Alice. 'Maybe we're looking at it the wrong way. We are trying to reach a decision that really belongs to him. Does he want us back in his life again?'

'It's highly unlikely.'

'It might also be very upsetting for him. Paul will feel ashamed to have let us down the way that he has.'

'I doubt if he has any sense of shame left, Alice. Remember what your father told us about his behaviour at that police station in Wells. Does that sound to you as if he cares what he does?' She heaved a sigh. 'We could be going all that way just to get a slap in the face from him.'

'I can't believe that.'

'I still can't believe the way he tormented Sally Redwood, but that's exactly what he did.'

'Yes,' said Alice, 'and he had no sense of shame afterwards.'

'He laughed about it.'

'That was so unlike Paul. When we were growing up together, he could be mischievous and wayward, but never cruel. He is different now. Perhaps we need another full day to think it through,' said Alice. 'At the moment, we're simply reacting quickly to a complete surprise.'

'I agree. We deserve time to let it sink in.'

Alice smiled. 'Is there any chance of food while we do that?'

'Are you hungry?'

'I'm starving, Mummy.'

'Let's see what's in the larder.'

'I'll be happy to do the cooking.'

'Then I'll be happy to let you,' said Ellen, gratefully. 'At the moment, I'm not sure that I could do anything properly. I'm still trying to come to terms with what's happened. And I'm so grateful that I've got company.' She put her arms around her daughter. 'Honestly, I've never needed you so much, Alice.'

They hugged each other for several minutes.

It was dark when the police car nosed its way through the streets of Camden Town. When it reached its destination, it pulled up at the kerb. Marmion and Keedy got out and looked at the dingy street around them. From what they could make out in the gloom, the houses were small, terraced and in dire need of repair. Evidently, art was not a lucrative source of money for Colin Voisey.

They walked along the street until they reached the address they sought. It was a basement flat in a house in the middle of the row. Marmion chuckled.

'What a disappointment!' he said.

'Why?'

'I always thought artists starved in garrets. This one lives in a basement that must get little natural light.'

'Let's find out, shall we?' said Keedy.

They opened the iron gate and went down the steps. As soon as they knocked on the door, they heard a shout of annoyance. Since nobody came to let them in, Keedy banged even harder. The protests were even louder, but they had at least aroused attention.

The door swung open to reveal a tall, dishevelled, scrawny man in his forties.

'Who the bleeding hell are you?' he demanded.

'We're detectives from Scotland Yard,' said Marmion.

The artist stiffened. 'Painting a picture is not against the law now, is it?'

'No, it isn't, Mr Voisey.'

'How do you know my name?' asked the other, warily.

'We're interested in your work,' said Keedy. 'That's to say, we'd like to look at a painting you exhibited recently.'

Voisey relaxed. 'Why didn't you say so? People who admire my work are always welcome. It's a pity there aren't more of them.' He stood back. 'Come in.'

Entering the living room, they were grateful for the light from the gas lamp. It allowed them to take a closer look at Voisey. He had a shaggy beard tinged with the same paint that they could see on his hands. A rag was dangling from his pocket. Pulling it out, he wiped his hands with it.

'I know what you're thinking,' he said, appraising each of them in turn. 'Why do I work down here in the dark? It's because it suits the kind of pictures I paint. They belong in the shadows. I could never create them in broad daylight.'

'Is this what you do for a living?' asked Marmion.

'It's what I do out of love. My stall in the market is what I do for a living. Art is my true vocation. Selling fruit and veg allows me to follow it.'

'We're really interested in a painting that was on display at the Arts

Theatre here. I'm told that it features the Battle of the Somme.'

Voisey narrowed his lids. 'Why pick that one?'

'My son was injured in that battle.'

'Really?'

'I took him to see the film that was made about the battle.'

'Yes, I saw that as well. It was terrible. Our lads were killed like flies.'

'Could we see your painting, please?'

'Only if you're thinking of buying it,' said Voisey.

'We are, we are,' pretended Keedy. 'At least, the inspector is, because of his association with the battle through his son.'

'Wait here while I get it from my studio.'

Voisey shuffled out and gave them a chance to study their surroundings. They were in the middle of a low-ceilinged room that was more like a junk shop than a place where anyone would choose to live. The only thing on which it was possible to sit was on an old leather sofa with an abundance of cushions, none of which matched the others in size or colour. For the rest, the place was given over to an array of items that ranged from a pair of china peacocks to a grandfather clock. Its tick was loud and sonorous.

When he returned, Voisey was carrying a large painting in a black frame. He placed it under the light so that it was shown to its best advantage. They stared at it with mingled curiosity and revulsion. The battle itself had been created with some skill and reminded them of images from the film. But their gaze was fixed on the golden cross that rose above the dead and dying soldiers. Nailed immovably to it, Christ was sharing in their agony.

Keedy was astounded. 'I can see what Mrs Mandeville meant.'

'She's a true lover of art,' asserted Voisey. 'I know that she hated it, but she recognised its quality. When others criticised it, she defended me to the hilt.'

'We're told that someone tried to buy it off you,' said Marmion.

'That's right. He came and found me at the refreshments table.'

'How much were you asking?'

'It was a fair price – fifty pounds.'

Marmion gaped. 'How much?'

'You heard.'

'Did he try to haggle with you?'

'Yes,' said Voisey, 'and I felt insulted. You can see how much work went into the painting, not to mention the skill. A labourer is worthy of his hire, gentlemen. An artist deserves respect.' He turned on Keedy. 'How much would you pay, sir?'

'I certainly couldn't afford fifty pounds, I'm afraid. It would take me years to save an amount of that size. It's an extraordinary piece of work, Mr Voisey, but it's far too expensive for me.'

'They all say that,' muttered the artist.

'Tell us about the man who wanted to buy it.'

'He knew nothing about art.'

'Did he make you an offer?'

'Yes, he did, and it was insulting.'

'How would you describe him?' asked Marmion.

'Why do you wish to know?'

'Because the sergeant and I are leading a murder investigation. We have reason to believe that the man who showed interest in your work may have been involved in that murder.'

Voisey goggled. 'Really?'

'Mrs Mandeville has given us a good description of him, but she did not get as close to the man as you obviously did. Also,' Marmion continued, 'she was on duty at the exhibition and distracted by the crowd.'

'That man was a killer?' said the artist in disbelief.

'He may have been. That's all we can say.'

'Then I'll do more than describe him.'

'What do you mean?'

'I can draw a portrait of him in pencil. Would that be of any use?'

'It might well be.'

'Then let's talk about money beforehand.'

'Why?'

'You can't expect me to work for nothing,' said the artist, plaintively.

'And you can't expect us to buy a pig in a poke,' argued Keedy. 'We'd need to see it before we could assess its worth. And don't you dare dash off a sketch that is nothing like the man you met. We can always show it to Mrs Mandeville for confirmation.'

Voisey was offended. 'There's no need to do that,' he said, earnestly. 'I'm an artist. I paint the truth. You'll get what I saw, I promise you.' He looked from one to the other and sucked his teeth. 'Could you manage a fiver?'

Claude Chatfield had a justified reputation for starting work at Scotland Yard early in the morning and for finishing it well beyond the appointed time of his departure. When he held another press conference, he had been on duty for over thirteen hours. Questions from the reports came at him from all sides but he remained calm. Sir Edward Henry had watched part of the event. When it was all over, he took the superintendent aside.

'You should have been a cricketer,' he said.

'I dislike sports of any kind, Sir Edward.'

'That's a pity. You played like an opening batsman. No matter how fast and furious the questions came, you kept a straight bat.'

'I just hope they have the grace to print what I told them.'

'We'll see,' said the commissioner. 'Any breakthrough yet?'

'There's a possible one. Inspector Marmion and Keedy have gone to interview someone who may have met one of the suspects.'

'That's reassuring news.'

'I stress the word "may". It's best to remain cautious.'

'Where exactly have they gone?'

'Camden Town.'

'That's better than charging off to the seaside without notice,' said the commissioner with a ghost of a smile. 'Did anything come of the Brighton episode?'

'It's a matter of opinion. Marmion believed that it did. I disagreed.'

'Going back to the press conference,' said Sir Edward, 'I couldn't help noticing that three different reporters asked why they couldn't question Marmion as well as your good self.'

'If you heard those questions, then you know my answer.'

'You dismissed the idea out of hand.'

'Marmion is far more use gathering evidence than being interrogated by the press. It can, as you know, be a gruelling process.'

'Yet he's always coped well with it in the past.'

'The decision stands, Sir Edward,' said Chatfield, meeting his eye. 'There's something that you seem to have overlooked.'

'What's that?'

'The inspector's son is in prison on remand. If that information gets out, Marmion would be under heavy fire at a press conference. He needs to be protected from that at all costs.'

'What chance is there of a leak?'

'You know what the pay rates are for lower ranks, Sir Edward. Someone might be tempted to make a phone call to a national newspaper to see how much his information might be worth.'

The commissioner nodded. 'It must be embarrassing for the inspector.'

'And for his daughter,' said Chatfield. 'She's in the Women's Police Force. If the word spreads, she may come in for some ribbing from her colleagues.'

'What about the son himself?'

'Sadly, I don't think he cares two hoots about his family.'

The prisoner lay contentedly on his bunk with his hands behind his head. When he heard a key being inserted in the lock, he stood up at once. The door opened and a prison officer came in with a tray of food. When it was placed on the little table in the cell, the prisoner gave it a cursory glance.

'It looks better than the horse shit they served in Wells,' he said.

During the drive back to Scotland Yard, it was too dark to see anything of the portrait they had bought from Colin Voisey. When they eventually returned to Marmion's office, they were able to scrutinise it properly.

'Voisey is very nifty with a pencil,' said Marmion, noting the detail. 'We have to admire him for that.'

'Yes,' said Keedy. 'I agree. I think it might be a good likeness. All the features that Mrs Mandeville and the lady at Pegasus Costumes picked out are there.'

'I'm interested in his clothing. He's quite well-dressed.'

'Neither of the two ladies said much about that.'

'All in all,' said Marmion, 'my fiver was money well spent.'

'Are you going to give Chat the bill?'

'Only if this sketch turns out to be of any use. It might be worth taking it across to the police station in Camden Town. Someone might recognise him.'

'Let's look through our own records first,' said Keedy. 'If he has a history of offending, we may have his photograph in our files. If not, I'll go back to Camden first thing in the morning.'

'I'll hold you to that, Joe.'

'Are you going to show it to Chat?'

'I'll have to,' said Marmion, 'but I won't mention that we had to pay to get it.'

'Thank goodness you had enough money on you. I'm almost skint.'

'Solve this crime and you can demand a pay rise.'

'Is there any point?'

'None at all.' They laughed. Marmion studied the portrait again. 'Voisey certainly has an eye for detail. Those eyes are so dark and menacing,' he noted. 'He could well be one of the killers. Voisey deserves credit. He's a clever artist.'

'I didn't think so when he showed us that painting of the Battle of the Somme. Frankly,' admitted Keedy, 'it turned my stomach. I can't believe that he had the cheek to ask fifty pounds for it.'

'That was only a starting point. He was ready to haggle.'

'Even at half that amount, it would be ridiculously overpriced.'

'Maybe that was his intention, Joe.'

'What do you mean?'

'Voisey loves that painting,' said Marmion. 'You could see that it was special to him. He wants to keep it. When someone shows an interest, he gives them a ludicrous price to frighten them off.'

'Mrs Mandeville told me that he had other paintings on display and that a couple of them sold for modest amounts. But the one featuring that cross at the Battle of the Somme scared most people away.'

'Not this chap,' said Marmion, looking at the portrait once more. 'From what you told me about him, this is close to a photograph.'

'I think that's true.'

'What do we know about him, Joe?'

'He's capable of murder and likes paintings filled with violence.'

'Then who, in the name of God, is he?'

The man with ugly features was seated at the table, counting out the last of the money. His friend soon came into the room. Older and stockier, he had the furrowed brow of someone who took life seriously. He glanced at his companion.

'How much is there altogether?' he asked.

'There's nearly two hundred in cash plus the jewellery, though why a man living alone needs so much jewellery, I don't know.'

'It's too late to ask him.'

'We're not thieves. We needed to convince the police that we were just to confuse them. It's time to get rid of it.'

'I agree.'

'I've just realised something,' said the younger man with a smile. 'With this much money, I could afford to buy that painting I liked.'

'The money is not ours,' his friend reminded him. 'You know what we agreed. We keep enough for our expenses and the rest goes to charity. As for that painting, you told me you rejected it.'

'I did.'

'Why?'

'It wasn't worth the asking price.'

'What appealed to you about it?'

'I liked the message it sent out. It was bold and assertive.' He sat back in his chair. 'What shall we do with all those photographs we took from the house?'

'We put them in a sack and drop it in the canal.'

'And then what?'

'We wait for our orders.'

'That could take time.'

'There's no hurry.'

'There might be if the police pick up our trail.'

'Fat chance of that happening!' said the older man with a derisive laugh. 'You saw the morning papers. The coppers are hopeless. They're running around in circles like headless chickens.'

'I've heard about Inspector Marmion. He never gives up.'

'Forget him. We're in the clear and ready for another assignment.'

'Where will the next one be?'

'I don't know but I hope it's easier than this one. It took us ages to find that bloody doctor. He covered his tracks well.'

'We got him in the end.'

'It's because we stuck at it,' said the other. 'There's no escape from us.'

Though it was almost nine o'clock in the evening when they went to the superintendent's office, Chatfield was still there, studying reports of other investigations. When Marmion and Keedy entered, he looked up with interest.

'Well?'

'We have something to show you, sir,' said Marmion.

'I hope it's worth looking at.'

'It is,' confirmed Keedy. 'It's a portrait of one of the killers.'

'Let me see.' He took the paper and examined the portrait at length. His eyes flicked up at them. 'It's well drawn.'

'Voisey is a good artist,' said Marmion, 'but, like so many of them, not good enough to make money at it.'

'What took you so long?'

'We spent a lot of time with him, sir,' said Keedy, 'then we did what you'd have wanted us to do.'

'Oh?'

'We came back here and trawled through the files to see if we could find a photograph that looked like the man in front of you.'

'And?'

'The cupboard was bare, Superintendent.'

'We don't think that he has a police record,' added Marmion.

'He may not have been successfully prosecuted,' said Chatfield, 'but he could still be known to the police in Camden Town.'

'Inspector Marmion has already asked me to go there tomorrow morning,' said Keedy. 'What we don't know is if he's a resident in the area or someone who just stayed there until he and his accomplice had committed the murder.'

'Camden and Edmonton are not a million miles apart, sir.'

'Neither are they exactly next-door neighbours, Sergeant.' Chatfield set the portrait aside. 'We need more than a hasty sketch from an impecunious artist.'

'I think it could be a good likeness, sir.'

'You might even release it to the press,' ventured Marmion.

'They've got enough to go on,' said Chatfield, fussily. 'I saw to that. I have doubts about this man being a suspect. If he is not, we will have wasted valuable time going down a blind alley. If, by chance, he is – and my reservations remain – then a glance at this portrait of him in the papers will send him scuttling away from Camden Town in a flash. We must never give warnings to villains,' he said, handing the portrait back to Marmion. 'It hands them an advantage.'

'Wise counsel, sir,' said the other.

'I agree,' added Keedy, dutifully.

Before he dismissed them, Chatfield had a question for the inspector.

'I take it that you've spoken to your wife and daughter about ...'

'Yes, sir. Thanks to you, I have.'

'And what have they decided to do?'

'I don't know,' said Marmion. 'If I manage to get home in time, I'm hoping to find out if they have made a decision.'

Having her daughter there for two consecutive nights was a treat that Ellen had not enjoyed for a long time. She was doing the best to make the most of it. Instead of debating endlessly the possibility of a visit to Shepton Mallet prison, they ranged over several subjects. Chief among them was the forthcoming marriage.

'What did Joe think of the house?' asked Ellen.

'He liked it, Mummy, much more than I did.'

'Was this the one you spotted in the evening paper?'

'Yes,' said Alice. 'We couldn't find a time to see it together. I went first and Joe sneaked a few minutes to pop in for a quick look.'

'What was the result?'

'He really liked it, but I didn't.'

'Why was that?'

'It had the smallest kitchen I've ever seen and no garden. There was just a yard at the back, filled with bins and a pile of junk. Also,' said Alice, 'there was a smell as if a drain was blocked.'

'Why did Joe react so differently to you?'

'A small kitchen didn't put him off because I'll do all the cooking. And he was glad there was no garden because it meant there was no grass for him to cut. As for the stench, someone could fix that.' Ellen laughed. 'What's so funny?'

'You sound just like me and your father. We look at the same thing from completely different angles. Not that we were able to own a house straight away, mind you,' recalled Ellen. 'After the wedding, your father moved into our house. A lot of awkward adjustments had to be made with my parents. When we did finally move out, my father was delighted, and my mother begged us to stay.'

'But you both wanted your independence.'

'Yes, we did.'

'So you know why it means so much to me and Joe.'

Ellen brought up a hand to stifle a yawn. 'I'm tired,' she said, glancing at the clock on the mantelpiece. 'Have you seen the time?'

'I'm usually in bed much earlier than this.'

'It's not a usual day, Alice.'

Getting up from the sofa, they were about to leave the room when they heard a car pull up outside. Ellen was delighted.

'That will be your father,' she said.

'I'll be glad of a word with him before I go to bed.'

'I'm so weary, I may need him to help me upstairs.'

They heard a key being inserted in the front door, then it opened wide. When she heard two voices, Alice was delighted. Her father had brought Keedy with him. She ran out of the room and into his arms. Marmion closed the front door.

'I brought you a present, Alice,' he said.

Keedy laughed. 'I've been called worse.'

'It's such a wonderful surprise,' said Alice.

'Yes, it is,' said Ellen, joining them. 'Hello, Joe.'

'I've been invited to spend the night on your sofa,' he told her.

She headed for the stairs. 'I'll get blankets right away.'

'How is the investigation going?' asked Alice.

'I'll let Joe tell you,' said Marmion. 'I'm off to bed.'

'Good night, Daddy.'

She took Keedy into the living room and kissed him. He pulled her close.

'This is the best thing that's happened to me all day,' he said. He looked down at the sofa. 'If I remember aright, it's not very comfy to sleep on.'

Alice laughed softly. 'You may not get much sleep.'

CHAPTER THIRTEEN

For those in law enforcement, there was no rest. Crime in Camden Town took place all day and night, so its police station never closed. It was five o'clock in the morning when a figure crept along the street with a small bag in his hand. Approaching cautiously, he reached the police station, eased open the door and pushed the bag inside. Then he sprinted off into the darkness. The desk sergeant had heard the door open and shut. When he came to investigate, he saw the bag and picked it up. Taking it back to his desk, he tipped out the contents. His jaw dropped involuntarily.

'Where the hell did all this come from?' he asked.

He was looking at a small pile of jewellery.

After an early breakfast at Marmion's home, he and Keedy were picked up by a police car and driven towards central London. A good night's sleep had revived Marmion but Keedy seemed as if he was only half-awake. For the first stretch of the journey, he let Marmion do most of the talking. He then made a conscious effort to join in the conversation.

'I agree with you, Harv,' he said. 'They made the right decision.'

'It was Alice who actually made it. Ellen took time to come round to the idea. My daughter can be very persuasive when she wants to be.'

'I've already found that out.'

'Drop me off at Scotland Yard,' said Marmion, 'then continue on to Camden Town.'

'I don't hold out much hope.'

'Why not?'

'Those men are professionals. Look at the way that they got into Dr Tindall's house. They did their homework beforehand. It's the reason we found no trace of them in our files. They've so far got away scot-free.'

'That will soon change.'

'I hope so, Harv. By the way, are you going to ring the prison?'

'No, I'll ask Chat to do that. Superintendents carry more weight.'

'What about Inspector Gale? Someone needs to explain to her why Alice is not available today.'

'I'll do that as soon as I reach my office.'

'Use your charm.'

'What charm?' asked Marmion with a hollow laugh.

'Oh, I've just thought of something,' said Keedy. 'Suppose the prisoner refuses to see them?'

'I can't see that happening, Joe. In my experience, anyone locked up behind bars usually jumps at the chance of a change of scene, if only for a short time. Apart from anything else, they like to stretch their legs.'

'But a prisoner can't be forced to leave his cell, can he?'

'That depends on the circumstances.'

'What if his mother and sister have come to visit him?'

'There's always the chance that it's not Paul,' insisted Marmion.

'They'd have to see him to make absolutely sure.'

'No, they wouldn't, Joe.'

'What makes you say that?'

'If he refuses to see them, then we know one thing for certain.'

'Do we?'

'Yes – it definitely is Paul.'

Breakfast was served by an impassive prison officer who made no comment. The prisoner ran an appreciative eye over the items on his tray.

'That looks good,' he said, cheerily. 'I came to the right place.'

Alice Marmion was annoyed with herself for having overslept. It meant that she had missed seeing Keedy leave. She blamed her mother.

'Why didn't you call me?' she demanded.

'I did, Alice, but you obviously didn't hear me.'

'Nobody told me that they'd have to be off so early.'

Ellen was philosophical. 'That's police work for you.'

'Oh, I'm so cross with myself.'

She attacked the boiled egg with her spoon. As she ate her breakfast, Alice slowly relaxed and accepted what had happened.

'I'm sorry, Mummy,' she said. 'It's my fault. I should have got up in time.'

'You're up now, that's the main thing.'

'Gale Force will be up as well. She'll soon be wondering where I am.'

'Your father promised to smooth her feathers.'

Alice spluttered. 'Then he's in for a shock. Gale Force doesn't have feathers. She's covered in spikes like a hedgehog. Yes, and she snuffles like one sometimes. If Daddy tries to stroke her, he'll get a nasty surprise.'

'Your father is more tactful than you know,' said Ellen. 'He'll have Inspector Gale eating out of his hand.'

'Count his fingers when he comes home. He might have one missing.'

'Alice!'

While her daughter carried on eating, Ellen sipped her tea reflectively. Her face was soon shadowed with doubt.

'I still don't know if we made the right decision,' she said.

'There's no point in delay, Mummy. That would give us an extra twenty-four hours of sheer misery, wondering if it is Paul. Remember what Daddy and Joe said. We must find out the truth as soon as possible.'

'I suppose so.'

'What's happened to that confidence you suddenly had last night?' asked Alice. 'You couldn't wait to get off to Somerset.'

'Things are different in the daylight.'

'Not for me. I'm going, even if you pull out.'

The telephone rang in the hall. Ellen leapt to her feet at once and ran out.

'That will be your father to tell us if the prison will let us in ...'

The car drew up outside the police station in Camden Town and Keedy got out. After looking up and down the street, he went into the building. The desk sergeant was glancing at a morning newspaper. When he saw Keedy, he put it away. The sergeant was a stout, grizzled man in his late fifties with a world of suspicion in his eyes.

'Can I help you, sir?' he asked.

'I hope so,' said Keedy, producing his warrant card and holding it up. 'I'm involved in the investigation into the murder of Dr Tindall.'

'I read about that,' said the other, his manner changing at once. 'It's not often that I'm shocked but I was when I learnt the details. The poor man was executed.'

'We're anxious to speak to someone from Camden Town who may be of interest to us. As far as we know, he has no previous convictions, but you might just have come across him.'

'What was the name?'

'We don't have one.'

'That's awkward.'

'What we do have,' said Keedy, taking the portrait from his pocket and unfolding it to put on the desk, 'is this. We're assured that it's a good likeness.'

The sergeant's eyebrows arched in approval. 'It's certainly a good drawing,' he said. 'This was done by a proper artist.'

'I'll come to him. Take your time – have a good look.'

Picking up the portrait, the sergeant held it near his face so that he could squint at it. It was almost a minute before he spoke.

'No,' he said, 'I'm sorry. I've never seen him before.'

'Are you certain of that?'

'I've got a good memory, Sergeant Keedy.'

'Fair enough.' Taking the portrait from him, Keedy folded it up and put it back in his pocket. 'Let's move on to the artist, shall we?'

'What artist?'

'His name is Colin Voisey.'

The sergeant chuckled. 'Oh, we know Colin very well.'

'Has he been in trouble?'

'He's spent the odd night in one of our cells, drunk as a lord.'

'I'm surprised he can afford it.'

'Last time we had him here was over an argument in the market. A customer claimed that some of the fruit Colin sold him was rotten. That was like a red rag to a bull. Colin threatened to kick lumps off the customer. They both ended up in here.' He peered at Keedy. 'What's your interest in Colin Voisey?'

'He drew that portrait I showed you.'

'Did he?' asked the other. 'He's got more talent than I thought.'

'There's someone else you might have come across,' said Keedy.

'Who's that?'

'Mrs Mandeville.'

'Oh, yes,' said the other, grinning. 'We've certainly come across Cassie Mandeville. She puts on a pantomime every year in the Arts Theatre. I took my granddaughter to the last one and she's still talking about it …'

Having enjoyed their day out together, Iris Goodliffe was looking forward to seeing her friend again so that she could thank her. She was therefore nonplussed when she was told by Inspector Gale that Alice Marmion was not there.

'Why not?' she asked.

'It doesn't matter,' said the older woman.

'It matters to me, Inspector. We walk the same beat.'

'Today, you will have a different partner.'

'Is Alice ill?' asked Iris. 'She was fine yesterday.'

'I'm not at liberty to tell you the reason why she's unable to be here,' said the inspector. 'When I spoke to her father, he stressed that it was a private matter.'

'There are no secrets between Alice and me.'

Thelma Gale glared. 'Stop pestering me.'

'I'm curious, that's all, Inspector.'

'Direct your curiosity at the streets you're about to walk. I've assigned Jerrold to your beat.'

'Oh, no!'

'Is there a problem?'

'I like Jennifer Jerrold,' said Iris. 'I like her a lot but ... she's not the person I'd choose to spend most of the day with.'

'You don't have the option of a choice,' warned the inspector. 'You go wherever I tell you and with whom I select. Is that clear?'

'Yes, Inspector.'

'In fact, I've been thinking of putting you with Jerrold on a permanent basis.'

Iris was aghast. 'You can't do that!'

'I can do whatever I wish.'

'Alice and I are best friends.'

'That's one of the reasons I'm splitting you up. Walking the beat is more of a social event for the two of you. You probably spend most of the time exchanging gossip instead of concentrating on the task in hand.'

'That's unfair.'

'Jerrold will be a steadying influence.'

'Alice and I have proved our worth as a team many times.'

'You'll do even better in harness with Jerrold.'

'But Jenny and I don't have the same ... understanding.'

'That will come in time.'

'There's no earthly chance of it happening,' said Iris in despair. 'I've nothing against Jenny. She's a nice woman. But – if I may be honest with you – she's too religious for me. She's always talking about her church.'

'Good,' said the other, crisply. 'A brush with Christianity might help to rub some of those rough edges off you. Now get out there and do your job.'

While he and Sergeant Keedy ventured outside Scotland Yard, Marmion had a small team of detectives who remained, for the most part, back at their base. One of them was Detective Constable Clifford Burge, a powerful, thickset man in his thirties with a face that even his best friends would never call handsome. He had already proven his worth when he dealt with some feral gangs terrorising the district where he had grown up. Marmion valued him highly. Once Burge was given an assignment, he worked tirelessly at it.

When he came into Marmion's office, the inspector was glad to see him.

'Good morning, sir,' said Burge, smiling.

'I hope that that look on your face means you have something for me.'

'I may have.'

'Sit down and tell me what it is.'

'Thank you,' said Burge, taking a seat and flipping his notebook open. 'You asked me to look at this case and try to find something similar in the files.'

'And did you?'

'I believe so.'

Marmion waved an arm. 'The floor is yours.'

'Right, sir.' Burge cleared his throat then launched into his report. 'Several months ago, a solicitor in Bristol was hacked to death in his office. He had been castrated.' He gave a grim chuckle. 'Even an angry client wouldn't go that far.'

'What did the police report say?'

'They believe that two men were involved but have no idea who they were. The search continues,' said Burge, 'but there is an interesting piece of information that came to light. The victim had a brother in the army – a Captain Tait.'

'So?'

'He committed suicide some time after his brother was killed.'

'Has any connection been made between the two incidents?'

'The police are still speculating, sir.'

'I'm sure they are,' said Marmion. 'Is that it?'

'No, Inspector. I telephoned the police in Bristol and asked for more detail about the case.'

'Good man.'

'It should arrive by post today.'

'I look forward to seeing it. Making a judgement without more detail would be foolish but, on the surface, there is a resemblance to the case in hand. First, a lawyer and now, an orthopaedic surgeon. Does someone bear a grudge against middle-class professional men?'

'I haven't finished yet, Inspector.'

'Oh, I'm sorry. Do carry on.'

'There's somebody we have to slip in between those two cases. The landlord of a pub in Stafford was murdered several weeks ago. Unnecessary violence was used. In this case, the head was cut off – and so was something else.'

'I can guess what it was,' said Marmion. 'Any leads?'

'Not really, sir. The police have drafted in additional manpower, but they have not dug up anything significant yet. And yes,' Burge went on, 'I did try to get more detail. I got in touch with a Superintendent Ash in Stafford. He was very helpful.'

'Put what he told you in a report so that I can read it.'

'I will, sir. If I keep on looking, I may find other similar murders.'

'Then do just that.'

'It's the degree of brutality that links all three cases.'

'That's true,' agreed Marmion, 'but that's not enough in itself to prove that the same killers were at work in all three cases. Why should anyone jump from Bristol to Stafford then on to London? Since the war started, most people have stayed where they are and kept their heads down. As for the excessive violence, I'm afraid that that, too, is a legacy of the war. It has pushed people to extremes. What used to be a fist is now a knife or a broken bottle. Well, look at those gangs you tackled for us. That turf war was incendiary.'

'Those lads were ready to kill,' recalled Burge. 'I couldn't believe some of the weapons we collected.'

'Thankfully, they've been taken out of action.'

'What shall I do next, sir?'

'Wait until the information arrives from Bristol then compare the details with those of the Stafford murder. I want a written report of both investigations.'

'Yes, sir.'

'Oh, and a word of warning,' added Marmion. 'Don't bank on the three crimes being the work of the same offenders. We've had close similarities before between cases that turned out to be unrelated.'

'I'll bear that in mind.'

'Off you go, then – and well done!'

Faced with a long journey, Ellen Marmion was determined not to spend it agonising about her son. Accordingly, she took a library book with her to read on the train and Alice bought a magazine from the bookstall at the station. As it was, the only seats they could find were in a full compartment, so a private conversation was impossible. Though Ellen tried hard to concentrate on her romantic novel, her mind kept gravitating towards her son. When Marmion had contacted her earlier on, he told her that Superintendent Chatfield had not only secured permission for the two women to get into Shepton Mallet prison. He was even able to pass on the news that – having been contacted by the governor – the prisoner had agreed to meet them.

What had at first been a source of optimism had now become one that made her increasingly uneasy. Even if the prisoner was her son, she was going to meet a stranger. It was a long time since they had seen each other and Paul would have changed in every way. While he may have agreed to see two members of his family, he might refuse to do so out of spite once they had arrived. It was a risk they had to take. And there was also the possibility that the prisoner was not even her son, and that he had used the invitation to meet the two women simply to enjoy some momentary freedom from being locked in his cell. If that were the case, Ellen wondered how she would react. Would she feel anguish or relief?

For her part, Alice was dividing her attention between a recipe in her magazine and warm thoughts about Joe Keedy. Time went quickly for her.

The two policewomen had walked side by side for several minutes without exchanging a single word. It was unusual for someone as garrulous as Iris Goodliffe to remain silent. At length, it was Jennifer Jerrold who spoke first. She was a lanky, fair-haired young woman with a pretty face, now disfigured by a frown.

'Have I done something wrong?' she asked, tentatively.

'No,' said Iris, 'of course not.'

'I get the feeling that you're cross with me.'

'That's not true, Jenny.'

'Then why haven't you spoken since we set out?'

'My mind was on other things.'

'In other words, you were thinking about Alice.'

'Yes, I was. I still can't work out why she didn't turn up this morning. We spent the best part of the day together yesterday, so she had plenty of chances to warn me that she was not feeling well or that she had another reason for staying away today. It's so unlike Alice.'

'The inspector says that she is the best policewoman we have.'

'It's true,' said Iris. 'It's a pity that Gale Force doesn't tell her that to her face. She never stops criticising Alice. I think she is jealous because Alice has got a father who is a detective inspector and because she's engaged to Sergeant Keedy. In other words, she rubs shoulders with real policemen.'

'We're real policewomen,' said Jennifer, proudly.

'Yes, but we don't have the power or the experience that men have.'

'All I know is that Alice saved me from resigning.'

'Thank goodness she did,' said Iris. 'In doing so, she proved what a good detective she is. Because she found out who was stalking you, you are still here with us. That's a bonus.'

'There's more to it than that. Because I felt that someone was watching me all the time, I withdrew into my shell. I can't tell you how horrible it was,' said Jennifer. 'My confidence drained away completely. How could I enforce the law when I was feeling like that?'

'It must have been an ordeal.'

'Because of Alice, I'm a new woman. I can't thank her enough.'

'I'm the same, Jenny. She has been a rock to me. When I had … problems, it was Alice who gave me moral support. That meant so much.'

Jennifer smiled. 'She's done something for the two of us as well.'

'Has she?'

'Yes, Alice has got the two of us talking to each other at last.'

They burst out laughing and walked on purposefully.

As soon as he returned to Scotland Yard, Keedy went straight to Marmion's office. The inspector glanced up from his desk.

'Take a pew, Joe,' he said. 'How did you get on?'

Keedy sat down. 'It was worth the visit,' he replied.

'Tell me why.'

The sergeant recounted the long chat he had with the duty sergeant at Camden Town police station. The man had been unable to recognise the face in the portrait. What he had been able to do was to tell Keedy how much Roland Mandeville and his wife contributed to the community. Keedy looked up from the notebook.

'I've saved the best bit to the end,' he said.

'I'm all agog.'

'Earlier this morning, someone sneaked up to the police station in the dark and left a bag inside the door. When it was opened, it was found to contain an assortment of jewellery. I'm no expert,' said Keedy, 'but it looked like the expensive kind.'

'Did the duty sergeant have any idea where it came from?' asked Marmion.

'No, he didn't.'

'Had there been any recent robbery that involved the theft of jewellery?' Keedy shook his head. 'So where did it come from?'

'I could hazard a guess.'

'Don't jump to conclusions, Joe.'

'Well, we know that valuables were taken from Dr Tindall's safe.'

'But we don't know which valuables,' stressed Marmion.

'Think about it,' urged Keedy. 'A man who keeps photographs of his late wife would be bound to keep her jewellery as a souvenir, especially as he had paid for it in the first place.'

'He may also have paid for her clothing, yet we didn't find a single dress hanging up in the wardrobe. And please do not tell me that the killers took those as well,' added Marmion. 'They may have enjoyed wearing an army uniform, but I fancy that they'd draw the line at ballroom gowns.'

'You're missing something, Harv.'

'Am I?'

'One of those men has been traced to Camden Town.'

'He's been traced to an art exhibition there, maybe. It does not prove that he lives in Camden. He might have been passing through the area, or he may have come off a barge moored in the canal. He might have been visiting a friend who does live there, and he happened to notice what was on at the Arts Theatre. No,' said Marmion, 'there are far too many "mights" here.'

'You may change your mind when that jewellery is valued.'

'Why is that?'

'We've already discovered that Tindall was a wealthy man. He would have bought stuff of the highest quality for his wife. If a jeweller puts a high valuation on it, I think it came from that safe in Edmonton.' Marmion looked dubious. 'It's a reasonable assumption.'

'Then why am I unable to make that assumption?'

'You're starting to sound like Chat.'

Marmion grinned. 'Insults will get you nowhere.'

'Let me remind you of something else,' said Keedy. 'Because we specialise in homicide, we rarely look closely at other crimes being investigated. If there is a big jewellery heist, however, we would get to hear about it, if only from the gossip in the canteen. Can you think of a recent case that was worth talking about?'

'No,' conceded Marmion, 'I can't.'

'Then don't just dismiss my theory.'

'I'm not dismissing it, Joe. I'm glad that you've woken up in time to think straight again. In the car on the way here, you were barely awake. A bag of jewellery has really brought you alive. From my point of view, that's good news.'

'Fair enough,' said Keedy. 'I've said my piece. I won't badger you any more about that jewellery.'

'Thanks.'

'What have you been up to here?'

'I've been considering what may turn out to be some new evidence.'

'Where did it come from?'

'I asked Detective Constable Burge to search for a lookalike crime.'

'Did he find one?'

'He may have found two,' said Marmion, 'though that has yet to be confirmed. Burge is a good detective. I'll be interested to discover what he has unearthed.'

After a long, tedious, and uncomfortable train journey, Ellen Marmion and her daughter endured a lengthy wait at the railway station before a bus finally arrived to take them to Shepton Mallet. As the vehicle struggled along bumpy roads, they were reminded how spoilt they were by living in the nation's capital where taxis, buses and an underground system made travel relatively easy. The one advantage of the second part of their journey was that they were able sit at the rear of the bus and converse freely without being overheard.

'I'm beginning to wonder if we'll ever get there,' moaned Ellen.

'Don't say that, Mummy. My nerves are shredded enough already.'

'I'm having second thoughts.'

'It's too late for that,' said Alice, firmly. 'We have to know the truth.'

'The fact is that Paul has avoided us like the plague.'

'I'm not sure about that. I wonder whether he's just too embarrassed to come back.'

'Embarrassed?' echoed her mother. 'By what?'

'By what he sees as his failure to build a new life. That must have been part of the reason why he left. Paul wanted to find something else,' said Alice. 'He knew he was causing all sorts of problems for us and we were probably doing things that maddened him.'

'I felt that sometimes. He hated being mothered.'

'Perhaps he's changed his mind.'

'There's only one way to find out, Alice.'

The bus eventually dropped them off in the middle of Shepton Mallet and they took their first look at the historic town. It was a world away from the crowded streets and permanent hubbub of the capital. After taking directions from a uniformed policeman, they walked to Frithfield Lane and found the prison. By comparison with the major prisons in London, it was small, but nevertheless forbidding. The idea that Paul was being held behind the high perimeter walls was a chilling one for both women. As they approached, they tried not to look up.

Getting into the prison took time. They were questioned at length, asked to produce proof of identity, and stared at by burly male officers. Eventually, they were taken to the governor's office. After introductions had been made, they sat down.

Gerald Scarman, the governor, was a tall, angular man in his fifties.

'How was your journey?' he asked.

'It was something of a trial,' said Ellen.

'When I spoke to Superintendent Chatfield yesterday, he told me that your husband was a detective inspector at Scotland Yard.'

'That's right. He is. Did he tell you that my daughter was in the Women's Police Force?'

'No, he didn't,' said the governor, turning his attention to Alice. 'I applaud you, Miss Marmion. In times of crisis, it is a case of all hands to the pump, even if some of them are soft, feminine hands.'

'We believe that Paul agreed to see us,' said Alice.

'Ah, well, he did at first, but he seems to have had a change of heart.'

Ellen was horrified. 'We've come all this way for nothing?'

'Not necessarily. The chaplain is talking to the prisoner. He can be very persuasive. What we want to avoid, of course,' said the governor, 'is having to drag him kicking and screaming from his cell. That's hardly the mood you want him in for a family reunion.'

'But we don't yet know that it is my brother,' said Alice.

'The prisoner was happy to confirm it. There is no doubt on that score. We will just have to wait to see if the chaplain can work his magic. Meanwhile,' he went on, 'may I offer you some refreshments?'

CHAPTER FOURTEEN

Claude Chatfield disliked criticism, especially when it came from the commissioner. Because it was delivered by Sir Edward Henry in such a polite, gentlemanly way, it somehow had more impact than a blistering tirade. The morning newspapers had given more extensive coverage on their front pages to the fate of Dr Tindall but – by means of misquoting the superintendent – had somehow conveyed the impression that Scotland Yard was baffled and had made virtually no progress in the investigation. The commissioner had, in effect, blamed the superintendent. As he walked off to his office, Chatfield was in no mood for conversation. When he was confronted by Marmion and Burge, therefore, he waved them aside with an imperious hand.

Marmion stood his ground. 'We need to speak to you, sir,' he said.

'Come back this afternoon.'

'This is important.'

'Don't you understand an order when you hear one?'

'As you wish,' said Marmion, moving aside. 'We'll have to take the information to the commissioner.'

'Don't you dare go above my head,' snapped Chatfield. 'And who are you?' he added, noticing Burge for the first time.

'Detective Constable Burge, sir,' replied the other.

'Are you part of this ambush?'

'It is not an ambush, sir,' said Marmion. 'We are simply trying to bring you what may turn out to be crucial information. If you have more important things to deal with, of course, we'll seek an opinion from Sir Edward.'

There was a long pause as Chatfield considered the threat.

'Follow me,' he growled.

He swept off down the corridor. Marmion winked at Burge and followed the quivering figure in front of them. Once inside his office, Chatfield swung round to issue a challenge.

'I need good news for a change. Give it to me.'

'It concerns a case in Bristol, sir,' said Marmion.

'Then I've no wish to hear about it. My only interest is in a murder that happened right here in London.'

'The men who killed Dr Tindall may have been active in Bristol beforehand.'

'And in Stafford, for that matter,' said Burge.

'We're talking about two remarkably similar murders, sir.'

Burge nodded. 'And there's a distinct echo of them in Dr Tindall's case.'

'You've been distracted,' said Chatfield, acidly. 'I can forgive someone like Burge but a man of your experience, Inspector, should not be led astray so easily.'

'Both murders feature brutality on a scale comparable to that in our case, Superintendent. To be more exact,' Marmion went on, 'both victims were hacked to death and castrated – just like Dr Tindall.'

'We believe the killers were making a point,' said Burge.

'They made the same one in Edmonton.'

'The inspector has told me what the post-mortem report revealed. It's very much in accord with what happened in Bristol and Stafford.'

'What are you trying to tell me?' asked Chatfield.

'If you care to sit down, sir,' said Marmion, 'we will explain.'

'I can hear perfectly well standing up.'

'So be it.' He turned to Burge. 'You take over.'

'Well,' said the other, 'this all came about because of an initiative launched by Inspector Marmion. He believes that the men who killed Dr Tindall were experienced. He therefore asked me to search for cases with the same modus operandi. I began digging in the recent past. The first murder that jumped out at me occurred in Bristol months ago. The victim was a respected solicitor in the city – Meredith Tait. They are still searching for the men who butchered him to death ...'

When they left London, the last thing that Ellen and Alice expected to do was to sit in the prison governor's office, drink tea, nibble biscuits and wonder if they would get to see the person calling himself Paul Marmion. Scarman was pleasant and attentive. He was particularly interested in what being a policewoman entailed.

'My daughter is somewhat younger than you, Miss Marmion,' he said, 'and finds it rather embarrassing that her father runs a prison. It's something she never dared to mention when she was at school.'

'I'm proud of what my father does,' said Alice.

'Rightly so, Miss Marmion.'

'This war has given us precious few benefits but one of them is that it has enabled women to play a more active role in society.'

'I couldn't agree more. As a matter of fact ...'

Whatever he was about to say died on his lips because there was a knock on his door. Scarman opened it to admit a prison officer who delivered a message in an undertone. After apologising to his visitors, the governor went out.

'Paul has turned us down,' said Ellen with an air of finality.

'Let's wait to see what the chaplain does.'

'He's had plenty of time to persuade him and he's failed. If you want my opinion, I think that Paul is playing games with us. He agreed to see us to bring us all the way here, then refused to leave his cell. He's probably sitting in there at this moment, laughing at us.'

'He's not that callous.'

'He is now, Alice.'

'We talked ourselves into believing that it is really him.'

'It is – I sense it.'

'Well, I'm starting to think that it's not my brother at all. It is someone he met along the way who got hold of Paul's papers. That is why he is refusing to see us face to face. We'd expose him as the fraud he obviously is.'

'All I want,' said Ellen, 'is to learn the truth. Is it really Paul?'

'No – he'd never treat us like this.'

'I'm horribly afraid that he would, Alice.'

Her daughter's face puckered. 'I blame myself for persuading you to come here,' she said. 'You wanted another day to think it over and you were right.'

'There's no need to be sorry,' said Ellen. 'I needed a good push from someone, and you gave it to me.' She looked around. 'This place gives me the shivers.'

'Imagine what it must be like to be locked up here.'

'I can't bear to think about it.'

Ellen sat up in surprise as the door opened and the governor came in.

'Your son has agreed to see you, after all,' he said.

'What a relief!' she sighed.

'Why did he change his mind?' asked Alice.

Scarman smiled. 'I did say that the chaplain was persuasive.'

She got to her feet. 'How do we know that it is Paul?'

'It seems that he anticipated that question, Miss Marmion. That's why he sent a message to both of you.'

'What is it?'

'He asked to be remembered to Sally Redwood.'

Ellen gasped and glanced at Alice. It was him.

Remaining on his feet throughout, Chatfield listened carefully. Clifford Burge referred to his notes throughout and marshalled his argument well. Marmion slipped in the occasional rider. The superintendent's face was so motionless that it was impossible to fathom his reaction. When it came, it was cold and clinical.

'Granted,' he said, 'there are surface similarities between the Bristol and the Stafford cases, but that is all they are. You should have started by listing the differences between the two, instead of the coincidences.'

'Both victims died in the same way,' Marmion reminded him.

'They appeared to have done, Inspector, but bear this in mind. Murders across the board have become more vicious. In the last century,' said Chatfield, 'poison was often the chosen weapon. It is far more likely to be a gun, a knife or a meat cleaver now. For some depraved individuals, it is not enough simply to kill. They have the urge to butcher the corpse until it is unrecognisable.'

'That is what happened in both cases,' said Burge.

'I know, but take a closer look at the victims. One was a solicitor with a glowing reputation while the other ran a pub in the Midlands. In the first case, theft was involved. Solicitors are well paid,' said Chatfield. 'When they opened the safe in his office, the killers knew that there would be rich pickings. Robbery played no part whatsoever in the second case. That is hardly surprising. What was there to steal in a pub except a barrel of beer?'

'In both cases,' said Marmion, 'their purpose was to kill. It was the same in Dr Tindall's case. The killers dumped the jewellery they stole at a police station.'

'That's purely hypothetical.'

'It came from a safe in Edmonton.'

'What proof do you have?'

'We can place one of the killers in Camden.'

'That's guesswork.'

'I believe we can see a pattern, sir.'

'Then let me tell you what I believe,' said Chatfield, icily. 'Neither of the cases that Burge has found are linked in any way with what happened to Dr Tindall. That has unique features that separate it from the Bristol and Stafford murders. Nor am I convinced that the same men chose to kill a solicitor in one part of the country and a publican in another. What were their motives?'

'They were obeying orders, sir,' said Marmion.

'From whom?'

'I don't know.'

'Then come back to me when you do.'

'I will, sir. That's a promise.'

'Can I add an interesting piece of information, sir?' asked Burge.

'Please do,' invited Chatfield.

'I told you that the solicitor's brother, Captain Tait, committed suicide.'

'Yes, he shot himself.'

'What I didn't mention was someone in the Stafford case. The police interviewed a woman named Molly Roper, who had worked as a barmaid at the pub for some years. From what I can gather, she had a small stake in the business. Superintendent Ash told me that she was devastated by the murder.'

'I hope this digression has a point,' said Chatfield.

'Mrs Roper's husband was fighting in France. He was killed in action. That, at least, is what his wife was told. Ash learnt more detail about his death. He discovered that Sam Roper, the husband, climbed out of the trench against orders and ran towards the enemy.'

'That sounds like a man who wanted to be killed,' observed Marmion.

'Not to me,' argued Chatfield. 'I think he simply went berserk out of sheer frustration. I can understand that all too easily. If you are stuck in a trench under constant bombardment, it must be like hell. Every day is the same – mud, rats, the stench of death, the noise of bullets and bombs, the sheer terror of it all. You must yearn to escape somehow, no matter what the danger is.'

'There's something I haven't told you yet, sir,' said Burge.

'Well, get on with it, man.'

'Captain Tait and Sam Roper were in the same regiment.'

Chatfield was silenced. His jaw dropped.

'Explain that away, sir,' said Marmion. 'If you can, that is.'

The visitors were taken to a cold, bare, cheerless room. Apart from a table and three chairs, there was no furniture. The whitewashed walls had faded badly over the years. There was a distinct smell of damp. Ellen and Alice sat beside each other on one side of the table. The third chair was opposite them. The governor stood behind the two women. There was a long delay. Ellen's heart was beating faster all the time and she was afraid that the sight of her son would be too much for her. Alice, too, was suffering, certain that Paul would reject them and even resort to abuse. The longer they waited, the more the women suffered.

When the door was finally unlocked, a prison officer led in a young man whose wrists were handcuffed behind his back.

'Paul!' cried Ellen, jumping to her feet.

'It's not him, Mummy,' said Alice, holding her arm.

'Yes, it is,' said the prisoner, defiantly. 'You ask Sally Redwood.'

Ellen stared at him. He looked like her son, though his face was largely obscured by his beard. Alice had no doubts.

'His voice gives him away,' she said to the governor. 'This man is only pretending to be my brother.'

'Alice is right,' agreed Ellen, sadly. 'I was mistaken.'

'Get him out of here,' ordered the governor.

As the prisoner was pushed out of the room, he was cackling.

'I'm sorry that we were tricked by him,' said the governor, 'but your visit was not in vain. You helped to expose him as the arrant liar that he is. We can now add an extra charge against him.' He saw the whiteness of Ellen's face. 'Are you all right, Mrs Marmion? Can I get you something – another cup of tea, perhaps?'

'No, thank you,' she said.

'We just want to get out of here,' added Alice.

'Yes, we do. I feel the need for fresh air.'

'There is one thing you might do for us, please.'

'What is it, Miss Marmion?' he asked.

'Make him tell you where Paul is. He obviously met my brother, but he has not explained when and how. We want the truth.'

The governor nodded. 'Leave it to us.'

Back in his office, Marmion was explaining how the superintendent had rejected the idea of three related murder cases. Keedy rolled his eyes.

'What else could you expect from Chat?'

'We'd have liked a fair hearing from him, Joe.'

'Was he in a bad mood?'

'Yes,' said Marmion. 'He shot down every theory we offered him. Burge was quite upset. He worked hard to collate all that information.'

'What are we going to do with it?'

'Follow in the direction it is pointing us.'

'In other words,' said Keedy, 'we defy the superintendent. I've no argument with that. We've done it before when he's been bone-headed.'

'What stands out in all three cases?'

'Sadistic violence.'

'That is present, I admit, but the link between them for me is the army. The Bristol case was linked to the suicide of an army officer. Another suicide occurred on the battlefield before a publican was murdered in Stafford. And,' Marmion went on, 'I need hardly remind you that Dr Tindall was working in an army hospital. In his case, we believe the killers were disguised as soldiers.'

'I'm convinced of it.'

'Put yourself in their position, Joe.'

'I don't follow.'

'Well, it's highly unlikely they happened to live in Camden Town – or in Bristol or Stafford. What would they have done?'

'Move into each of those places in turn to familiarise themselves with it,' said Keedy. 'Look at the amount of preparation needed for Dr Tindall's murder. They might have watched him for weeks.'

'How would they do that?'

'They'd find a base nearby.'

'Exactly,' said Marmion. 'They would have rented a small house or bedsit.'

'What would that entail?'

'Think hard.'

'Ah,' said Keedy, realising. 'You want me to get in touch with estate agents in Camden Town and adjoining districts.'

Marmion grinned. 'You've read my mind at last.'

'I've had plenty of practice over the years.'

About to reply, the inspector looked at his watch instead.

'What's up?' asked Keedy.

'They should have reached the prison by now.'

'I'd forgotten about that.'

'I hadn't. It's far too important to forget.'

'You're right.'

'I just hope that Ellen bears up under the pressure.'

'What are you expecting?'

'The truth, Joe,' said the other. 'I want to know exactly what my son has been doing since he ran away from home.'

On the bus journey, they sat in silence. Ellen was too stunned to say a word and Alice was simmering with rage. They were on the station platform before they finally broke the silence.

'It was my own fault,' admitted Ellen.

'That's not true, Mummy.'

214

'I dared to hope. I dared to believe that Paul would be at the prison, and that he would be touched by the fact that we had gone all that way to see him. Instead of that, we were humiliated by that … dreadful young man.'

'He enjoyed it,' said Alice. 'That's what made my blood boil. First, he deliberately kept us waiting then he played a cruel trick on us. How could anyone behave that way?'

'I thought it was Paul. He fooled me at first.'

'I knew that he was an impostor as soon as I saw him.'

'Oh, I feel so disappointed, Alice.'

'I'm just furious,' said her daughter. 'When he mentioned Sally Redwood, I really hoped it was him, but it was simply a means of taunting us.'

'He must have heard about Sally from Paul, who probably boasted about what he did to the poor girl. I daresay the two of them sniggered about her.'

'I'm afraid that might be true.'

'Who is that wicked young man, Alice?'

'I wish I knew.'

'Did Paul choose someone like that as a friend?' asked Ellen.

'I hope so, Mummy.'

'That's a terrible thing to say. He is a criminal. Are you happy that your brother is close to someone as revolting as that?'

'I'd much rather he was Paul's friend than his enemy.'

'I don't understand.'

'How do you think he got hold of Paul's papers?' asked Alice, worriedly. 'If he was not a friend, he might have killed to get his hands on them.'

* * *

When the younger man got back to the house, he put the food on a shelf in the larder. His companion came into the kitchen.

'How did you get on?' he asked.

'The market was as busy as ever.'

'Did you see that so-called artist?'

'Yes,' said the other. 'He was selling fruit and veg as usual. I asked him how much he would charge for a couple of apples and that painting I fancied.'

'What did he say?'

'His price is still stupidly high.'

'Nobody will ever pay that much,' said the other with contempt. 'He's not a real artist. He's just a market trader who dabbles in art.'

'Voisey thinks it's the other way round.'

'He's simply playing at being an artist. I should know.'

'Yes, you make a living at it.'

A sudden noise startled the younger man.

'Relax,' said the other. 'It's only the letter box.'

He went into the passageway to pick up the mail. When he came back, he was opening an envelope. His friend was hopeful.

'Is it from him?'

'No,' said the older man, reading the letter. 'It's from the estate agent, reminding us we leave at the end of the week. Someone will come to pick up the key.'

The gates of Edmonton Military Hospital were opened so that two ambulances could drive in. Looking down from the window of his office, Major Palmer-Loach clicked his tongue. Neil Irvine was standing beside him.

'Is this another batch from Cambrai?' he asked.

216

'Yes – they keep coming.'

'Casualties were appallingly high, Howard, but that applies to the Germans as well. Our tanks drove them right back.'

'It seemed so at the time perhaps,' said the major, sadly, 'but reports are now coming through that suggest the Germans have recovered much of the territory they lost to us. Meanwhile, this hospital is having to find beds for those wounded in the battle.'

'You sound weary. That's unlike you.'

'I'm not so much weary as pessimistic,' said Palmer-Loach. 'I just can't see an end to this war. We keep winning ground we are unable to hold and losing good men by the thousand. It is so pointless.' He turned away from the window. 'I'm sorry, Neil. I'm talking like a civilian and not like the soldier I've been for all these years. Victory will be within sight one day and we'll celebrate it together.'

'I'll hold you to that, Howard. We'll raise a glass to the Gordon Highlanders. I've a cousin serving in that regiment. They fought at Passchendaele, an even bloodier battle than Cambrai.'

'Scots regiments have distinguished themselves.'

'They always do. Oh,' said Irvine, remembering something. 'Any word from Inspector Marmion?'

'No – he's been eerily silent.'

'I'm sorry to hear that.'

'He did warn us that it would take time.'

'He also said that he'd keep in touch.'

'When he had something of moment to report – that's what he meant. Evidently, there has been no real progress. But I remain confident that there will be in due course. Marmion is tenacious,' said the major. 'I have faith in him to solve the murder of George Tindall and put all our minds at rest.'

* * *

On the train journey back to London, there was no need for a romantic novel or a magazine. All that Ellen and Alice wanted was to be left alone with their thoughts. The visit to Shepton Mallet had been more than a disappointment. It had raised the possibility that Paul might not even be alive. Ellen struggled to hold on to the idea that her son was safe and well. There was something so vile and knowing about the prisoner they had met. He had deliberately made their ordeal more difficult to bear, agreeing to meet them for the sole purpose of shattering their hopes. Now that Alice had put the idea into her head, Ellen was in agony. Paul was dead. He had been murdered by someone who stole his identity and used it as a way of tormenting his mother and his sister.

Alice was trying hard to believe that her brother might still be alive, after all. Paul had somehow managed to keep well clear of the police, knowing that his family would have reported him as a missing person and that a description of him would have been circulated to every police station. Arrest meant that they would know where he was. Paul had wanted to avoid that at all costs. Alice had assumed that her brother had drifted from place to place, searching for casual work and, if driven to it, begging for food. What she had never considered was the sort of people he might meet along the way. Now that she had done so, she realised just how dangerous a life on the road could be.

The impostor they had met at the prison was an unapologetic criminal, taking anything that he could get his hands on. He must have wormed his way into a friendship with Paul and got him to talk openly about his family. When she first saw the prisoner, Ellen had believed it was her son. Alice was not deceived for a second. What she noticed was the way that he leered at her. It made her wonder what exactly Paul had told him about his sister. At all events, the visit to the prison had been an ordeal from start to finish. She clung to one slim hope – that Paul was alive. Alice now had to convince her mother that it might be true.

While he had been unfairly misquoted in some of the newspapers, Claude Chatfield saw the benefits of publicity. There was an immediate response. Those who manned the switchboard at Scotland Yard took several calls offering information regarding the murder. Some of it was clearly bogus, aimed at confusing the police investigation, but a lot of reliable facts about George Tindall also came in. From time to time, it was collated and taken to the superintendent's office.

He was busy separating the wheat from the chaff when he was interrupted by a detective constable. The man held out a sheet of paper.

'What's that?' asked Chatfield.

'It's a telephone number, sir.'

'If it's another hoax call, you can tear it up right now.'

'I'm convinced that it's genuine.'

'Let me see.'

Chatfield took the paper and read the name on it. The impact made him reel. When he recovered, he snatched up the receiver immediately.

Keedy was restive. Instead of being out in pursuit of suspects, he was stuck in Marmion's office, ringing estate agents in turn. Time and again, he spoke to someone who was unable to help him, leading him to believe that the suspects might be living nowhere near Camden Town. After another call proved fruitless, he slammed the receiver down.

'Steady on, Joe,' said Marmion. 'That phone is a vital tool for us. Don't smash it to bits.'

'I'm sorry, but it's so frustrating. I'm getting nowhere.'

'How many costume hire companies did you contact before you

found one that gave you vital evidence?'

'Quite a few,' admitted Keedy.

'I rest my case.'

'I'm sorry to complain, Harv, but this is getting on my nerves. I'd much rather be in Camden Town, searching for them.'

'Where would you start? You'd be like a blind man in a dark cellar.'

'I could take that portrait of one of the killers with me and show it around. At least, I'd have the feeling of doing something.'

'You are doing something,' said Marmion, 'and it's important work. Grit your teeth and keep going. Who knows? The next estate agent you speak to might be the one who can actually help us.'

'I've been telling myself that for the last half an hour.'

'Perseverance is a virtue.'

Keedy sighed. 'If you say so …'

The door suddenly opened, and Chatfield came in.

'I've been on the telephone,' he announced.

'So have I, sir,' complained Keedy, 'and I'm getting nowhere.'

'As a result of the newspaper coverage, information has been coming in from all over the place. This is a summary of it,' he went on, handing a sheaf of papers to Marmion. 'There are people who worked alongside Dr Tindall in Brighton and others who knew him as a medical student in St Thomas's Hospital.'

'Thank you very much, sir,' said Marmion.

'It will help to fill in some of the gaps.'

'They're not gaps – they're chasms.'

'Whatever you're doing, I want you to drop it at once.'

'Why?'

'You and the sergeant must go to Kent immediately.'

Marmion was taken aback. 'Has something happened?'

'I spoke to a woman on the telephone,' explained Chatfield. 'She was in such a state that I couldn't make out what she was saying at first. When I did manage to calm her down, she made a remarkable claim.'

'What was it, sir?'

'She said that she was George Tindall's wife.'

'But his wife is dead,' said Marmion.

'She sounded very much alive to me.'

'What name did she give, Superintendent?'

'Eleanor Tindall.'

'That was the name of his late wife.'

'He kept photographs of her all over his house,' recalled Keedy. 'For some reason, the killers stole them.'

'How convinced were you she was telling the truth?' asked Marmion.

'Completely,' affirmed Chatfield. 'She provided so much detail that it was impossible not to believe her. She was in great distress. Only two weeks ago, Mrs Tindall saw her husband alive and well. He paid a fleeting visit to her.'

'What's her address?'

'It's on the top page I just gave you – so is her telephone number.'

'Well,' said Keedy, 'this sounds promising.'

'Go by train to Tonbridge and take a taxi from there.'

Marmion was puzzled. 'Why on earth did Dr Tindall tell everyone that his wife had died?' he wondered. 'That's an extraordinary thing to do.'

'I agree,' said Chatfield, 'but we are dealing with an extraordinary man.'

CHAPTER FIFTEEN

When their train stopped at Reading station, the other passengers in their compartment got out. Ellen and Alice were able to talk freely at last and release emotions that had been bottled up throughout their journey.

'I thought that we'd never be alone,' said Ellen with relief.

'I felt the same, Mummy. We've had to suffer in silence.'

'Being able to talk to you like this is a luxury.'

'How are you feeling now?' asked Alice.

'To be honest, I feel more depressed than ever. I could not believe that anyone could be so cruel. He dragged us all the way there on purpose. If he can do something as wicked as that, he's got no conscience.'

'He will pay for it, Mummy. As a result of what he did, time will be added to the length of his sentence. In torturing us, he gave himself away. They know that he was lying about his identity now and will do their best to find out who he really is. Anyway,' said Alice, 'forget about

222

him. We still have our freedom. He's going to be locked up for a long time.'

'Do you really believe that he did kill Paul?'

'No, I don't.'

'But you thought he was capable of it.'

'That was my immediate reaction.'

'What has changed your mind?'

'I've been thinking,' said Alice. 'If he had murdered Paul, he wouldn't have been stupid enough to see us because he knew that his deception would be revealed immediately. How he got hold of those papers, I have no idea, but they're worthless now and that didn't worry him.'

'Nothing did,' said Ellen. 'Even though he was handcuffed, he seemed completely at home in that prison. Obviously, it is not the first time that he's been locked up. It may well be the story of his life.'

'Let's hope that Paul was not led astray by him.'

'You know what they say about birds of a feather.'

'I refuse to believe that my brother would sink that low,' said Alice with sudden passion. 'He had his faults, but he was brought up to know the difference between right and wrong. Have more faith in him.'

'I wish that I could,' said Ellen, uneasily.

'What do you mean?'

'Running away from home is wrong. Refusing to contact your parents is wrong. Deliberately letting us suffer is wrong. Paul might have been able to tell the difference between right and wrong once,' said Ellen, sharply, 'but he's forgotten how to do it now. We've lost him, Alice.'

They sat at the kitchen table over the remains of their meal. The older man was reading a newspaper. When he broke off, he tapped the photograph on the front page.

'Look at him,' he said. 'Tindall was a handsome man in his prime.'

'He wasn't very handsome by the time we finished with him,' said the other with a snigger. 'He got what he deserved.'

'We stopped him for good – and not before time.'

'What does the article say?'

'Oh, it's full of threats by someone called Superintendent Chatfield. He reckons that his detectives will soon run the culprits to earth.'

'Is that what we are – culprits?'

'We are much more than that,' said the older man, seriously, 'but this superintendent would never understand why. He thinks we're no better than wild animals.'

'What evidence do they have?'

'None at all, Brian. The police know absolutely nothing.'

'Nevertheless,' admitted the other, 'I'll be glad when we move away from here. I'll feel safer then.'

'We're perfectly safe where we are.'

'I'm not so sure now. We're strangers here, remember. People still give us funny looks in the street. What if someone reports us to the police?'

'Calm down,' said the other. 'I thought you liked this area. Where else would you have found that painting you liked so much? In art galleries, all you can do is look. At that exhibition in the Arts Theatre, everything was for sale.'

'The only painting I wanted was too expensive.'

'You could always steal it,' teased the older man.

'We don't steal. That's why we gave that jewellery back.'

'I wonder what the police thought when they found it.'

'They'll know something funny is going on. It's one of the reasons I'd like to move on.'

'We rented this place until the end of the week,' said the other, calmly. 'It's been perfect for us. I hope we find somewhere like it when we move on and leave the police floundering yet again.'

As they alighted from the train at Tonbridge station, Marmion and Keedy headed for the exit. They soon joined the queue at the taxi rank. Keedy was sceptical.

'Are we certain that this woman really is Mrs Tindall?' he asked.

'Who else might she be?'

'Some people love making fake calls.'

'Not in this case, Joe,' said Marmion. 'Chat would never be fooled like that. If he says that she is genuine, then I accept that she must be. I'm just surprised that she lives in Kent.'

'But we knew that he owned a house here somewhere.'

'He used to own one. I assumed that he sold it when he moved to Edmonton. We were told that he wanted to get away from a place with so many associations with his late wife.'

'There is no late wife. Mrs Tindall is alive and kicking.'

'Yes – and he even found time to visit her recently.'

'Whatever is going on?' asked Keedy, bemused.

'I think the doctor must have been leading a double life.'

'How did he manage that? I can't afford to live one on police pay.'

'I've just remembered something,' said Marmion. 'We were told that he owned a property in Brighton.'

'Yes, we saw it – that large flat of his.'

'I'm talking about the house we visited.'

'Hipwell Manor?'

'Yes, that's the place.'

'It was a big mistake. We got kicked out straight away.'

'I know. Mrs Langford was furious with us.'

'I'll never forget that look on her face.'

'Do you remember what she threatened to do?'

'Yes,' said Keedy. 'She was going to complain about us to Chat.'

'Then why didn't she?'

'She must have changed her mind.'

'I doubt that, Joe. There must be another reason.'

'Her letter might have got stuck in the post.'

'When we left her,' recalled Marmion, 'she was in a mood to deliver it in person to Scotland Yard. She claimed that we'd violated her privacy, yet all we did was to ask a few simple questions.'

'Some women are like that.'

'Mrs Langford is not one of them, Joe. I've got a strange feeling that we haven't heard the last of her somehow.'

'No,' said Keedy. 'When that husband of hers gets back from his latest deployment, she'll probably set him on to us. That means we'll have the Admiralty on our tails – and all for asking a few simple questions.'

Before they left Scotland Yard, Marmion had delegated the job of ringing estate agents to Clifford Burge. Having already contributed evidence to the investigation, Burge was delighted to be trusted with an important task. Unlike Keedy, he was not disheartened by lack of success. As he drew a blank with one estate agent, he simply moved on to another. The sergeant had started with companies based in or near Camden Town before shifting slowly away from it.

Burge followed his example, moving slightly north, then east and then south before completing the circle by pushing to the west. When he telephoned someone in Acton, he finally got a positive result.

'I may have found what you wanted,' said the estate agent. 'It's a three-week rental in Camden Town that terminates this weekend.'

'Could I have the address, please?'

The man gave him the details and described the house as small but with a garden at the rear. It was something the client had stipulated.

'I'd like his name, please,' said Burge.

'It was Anthony Brown, sir.'

'Did he give you his home address?'

'No,' said the other, 'but there was a sort of rustic burr in his voice. The rental address is as follows.'

Burge jotted it down. The estate agent anticipated the next question.

'He paid the full amount in advance, sir. He came here and paid in cash.'

'Can you recall what he looked like?'

'He was an older man, perhaps in his late fifties. He was well-built and wore a suit. He gave no reason for moving to Camden Town for such a short time. I assumed he had business in the area. He was anxious to view the property before handing over the money.'

'Any distinguishing features?' asked Burge.

'Yes, he had a beard. He was quiet, polite and had the kind of eyes that seem to look right through you. Oh, and he was broad-shouldered. Somehow he didn't look as if he belonged in a suit.'

'Do you have any idea what he did for a living?'

'If I had to guess,' said the estate agent, 'I'd say that he had something to do with the land. He was definitely not a city person.'

The taxi took them to a country lane near Hadlow and the driver agreed to wait until the detectives had finished their business there. Marmion and Keedy appraised the house. It was a sprawling cottage set in the middle of a garden large enough to boast a lawn tennis court. They admired its charm and serenity.

'It's idyllic, Joe,' said Marmion. 'I'd move in tomorrow if I could.'

'You hate gardening.'

'I'd expect you to do that in your spare time.'

Keedy laughed. 'What spare time?'

Before they reached the front door, it was opened by a nervous young maidservant who all but curtseyed to them. As they entered the house, she told them that Mrs Tindall was unwell and being looked after by her mother. When they removed their coats and hats, the servant hung them on pegs in the hall. She then conducted them into the lounge.

Eleanor Tindall was seated on the sofa with a blanket draped across her lap. She was a beautiful woman in her thirties turned into a pale, fragile shell of her former self. Sitting beside her was the person from whom she had inherited her good looks. Romilly Staynes was a handsome, well-dressed woman who had retained her figure into her early sixties. When the detectives entered the room, she rose at once to introduce herself and her daughter, speaking in a clipped, educated voice. Marmion performed introductions in return. Keedy, meanwhile, was glancing around the room and taking note of the expensive furniture and fittings.

As the three of them took their seats, Romilly explained that her daughter was still reeling from the shock she had received, and that the detectives had to be gentle with her.

'I'm fine now, Mama,' said Eleanor.

'Let me do the talking, dear,' suggested her mother. She turned to Marmion. 'You can guess what I'm about to ask you, Inspector.'

'Yes, Mrs Staynes,' he said, 'and the simple answer is that we are absolutely certain that the deceased is Dr George Tindall.'

'But he wasn't a doctor,' protested Eleanor.

'What did you think he was, Mrs Tindall?'

'I can't tell you that.'

'Why not?'

'It's … classified information.'

'That is what we were tricked into believing,' said Romilly, spitting the words out. 'The simple truth is that my daughter married a man who deceived her in the most appalling way. What we need from you, Inspector, is a promise that we will be protected from any intrusion by the newspapers. Above all else, my daughter needs privacy. She sustained a fearful blow – and so, of course, have I.'

'What about your husband, Mrs Staynes?' asked Keedy.

'He died some years ago. If he had been alive at the time, the marriage would never have taken place. He had a nose for bounders.'

'That's not what George was, Mama,' pleaded Eleanor. 'He loved me truly. I still think that a grotesque mistake has been made.'

'Unfortunately, we made it.'

'To answer your question, Mrs Staynes,' said Marmion, 'I am unable to guarantee complete immunity from the press, but there are ways in which we can help you in that regard. What we don't understand is why Dr Tindall and his wife chose to live apart.' The two women exchanged a rueful glance. 'Sooner or later, the truth will come out. Furthermore, it would help our investigation if we understood how your daughter came to meet and marry George Tindall.'

Alice Marmion waited at the bus stop with her mother so that she could wave her off. They were both reassured to be back in London again.

'It's funny, isn't it?' said Ellen.

'What is?'

'On any other day, it would have been a pleasure to visit a lovely town like Shepton Mallet. When we first got to meet, your father and I sometimes went for a walk in the country. The peace was wonderful and there were always animals to see in the fields.'

'It might have been the same for us today, Mummy. We went at the wrong time to a place we would otherwise have enjoyed. It was so pretty – until we saw its prison.'

'Let's put that all behind us, Alice.'

'I agree.'

'It's caused us enough heartache already.'

'Are you going to ring Daddy when you get home?'

'No, I won't do that.'

'He'll be dying to know what happened.'

'I can't interrupt him in the middle of a murder investigation,' said Ellen. 'Besides, I'm not supposed to contact him unless there's an emergency.'

'That means he won't know what happened until he gets home late.'

'Oh, I think he will. In fact, he may already have been told.'

'How?'

'Superintendent Chatfield may have spoken to your father. It was only because of him that we were able to visit the prison. I'm fairly certain that the governor would have contacted the superintendent to tell him all about our visit.'

When he discovered what he felt was to be crucial information, Clifford Burge had wanted to pass it on immediately so that he could accompany Marmion and Keedy to the address in Camden Town. Unfortunately, they were no longer in Scotland Yard. He was therefore forced to report to Chatfield instead. The superintendent listened carefully but was unconvinced.

'Remember your mathematics,' he warned.

'What do you mean, sir?'

230

'Things have to add up properly. You put two and two together and ended up with twenty-seven. If I had a dunce's hat in here, you'd be wearing it.'

Burge was deflated. 'That's unfair, sir,' he protested. 'I spent a long time on the telephone to get that address and I still think it could be significant.'

'Why?'

'Our suspects could be living there.'

'What are the chances of that?'

'I'd say that they were quite strong.'

'Well, I'd say that they were minimal. Sergeant Keedy has an obsession that those men are living in Camden Town, but he has no conclusive proof that it is true. All that you established with your phone call is that an estate agency in Acton rented a property in Camden. It was a perfectly legal transaction.'

'It was also a strange coincidence.'

'We're back to your faulty mathematics again.'

'The inspector believes that our suspects would have found somewhere to stay weeks before they actually committed the murder.'

'I agree with him,' said Chatfield, 'but why stay some distance away from Edmonton when that is where they should have been doing their reconnaissance?'

'I don't know,' admitted Burge.

'Start asking estate agents if they have rented property in Edmonton recently. That's a much more promising line of enquiry.'

'I was only following orders, sir.'

'Then let me give you some more to obey. One – forget about Camden Town.'

'Yes, sir.'

'Two – don't get infected by Sergeant's Keedy's overenthusiasm.'

'That's unkind, sir.'

'Three – don't bother me again unless you have cast-iron information.'

'It may still turn out to be exactly that,' insisted Burge.

'Four – abandon hopeless positions like the one you're in now. I'm sorry to be so harsh on you,' said Chatfield. 'You have the makings of a good detective. I expect big things of you – once you've learnt that brainwaves of the kind that some of my officers have from time to time bear no comparison with factual evidence gathered by means of hard graft.' He gave a steely smile. 'Pass that message on.'

Marmion and Keedy were spellbound by the story they were told. It was essentially a confession by Eleanor, though her mother interrupted her so often that it began to seem like a joint effort. With his notebook perched on his knee, Keedy was having trouble keeping up with the narrative.

It had all started before the war when Tindall had met the two women at a dinner party. He had sat between them and, with wine flowing, had ample time to ingratiate himself with them. The friendship forged there had developed slowly. What he had told them was that he was the administrator of a large hospital in Birmingham and that he was only able to get away from time to time. While his main interest had been in Eleanor, it was obvious that he had charmed the mother as well, conscious that he could make no headway without her approval.

Social events always involved the three of them. They went to plays, concerts and operas together. The fact that he insisted on paying for everything worked in his favour. When he visited the house, Romilly made sure that he spent time alone with her daughter. The friendship between them deepened into love. Then came the bombshell. Tindall told them that he could no longer deceive them. His job as a hospital administrator did not exist. It was a convenient mask for the work that he really did with British intelligence.

'First,' recalled Eleanor, 'he swore us to secrecy, then he told us about work he'd done abroad. War seemed inevitable at that point so – because he was fluent in German – he was about to be sent behind enemy lines.'

'He then told us,' added Romilly, 'that we had become his closest friends and that it had pained him to go on deceiving us. When he confided in us that he would have to disappear from our lives, we were thunderstruck. George had seemed everything I had ever hoped for my daughter.'

'We had ... talked about marriage,' murmured Eleanor.

'But he felt that the burden on us would be too great to bear. He would be away for long periods, unable to remain in constant contact.'

'I didn't mind that,' confessed Eleanor. 'In fact, I felt rather excited by the idea of a secret marriage to a wonderful man, facing danger for the benefit of his country. I was ready to accept him on those terms.'

'To my chagrin,' said Romilly, 'I agreed. I let my only child marry someone I admired as the secret agent he claimed he was. How reckless could a mother be?'

'What did you tell your family and friends?' said Keedy.

'We told them as little as possible,' replied Romilly. 'It was a quiet wedding. They were married in a civil ceremony and spent their honeymoon in the Lake District. A couple of weeks later, war broke out and George disappeared.'

'How often did you see him after that?' asked Marmion.

'No more than a dozen times or so. Often, it was only for a couple of days. On their first wedding anniversary, he managed a full week.'

'It was heavenly,' said Eleanor. 'Or so I thought at the time.'

'Do you have any children?' asked Keedy, softly.

'We have a son, Peter. He's almost three.'

'Imagine the kind of shock that awaits him,' said Romilly. 'The day will come when he has to know the truth about his father. He will carry the shame of it for the rest of his life. George was a barefaced liar. I find myself quite unable to have any sympathy for the way that he died.'

'Mama!' exclaimed her daughter.

'We have to be honest.'

'Even so ...'

When he saw tears forming in Eleanor's eyes, Marmion decided that it was time to bring the interview to an end. After a few more questions, he thanked both women for being so open with him and promised to keep in touch with them. He and Keedy then left the house.

'What did you make of that, Joe?'

'I can't wait to see the look on Chat's face when we pass on the information.'

'He'll be outraged,' said Marmion. 'He believes strongly in the sanctity of marriage – and so, for that matter, do I.'

Keedy was amused. 'Am I being warned by my future father-in-law?'

'It's more of a gentle nudge than a warning.'

'Fair enough.'

'Unlike Dr Tindall, you'll be married in the sight of God.'

'As it happens,' said Keedy, seriously, 'it's what Alice and I want more than anything else.'

Back at his desk, Clifford Burge was still feeling bruised after his argument with the superintendent. His frustration was compounded by the way he had been mocked, then summarily dismissed by Chatfield. Hoping for praise, he had met with condemnation instead. He felt certain that he would get a more sympathetic hearing from Marmion.

Until the inspector returned, Burge decided to take a second look at the evidence he discovered about the murders in Bristol and Stafford. What linked them was the suicide of two men in the North Staffordshire Regiment. Captain Tait had shot himself and Private Samuel Roper had deliberately broken cover to run towards enemy fire. Burge knew that they were by no means the only soldiers to commit suicide. Men who lost limbs or suffered disfiguring injuries had elected to die by their own hand rather than lead what they feared would be miserable lives. Those with severe mental problems or permanent shellshock also found death a tempting alternative to what lay ahead.

It was not in the interests of morale – at home as well as in the ranks – for the British Expeditionary Force to give full details of suicides. The terse telegrams sent to waiting families on the Home Front made no mention of the intolerable pressures that had forced someone to take his own life. They had died in action, an honourable way to serve their country. That was all that parents needed to be told.

The suicides he had located were two among many. Other soldiers had shot themselves or used enemy ammunition as a means of escape from hell. Yet the two deaths in the North Staffordshire Regiment continued to burrow into his mind. They were connected in a way he was unable to comprehend. Checking his notes once more, Burge gave the two victims his full concentration, convinced that they might somehow hold the key to the savage murder of George Tindall.

When evening shadows darkened the streets of Camden Town, the two men felt able to leave their hiding place without fear. They walked side by side along a high street now largely deserted. The older man turned to his companion.

'How do you feel now, Brian?' he asked.

'All the better for knowing we'll soon leave,' said the other.

'I was beginning to get bored with this place.'

'I can't wait to go.'

'Even though you can't take that painting with you?'

'I can live without it.'

'The main thing is that we obeyed our orders to the letter.'

'And we got away with it.'

'Remember to offer thanks in your prayers.'

Turning a corner, he led his companion towards the church.

As they walked across the concourse at Charing Cross Station, they were able to have a private conversation at last. That had been impossible in the taxi that took them to Tonbridge and the train that brought them back to London.

'What are you going to tell Chat?' asked Keedy.

'You were the one taking notes, Joe. I'll rely on you to give him an accurate account of what we learnt.'

'He's going to be appalled.'

'I agree,' said Marmion, 'and with good cause. Chat has got daughters of his own. The idea that one of them might suffer the fate of Eleanor Tindall will be horrifying to him.'

'If he'd been Eleanor's father, this would never have happened. He would have been suspicious of George Tindall from the very start. Unfortunately,' said Keedy, 'the poor woman didn't have a father.'

'That was one of the reasons Tindall was attracted to her.'

'It was easy to see why. Eleanor was beautiful, intelligent and came from a good family. The only problem was that hawk-eyed mother of hers. Tindall had to win her over first and he obviously did that.'

'I felt sorry for Mrs Staynes. She knows she failed her daughter.'

'It's the child I worry about,' said Keedy. 'There's going to be an awkward moment in his life when he learns what a ruthless man his father was.'

'Chat will be quick to make that point, Joe.'

'Is there anything you're not going to tell him?'

'Yes, there is.'

'What is it?'

'Attractive as she was,' said Marmion, 'I don't believe that Eleanor would ever be enough for Dr Tindall. He was a man of great cunning and, I fancy, great appetite. The tricks that he played on one woman would work equally well on others.'

Keedy was startled. 'You think that he had another wife?'

'I'd go even further, Joe. I believe that we may have met her.'

Donald Hepburn was a tall, dignified man in his sixties with long, curling grey hair giving him a slightly leonine appearance. He paced the lounge at Hipwell Manor, shifting between fury and concern. Above his head, he could hear footsteps in the main bedroom. When they began to descend the stairs, he rushed into the hall.

'How is my daughter?' he asked.

'I've given Mrs Langford a sedative,' said the doctor with a sad smile. 'Sleep is what she needs more than anything else.'

CHAPTER SIXTEEN

As soon as they got back to Scotland Yard, they went straight to Marmion's office. An envelope was propped up against the inkwell on his desk. Slitting it open with a paperknife, he read the message.

'Who is it from?' asked Keedy.

'Cliff Burge.'

'What does he want?'

'He thinks he's found something interesting,' said Marmion, 'but, when he discussed it with Chat, his theory was shot down in flames.'

'We've all had that happen to us,' moaned Keedy.

'Read this for yourself.'

Marmion handed him the letter and waited for his response. It took only seconds before the sergeant's face lit up with pleasure. He read on to the end of the letter then waved it in the air.

'This is wonderful news,' he said.

'And how was it achieved?'

'Cliff Burge used his intelligence.'

'There's something you've missed out, Joe. He used his intelligence by ringing estate agents until he found the right one. Then he got vital information. In other words,' said Marmion, 'he persisted at a task that you found boring.'

Keedy spread his arms. 'I admit it freely.'

'It's the boring tasks that often deliver the goods.'

'I'd love to put this new information to the test.'

'It's exactly what I want you to do,' said Marmion. 'Find Burge and get the full details from him. If you think his discovery merits acting upon, take him with you to Camden Town.'

'Don't I need Chat's permission?'

'Let me worry about the superintendent.'

'Won't he ask what I'm doing?'

'No, he'll be far too busy coping with the shock of what we discovered in Kent. Chat will be wondering how he can keep the full truth out of the newspapers. Think of the headlines,' said Marmion. 'Murder victim turns out to be a cruel confidence trickster – the press would love a story like that.'

Eleanor Tindall was sitting up in bed, reading wistfully through a pile of letters she had received during her courtship. They were so affectionate and touching that she could still not wholly believe her future husband had exploited her. Their intimate moments together were memories she had treasured. Could they really have been so many mirages? Were all his promises grounded in deceit? Had Tindall's joy at the birth of their son simply been an act for her benefit?

While she tried desperately to persuade herself that he had really loved her, she remembered the visit of the two detectives. They told her things about her husband that shattered her fantasies. Yet even as she kept telling herself to accept the harsh truth, she kept reading the honeyed words of his letters.

When the door suddenly opened, she was startled. Her mother had just come into the bedroom. It took Romilly only seconds to realise what her daughter was doing. Snatching the letters away from her, she walked across to the fire crackling in the grate and threw them one by one into the flames. Romilly's teeth were exposed in a silent snarl. She ignored Eleanor's squeals of protest and watched the false promises curling up the chimney in smoke.

It was uncharacteristic of Claude Chatfield to sit in his chair and listen to a report without interrupting it with endless questions. But the story that Marmion told him had rendered the superintendent speechless. He took a long time to absorb all the details. There was a note of incredulity in his voice.

'Can all this be true?' he asked.

'Mrs Staynes and her daughter gave us an honest, unvarnished account.'

'My heart goes out to them. What must they have thought when they saw that photograph of Dr Tindall in the newspapers? It came as a hammer blow to them.'

'They're still rather dazed by it all, sir.'

'The pair of them were bamboozled for years.'

'Tindall knew exactly how to worm his way into their affections,' said Marmion. 'I don't believe that they were his first victims.'

'What makes you think that?'

'He was obviously so confident and practised.'

'It's the wife that I feel the greatest sympathy for,' said Chatfield. 'After years of what she believed was a happy marriage, she learns that it was a complete sham.'

'Her mother suffered as well, sir. She blames herself for not protecting her daughter better. When her husband died, she took the duty of care onto her own shoulders. Mrs Staynes struck me as an intelligent, loving, watchful woman. It says a lot for Tindall's manipulative skills,' Marmion contended, 'that he was able to convince her that his attentions were entirely honourable.'

'You make him sound like a puppeteer.'

'That is exactly what he was, sir. He controlled their movements by twitching the strings. His wife and mother-in-law were ready to endure the many constraints and absences because he made up for them when he came back into their lives again.'

'And it was always at a time of his choosing,' said Chatfield, bitterly.

The superintendent fell silent. As a devout Roman Catholic, he had a clear idea of the virtues of family life. He could not understand how a talented man like George Tindall could jettison every principle of fatherhood and, indeed, of sheer decency. While it was necessary to discuss the ugly details of the case with Marmion, he would never dare to do so with his wife.

'One is bound to feel sorry for any murder victim,' he said, sonorously, 'but I feel that my sympathy for Dr Tindall is beginning to wane.'

'He was a vicious predator, sir.'

'Bigamy is a disgusting crime and a heinous sin.'

'I couldn't agree more, sir.'

Chatfield went off into a kind of trance as he considered the implications of Tindall's behaviour. When he had finished, he looked at Marmion as if seeing him for the first time. His memory was jogged.

241

'Oh,' he said, 'forgive me. I have a message for you. The governor of Shepton Mallet prison was kind enough to telephone me.'

'Is he holding my son in his prison?'

'No, Inspector.'

Marmion was relieved. 'Then who is using Paul's name?'

'His identity is still unknown.'

'What exactly happened at the prison?'

'To find that out,' said Chatfield, 'you will have to speak to your wife.'

When she alighted from the bus, Ellen Marmion still had to walk several blocks to reach her home. Her fear was that she would bump into Patricia Redwood once again. The most memorable thing about her visit to Shepton Mallet was the jeering reference to Sally Redwood. It had been made by the prisoner and it proved that he had met her son. Ellen was horrified that Sally's name had been used in the crude banter between two young men who were living rough. Much as she disliked the mother, she felt sorry for the daughter and was glad that Sally was unaware of what had happened.

It had been a long and disappointing day. When she got to the house, Ellen promised herself, she would make herself a cup of tea and flop into an armchair. The streets were cold, dark and deserted. Because a blackout had been imposed, there were no friendly gas lamps to guide her home. By the time she finally got there, her feet were sore. Letting herself into the house, she went straight to the kitchen, filled the kettle and set it on the stove. When the kettle had boiled, she used some of the hot water to warm the teapot. Minutes later, she went into the living room with her cup of tea and sat down.

Only then did she realise that she was still wearing her hat and coat.

Before she could laugh at herself, she heard the telephone ring. Putting her cup aside, Ellen hauled herself out of the chair and went into the hall. She put the receiver to her ear.

'Hello …'

'It's me, love,' said Marmion. 'How did you get on?'

It took Keedy only a couple of minutes to decide that Burge's argument was compelling. The two of them left the building at speed. As they sat in the rear of a police car, Burge was worried.

'Does the superintendent know about this?' he asked.

'He will do when we take two prisoners back with us.'

'We can't be sure that we will,' said Burge. 'I don't want to give him another chance to rap me over the knuckles.'

'Don't worry, Cliff. I take full responsibility for what we do.'

'The superintendent was so contemptuous. It made me feel that all my research had been a waste of time.'

'I take the opposite view – and so does the inspector. The information you discovered about that regiment could be vital.'

'I've learnt a bit more about them,' said Burge. 'The Prince of Wales's North Staffordshire Regiment has been involved in some of the toughest battles in the war – the Somme, Passchendaele and Cambrai, for instance. They've suffered huge losses.'

'We need to find out even more about those two cases of suicide,' said Keedy. 'Right now, however, our priority is that house in Camden Town.'

'Do you know where it is?'

'No, but we can get directions from the local police.'

'One thing puzzled me about the place they rented.'

'What was it?'

'The man insisted that it had a garden at the rear. Why was that?

243

They can't plant anything in the short time they are there.'

Keedy chuckled. 'They weren't thinking about gardening,' he said. 'They wanted a second exit in case people like us come knocking on the front door. We must split up, Cliff. While I do the knocking, you watch the back of the house.'

'Wonderful!' said Burge. 'I'm dying for some action.'

Though they sneered at police attempts to track them down, they nevertheless took precautions. While they were in the house during the day, they glanced through the front and back windows on a regular basis. At night they took it in turns to sleep for four-hour shifts, with one man on sentry duty in the front bedroom.

'What will you miss most about this place?' asked the older man.

'The painting I wanted to buy.'

'You can wave goodbye to that – unless you have fifty quid.'

Brian laughed. 'I don't have a fraction of that.'

'It's a pity you couldn't take a photo of it.'

'That would be pointless. It wouldn't be the same in black and white. What made it special were the colours Voisey chose.'

'I will miss the feeling of safety we have here,' said the other. 'We didn't really have that in Stafford. We were always on edge. I was glad when we finished our business there and moved on.'

'I liked the place. That pub served good beer.'

'We were there for a higher purpose than drinking beer.'

Brian nodded. 'Yes, I know.'

'Never forget it. We were doing God's work.'

When they stopped at the police station, they not only got directions to the house. They acquired two uniformed constables as well. The four passengers squeezed into the car and the driver followed Keedy's instructions.

'You were right about that garden,' said Burge, impressed. 'The duty sergeant said that there's a lane at the bottom of it.'

'That's their escape route.'

'We'll block it off.'

'Be careful, Cliff. These men are dangerous.'

'Yes, but we'll have the advantage of surprise.'

'That's true.' Keedy spoke to the driver. 'Get a move on.'

It was a relatively short journey. Turning into the street, the driver stopped the vehicle outside the house number they'd been given, then got out with the others. The five of them moved forward in the dark. After they had sized up the house, Keedy sent Burge off with the uniformed policemen to the lane at the rear of the property. He and the driver gave them five minutes to get in position. During the wait, Keedy's excitement was building. The promise of action was one of the things that had drawn him to the Metropolitan Police Force in the first place. He felt a surge of adrenalin.

'Right,' he said. 'Let's go.'

He and the driver walked up to the door of the house. Keedy used the knocker with as much force as he could, then waited for a response. None, however, came. Because the blinds were drawn, he was unable to see whether there were lights on inside. He banged on the door with his fist.

'Police! Open up!'

The driver joined in the shouting. After a while, the door opened wide to reveal Clifford Burge. He shrugged his shoulders.

'When we reached the garden gate,' he explained, 'it was wide open. I'm sorry, Sergeant. They got away.'

* * *

245

Alone in his office, Marmion was trying to digest what his wife had told him about the visit to the West Country. He was immensely grateful that his daughter had also been there. Her support and practicality would have been an asset to her mother. Even though he was preoccupied by the demands of his job, he never forgot Paul and frequently wondered what he was doing. The fact that his son had not, in fact, committed a series of crimes in Wells gave him solace. He was less comforted by Ellen's description of the young man who had clearly known Paul. Evidently, his son was moving in dangerous company.

His mind was still fixed on Shepton Mallet when the telephone rang.

He picked up the receiver. 'Inspector Marmion …'

'Ah,' said a hesitant voice, 'I was hoping to speak to you in confidence.'

'Do you have information regarding the murder, sir?'

'In a sense, I do.' There was a lengthy pause. 'My name is Donald Hepburn. I understand that you and a Sergeant Keedy came to Hipwell Manor and met my daughter, Caroline.'

'That is right, sir. We called on Mrs Langford some days ago.'

'You were given rather short shrift, I gather.'

'We were not made to feel entirely welcome,' said Marmion, tactfully.

'Caroline regrets that now.'

'We took no offence, sir.'

There was another pause. Feeling sorry for him, Marmion tried to make the conversation less painful for him.

'I believe I know why you have contacted me, Mr Hepburn,' he said, 'and I assure you that this is a private conversation between the two of us. Nothing of what you say needs to be made public.'

'Thank God for that!'

'It might interest you to know that Mrs Langford is not his only victim.'

Hepburn was rocked. 'Really?'

'We are learning some strange things about Dr Tindall.'

'Is that who he is?'

'Yes, sir.'

'He didn't even tell us his real name,' complained the other. 'When they were married in a register office, he was posing as a Michael Langford. He had documents that seemed to prove his identity.'

'How is your daughter now?' asked Marmion, quietly.

'She was hysterical when she learnt the truth, Inspector. We had to call in the doctor to give her a sedative. Look,' he went on, 'I hope that you will accept my version of events. Caroline could never withstand being questioned by you. She has been wounded far too deeply.'

'There will be no need for us to speak to her, Mr Hepburn.'

'That's a huge relief.'

'I suspect that you are able to tell us all that we need to know.'

Hepburn took a deep breath. 'The situation is this, Inspector …'

Roused by the noise in the street, one of the neighbours came out to investigate. He was a short, tubby old man in a dressing gown and slippers. Keedy explained who they were and asked if they might step inside his house. Glad to get out of the cold, the old man led the way. Keedy and Burge followed. When all three of them were indoors, Keedy took the folded portrait from his pocket and opened it out.

'Do you recognise this man, sir?' he asked.

'Yes, he's been living two doors away for weeks.'

'Do you know his name?'

'He told us it was John,' said the other, 'and his friend is Anthony.'

'John Morris and Anthony Brown,' said Keedy, thoughtfully. 'Those are not their real names, sir.'

'Why not? Are those men criminals?'

'Oh, yes and they need to be caught as soon as possible.'

'What can you tell us about him?' asked Burge.

'Not very much,' admitted the old man. 'Most of the time, they just stayed in the house. The only time I bumped into the younger one was in the market. He didn't really want to chat.'

He went on to tell them the little that he knew about the two men who had been his neighbours until that evening. He added one significant detail.

'They rented the house and a lock-up garage two streets away.'

'What did they want that for?' asked Keedy.

'Their motorbikes …'

It was the second conversation they had had about betrayal and it was just as upsetting for Claude Chatfield as the first. Marmion's account was slow and measured. He paid tribute to the father's courage in coming forward to explain how he, his wife and his daughter had been duped by a man he now knew as Dr George Tindall.

'What did they believe his name was?' asked Chatfield.

'Michael Langford.'

'Did he claim that he was a hospital administrator this time?'

'No,' replied Marmion, 'he invented another role for himself as a captain of a destroyer who spent most of his time at sea.'

'But from what you tell me about the father, he seems like a highly intelligent man. Why was he taken in so easily?'

'Oh, he had grave reservations about Tindall at the start. It took years before he accepted him as a suitor for his daughter. At that point – after Tindall had sworn him to secrecy – he believed that she was about to become the wife of a brave man who was engaged in the war at sea.

Mr Hepburn was so proud of him that he gave them Hipwell Manor as a wedding present.'

'I do wish people were not so gullible,' said Chatfield. 'I'd never have been persuaded to believe in that nonsense.'

'You are a trained policeman, sir. Suspicion is part of our stock-in-trade. It is unfair to blame hapless victims. They were exploited by a master of his art.'

'He was a master of his art as a surgeon as well.'

'There's no disputing it.'

'Wasn't that enough for him?'

'Apparently not, Superintendent.'

'The man was incorrigible.'

'I did tell you that Eleanor Tindall was not the only one,' Marmion reminded him. 'There could be others, though they may be too embarrassed to come forward.'

'Why do you say that?'

'We have to be realistic, sir. There may well have been relationships where Dr Tindall felt that matrimony was unnecessary. In other words, he could get what he wanted without a marriage proposal.'

'That's disgraceful!' hissed Chatfield.

'It may have been the reason why he rented the flat so near to the hospital in Brighton where he worked.'

'Are you telling me that he was entertaining women there while he had a wife just down the road in Hipwell Manor?'

'Technically, Mrs Langford was not really his wife. That honour – if I dare call it that – went to Eleanor Staynes. The second marriage was bigamous.'

'Is there no end to this man's lust?'

'We may never know.'

Chatfield was fuming. Leaping to his feet, he marched up and down his office several times before he controlled himself. He looked at Marmion.

'You say that you had doubts about Mrs Langford?'

'I did, sir.'

'How did they arise?'

'She was far too anxious to get us out of the house,' said Marmion. 'If she had been more cooperative, we would have gone on our way and forgotten all about her. The big mistake she made was to show us a photograph of her husband.'

'Why was it a mistake?'

'Her change of tone was too sudden, sir. One minute she was trying to throw us out, the next, she was taking the photograph off the piano and thrusting it at us. It worried me for some time,' confided Marmion. 'Then I began to wonder if she really was married to the bearded man she pointed out, or simply using the photograph of someone else in a bid to remove our suspicions.'

'Your instincts were sound,' said Chatfield, managing to make the compliment sound more like a reproach. 'Thank you for telling me all this. We must be as discreet as we can about Dr Tindall's ... entanglements.'

'He was so irresponsible.'

'I can think of a stronger word than that for his antics. He has fathered at least two children. Imagine the shock that awaits them in due course.'

'He may have left them something in his will.'

'Nothing can make up for the damage and misery he has caused. Thinking about it makes my stomach heave. Let's talk about something else,' he decided, changing tack and lowering his voice. 'I take it that you spoke to your wife?'

'I did, sir.'

'How did you find her?'

'I don't think she's fully recovered from the experience. It may take time to adjust to it. My daughter will have the same problem.'

'I meant to tell you what Inspector Gale said about her.'

'Oh?'

'When I explained to her that Alice needed a day off to visit someone in prison who might be her brother, the inspector agreed instantly. She said that your daughter was the best policewoman under her command. That's high praise.'

'It is, indeed,' said Marmion. 'I'm pleased that one member of the family is getting some recognition for their efforts.'

Turning on his heel, he left the room quickly.

Keedy's anger at their failure to make two arrests was tempered by the fact that they had tracked the suspects to their hiding place. That was an achievement. He and Burge started a thorough search of the house. While the sergeant went from room to room on the ground floor, his colleague did the same upstairs. After a few minutes, Keedy was alerted by a shout from above. He trotted up the staircase.

'I'm in the front bedroom,' said Burge.

Keedy joined him. 'Why have you got the light off?'

'I want to show you something.' He pointed to a hole cut in the blind. 'They took no chances. When the light was off in here, they could keep watch through that hole without giving themselves away.'

'No wonder they made a run for it,' said Keedy. 'When one of them saw five men coming out of the gloom towards the house, he guessed who we must be. They had their bags already packed for an emergency dash.'

251

'What did they leave behind?'

'Almost nothing, Cliff – just a couple of things in the larder.'

'They must have sprinted down the garden.'

'Thirty seconds was all they needed, and we were stupid enough to give it to them. Bugger!' exclaimed Keedy. 'I'm so annoyed we let them slip through our fingers. We knew they were professionals. We should have made allowances for that.'

'What about that lock-up garage?'

'We won't find any clues there, Cliff. It will be just like this house – nothing at all to give them away. Remember what the estate agent told you about the man who rented this house?'

'He looked powerful.'

'I fancy that he might well have served in the army. That is why they escaped. Everything was planned with military precision. Even though they felt safe here, they probably alternated as sentries. It's what saved them.'

'Where are they now?'

'Haring along on those motorbikes with a big grin on their faces.'

Burge sighed. 'So much for my hope of some real action.'

'I was fired up for it as well.'

'What are we going to tell the superintendent?'

'We have to tell him the truth.'

'I don't relish that.'

'It was my decision to come here,' admitted Keedy, 'so I'll bear the brunt of Chat's anger. You'll come out of it much better.'

'Why?'

'Well, it was your hard work on the phone that helped to find their hideaway. Chat is bound to give you credit for that.'

Burge was dubious. 'Is he?'

'Ah,' said Keedy, changing his mind. 'I see what you mean. Perhaps you ought to wear a bulletproof waistcoat just in case.'

During his long tenure as commissioner, Sir Edward Henry had introduced many improvements at Scotland Yard and built a reputation as a man with a steady hand on the tiller. He was at heart a realist and knew that major crimes were never solved easily. When he went to the superintendent's office that evening, all that he was hoping for was news of progress in the murder investigation. In the event, he was given far more information than he had expected.

'Tindall was married twice?' he gulped.

'The inspector believes that the two unfortunate women may not be the only victims of his carnal appetite.'

'Are you telling me that he had some sort of harem?'

'Some of the details made my hair stand on end,' confessed Chatfield. 'I feel that we must keep these unsavoury discoveries out of the newspapers.'

'Quite so, Superintendent. We must protect the unfortunate victims.'

'Inspector Marmion gave me a full report earlier on. He has dealt very tactfully with the two families who got in touch with us.'

'Were there children from these marriages?'

'I'm afraid so. The first wife had a boy and the second – who is not legally his spouse, of course – produced a girl.'

'Dear God!'

'The inspector spoke at length to the latter's father. According to the gentleman, Tindall – or Langford as he called himself – had always seemed so considerate towards his family.'

'It's a pity his concern for others didn't keep him within the bounds of the law,' said the commissioner. 'The War Office holds Tindall up as an example of dedication to duty in that military hospital, yet the fellow is nothing but a rampant Lothario.'

'Let us not deprive him of his due reward, Sir Edward,' advised Chatfield. 'His surgical expertise has saved lives. On that account, we owe him respect. As for his private life, however …'

'We must put that aside. I agree with you. What I came for is something that will show the War Office that your detectives are getting closer to the men who committed the murder. May I report that they are?'

'You may,' said Chatfield, conjuring up a smile behind which to hide his misgivings. 'Tell them that my detectives are getting closer every day to the two suspects responsible.'

CHAPTER SEVENTEEN

Keedy and Burge returned to Scotland Yard empty-handed. They told Marmion about the abortive raid in Camden Town. The inspector was very unhappy about what he was hearing.

'Enthusiasm got the better of us,' admitted Keedy. 'When we raced to the house in the car, the noise of the engine must have alerted them. By the time we got on to the pavement, they were probably running away.'

'It was the reason they rented a house with a rear exit,' explained Burge. 'The garden gate was wide open when we got there.'

'Didn't you search the streets for them?' asked Marmion.

'We tried, sir, but they'd already escaped on their motorbikes. The local police station sent out two cars to scour the area, but the suspects had a head start.'

'Had they left anything behind them?'

'Two apples and some tins of baked beans,' said Keedy. 'We searched the place from top to bottom.'

Marmion was dismayed. 'You should have parked streets away,' he said, 'and sneaked up on them.'

'We know that now. Because we were too hasty, we lost them.'

'And you probably threw away the one chance you had of catching the pair. This is unlike you, Joe. I'm disappointed.'

'I'm to blame as well, sir,' confessed Burge. 'When we had the support of those two constables, I was raring to go.' He grimaced. 'Do we have to tell the superintendent that we failed?'

'There's no way we can hide this from him.'

'I was afraid you'd say that.'

'It was my call,' said Keedy.

'Yes,' agreed Marmion, 'but you were acting on my instructions. We'll speak to Chat together and keep Cliff out of this.'

'I deserve to face the music as well,' offered Burge.

'There's no point in all three of us getting a reprimand. Besides, you provided the crucial address. That needs to be recognised.'

'Thank you.'

'Keep your head down and say nothing.'

'Yes, Inspector.'

'Just pray that we come out of Chat's office alive,' joked Keedy. 'By the way, I showed that portrait to one of the neighbours. He said it was a good likeness of the younger man, who called himself John Morris.'

'It's a common enough name,' said Marmion.

'So is Anthony Brown. There must be hundreds of men in London with that name. You can see why they both used an alias.'

'It's further proof that they are experienced.'

'And very brave,' said Keedy with a chuckle. 'Who else would want to live on a diet of apples and baked beans?'

'We're learning more about them all the time,' said Marmion. 'Morris is the one who likes scary paintings and Brown may have served in the army.'

'We need a lot more than that to run them to earth.'

'We found them once and we can find them again.'

'How do we do that?' asked Keedy.

Marmion puffed out his cheeks. 'There must be a way somehow.'

Romilly Staynes sat on the edge of the bed with an arm around her daughter, offering what comfort she could. As a result of the revelations about her husband, Eleanor was close to despair. Every so often, a memory helped to ease the pain.

'I can't believe that my marriage was completely hollow, Mummy.'

'No,' said Romilly, 'I accept that. There were good times. The problem was that they were few and far between.'

'What was George doing when he wasn't there?' asked Eleanor.

'It seems that he was working in a hospital as a surgeon.'

'I wasn't thinking about his job. Where did he live? How did he spend his free time? Was he alone or ... did he have someone else?'

'Don't ask such questions, darling. It only makes things worse.'

'I must know the truth.'

'And you will,' said her mother, 'in due course. Now is not the time to torment yourself. There is a long way to go before the police investigation is complete. Only then will we know the full truth.'

'He told me that I was the only woman he ever loved.'

'I think you should try to forget anything he ever said to you, Eleanor. That's why I burnt those letters of his. They were full of lies.'

Her daughter brooded. 'I should have spotted the signs,' she said at length.

'What signs?'

'It happened more than once,' remembered Eleanor. 'We moved here because George knew that I wanted a big garden. When I told him that we could potter about in it together, he made it clear that he would never actually do anything like digging or even mowing the lawn. I couldn't understand why he emphasised that.'

'His hands,' said Romilly, realising. 'A surgeon has to protect his hands. He was ready to play tennis with you, but he could not risk doing manual work.'

'Why were we both so blind, Mummy?'

'It was because he made us trust him,' said Romilly. 'He worked on the pair of us slowly and cunningly. I was taken in by him just as you were.' She bit her lip. 'There may well be horrid revelations to come. We must brace ourselves for that.'

'People will laugh at us.'

'We must ignore them.'

'Do you think we should move away from here?'

'No,' said her mother, decisively. 'Our family and friends won't laugh. We will be drawn closer to them. Besides, where would we go?'

'I've no idea.'

'We must wait until the whole thing blows over.'

'But it's never going to do that, is it?' said Eleanor.

Romilly sighed. 'No, I suppose not.'

'The stigma will be there for ever.'

She burst into tears and her mother hugged her close for minutes.

'Do you know what I really hate him for?' said Romilly.

'What?'

'If George had been honest about his work as a surgeon, I would have admired him. He was saving lives.' Her eyes flashed. 'Yet he ruined ours.'

* * *

When he and Keedy faced the superintendent in the latter's office, Marmion had no opportunity to give the full account he had rehearsed. As soon as the failure to catch the suspects was admitted, Chatfield swooped like an eagle on Keedy, digging in his talons with relish.

'You let them get away?' he demanded.

'I misjudged the situation, sir,' said Keedy.

'Five of you against two of them – and they escape without a scratch.'

'They were alert and prepared for anything.'

'That's more than I can say about you, Sergeant. I cannot believe that an officer of mine was so inept. It's almost as if you wanted them to escape.'

'That's not true at all, sir,' said Marmion, interrupting. 'The fact is that the sergeant and Detective Constable Burge did actually find out where these men were hiding. That took intelligence and persistence.'

'It's a pity those qualities were singularly lacking once they got to Camden Town,' said Chatfield. 'The operation was a disaster. Keedy and Burge must take the blame for that – but you were responsible for encouraging them, Inspector.'

'And I'd do the same again. All the evidence pointed to the fact that the suspects were hiding in Camden Town – a claim that you rejected with scorn.'

'That's right,' added Keedy. 'When Burge told you that he had found their address, you sent him packing.'

'I also told him to take no further action,' said Chatfield, vehemently.

'I felt that you were wrong to do so, sir.'

'An order is an order.'

'I chose to disobey it on this occasion,' said Marmion, 'because it meant disregarding sound evidence. If we had listened to you, we would never have confirmed that those men were hiding in the

259

very place Burge had identified.'

'I may have made a slight error of judgement,' confessed Chatfield, 'but it pales beside the idiocy that the sergeant showed this evening.'

'He rushed in where he should have crept up, but you have to applaud his bravery. The sergeant and the others were unarmed. Yet they were ready to tackle men who were proven killers.'

'We have armed officers at our disposal. They should have been used.'

'Impossible,' declared Keedy. 'You'd already dismissed the idea that the suspects were at the address we had. If we had appealed to you for armed support, we'd never have been allowed to leave this building.'

'It all comes back to your intransigence,' said Marmion.

'Be quiet!' snapped Chatfield.

'If you had had the sense to—'

'Quiet, I said!' yelled the other.

There was a tense silence. Chatfield took time to compose himself.

'Earlier on,' he told them, 'the commissioner asked me for signs of progress in this case. Because I trusted my officers, I told him that everything was in hand. What is he going to say if he learns that an inspector blatantly defied my orders and a sergeant, who had the suspects cornered, allowed them to get away scot-free?'

'If you wish to take us off this investigation,' said Marmion, stoutly, 'we will appeal to the commissioner. He will appreciate the amount of intelligence we have already gathered.'

'And he has always supported us to the hilt,' Keedy reminded him.

'What is your decision, sir?'

Chatfield looked from one to the other. Their threat was not an idle one. The commissioner's faith in Marmion was unshakeable. If the superintendent chose to take the inspector off the case, Sir Edward Henry would demand to know why.

'Get out and do your job,' snapped Chatfield.

'Can we have more of a free hand?' asked Marmion.

'It would make things so much easier,' said Keedy. 'If we have to come to you for permission whenever we want to take action, we're hampered.'

'What do you say, sir?'

'I remain in charge, Inspector,' affirmed Chatfield.

'We accept that. All that we ask for is some ... leeway.'

The superintendent sniffed. 'I'll think about it.'

It was a small concession but an important one. The balance of power had shifted slightly. Marmion and Keedy left the room with a spring in their step.

Since she had had two days off work in succession, Alice Marmion made sure that she reported for duty early the next morning. Thelma Gale was pleased to see her.

'Welcome back,' she said.

'Thank you, Inspector.'

'I gather that the prisoner was not, after all, your brother.'

'No,' replied Alice. 'He was simply using Paul's name.'

'Your father was considerate enough to ring me as soon as he'd heard details of what happened. He stressed how taxing an experience it had been for you and your mother.'

'That's true.'

'Are you sure that you feel able to go out on patrol today?'

'It's kind of you to ask,' said Alice, surprised by the kindness in the inspector's voice. 'I'm not only fit for work, I'm anxious to keep my mind occupied. Otherwise, I'd spend the whole day worrying about my brother.'

'You won't be able to forget him completely, I'm afraid.'

'Why not?'

'Iris Goodliffe is certain to bombard you with questions about your absence yesterday. You know how inquisitive she can be.'

'Iris understands the situation. I'll be happy to confide in her.'

'She was partnered by Jennifer Jerrold yesterday.'

'The two of them would have got on well together.'

'That's not what Goodliffe said – but I'm sure she'll give you full details.'

'Yes,' agreed Alice with a grin. 'I'm sure that she will.'

Breakfast at Hipwell Manor was a muted affair. Donald Hepburn buttered his toast and looked across at his daughter. She was pale, drawn and listless. Head down, Caroline was picking at her food but eating little of it. Her father was concerned.

'How do you feel now?' he asked.

'I just feel so stupid,' she replied. 'I can't think properly and it's an effort to move. All I want to do is to stay in bed and cry.'

'I can understand that but it's not the answer. Also, it is out of character. You have always been so strong and independent. Nothing seemed to get you down. You must fight back, Caroline,' he urged. 'It's what we must both do.'

'I know, Papa.'

'It will be a different life from now on. Adjustments will have to be made.'

'Adjustments?' She gave a weary laugh. 'Is that what you call them? My husband has been murdered and I have discovered that I might not even have been legally married to him. I have been living under a false name for years and our daughter, it now transpires, may be illegitimate.

How can I adjust to things like that?'

'It will take time.'

'Everything I believed in has been shattered to pieces.'

'You still have people who love you and you still have the most beautiful daughter in the world. For her sake – as well as for your own – you must fight against despair.' He reached out to take her hand. 'I know that your whole world looks black and pointless, but it will not always be like that. We must show some fighting spirit.'

'It's been drained out of me, Daddy.'

'I don't believe it,' he said. 'It's been bruised, perhaps, but it's still there to be called upon. Have you forgotten that tennis tournament you won?'

'It was years ago.'

'Your mother and I were so proud. When you came back on court for the deciding set, you looked exhausted. As soon as the ball was served at you, however, you came back to life with a vengeance and completely overpowered your opponent. We'd never seen you play so well.'

'This is different,' she said. 'It's not a game. It's a form of death sentence.'

'Caroline!' he exclaimed.

'It's true. Everything I valued has fallen apart. I've lost my husband, my reputation, my place in society and my will to live.'

'Don't talk like that. It's frightening me.'

'I'm sorry,' she said, 'but that is how I feel. I simply can't believe that it will ever be any better.'

'You just need care and attention to get over the shock.'

'I also need to apologise to you.'

'Why?'

'I was the one who let Michael into the family. You never liked him.'

'That was only at the start. I am ashamed to say that I lowered my defences. I came to be impressed by him. I'm the one who should apologise to you, Caroline,' he said. 'I should have sensed that there was something funny about him. Michael Langford was rotten to the core.'

'That was not even his real name.'

'He lied to you about almost everything.' Releasing her hand, he sat back. 'That conversation I had on the telephone with Inspector Marmion was one of the most difficult I've ever had in my life. I had to summon up all my courage to lift the receiver. I am so glad that I did, however. The inspector was kind and understanding. He actually managed to soothe me.'

Caroline was penitent. 'I feel so ashamed of the way I spoke to him,' she said. 'I just wanted to get him out of here. I still thought my husband was alive then. I was beastly to both of the detectives.'

'They'll forgive you,' he said. 'What you must do is to start forgiving yourself for things that were not really your fault. We are two of a kind – we were both victims of a clever impostor. Now that he is gone, we can live a better, more honest life.'

'I hope so,' she said.

But there was no conviction in her voice.

After sifting his way through a mound of material, Keedy went off to Marmion's office. As he entered the room, he saw that the inspector was on the telephone. Keedy mimed an apology and offered to leave. Marmion indicated that he should sit down. Within a few seconds, he replaced the receiver.

'Sorry to interrupt,' said Keedy.

'We'd almost finished. I got in touch with the hospital again.'

'Did you talk to that major?'

'No, I wanted another word with Dr Irvine,' said Marmion. 'Insofar as George Tindall actually had a friend, Irvine was him.'

'Did he have anything interesting to say?'

'Yes, Joe – he told me about Tindall's time in France.'

'I'd forgotten that,' said Keedy. 'He worked in a field hospital, didn't he?'

'It may be the link we need. However,' said Marmion, 'before I start theorising, let me hear what you found.'

'Reading all the letters that came in, I was staggered. Dr Tindall had a secret life. Most of the information came from women in his past who preferred to remain anonymous. I suspect that some of them were nurses.' He handed over a letter. 'This is from one in that Brighton hospital who thought she was engaged to him.'

Marmion gave it a glance, then handed it back.

'He's left a trail of disappointed women behind him,' he said.

Keedy squirmed slightly. Before he became engaged to the inspector's daughter, he had enjoyed a full social life and was noted for his success among nurses. Marmion gave him a long, hard look.

'But there was a lot of praise for him as well,' added Keedy, anxious to move the conversation in another direction. 'I read letters from some wounded soldiers. When they were sent to Edmonton Hospital, Dr Tindall not only saved their lives in the operating theatre, he kept an eye on them throughout their convalescence.'

'In other words, he was a saint as well as a sinner.'

'Nobody can be both.'

'That's what he found out in the end,' said Marmion. 'There's a price to pay for taking advantage of young women.'

'Are we sure that that is the reason he was murdered?'

265

'I'm ninety-nine per cent certain.'

'You mentioned a theory.'

'Let me tell you about it …'

Alice was glad to be back at work again even if it meant pacing the streets in a fine drizzle. Iris Goodliffe was thrilled to see her again and was primed with questions. She was fascinated to hear about Shepton Mallet prison.

'What was it like inside?' she asked.

'I don't think you would have enjoyed it.'

'Did they show you the place where they hang killers?'

'No, they didn't, Iris. We were not there for a tour. We just wanted to meet the prisoner named Paul Marmion.'

'Yet it wasn't him.'

'It was very much like him, and my mother jumped to her feet when they brought him in. Then she realised that it was not Paul.'

'Was she disappointed?'

'Mummy was in the same frame of mind as me,' said Alice. 'She just wanted to get out of there.'

Iris broke off as she noticed a blind man waiting patiently at the kerb. Putting a hand on his elbow, she waited for the traffic to stop before she took him to the safety of the opposite pavement. They exchanged a few words. When she came back, she was giggling.

'What's so funny?' asked Alice.

'He said that, if he was twenty years younger, he'd marry me.'

'That's your first offer of the day, Iris.'

'He loved the sound of my voice – that's what he said.'

'Blind people tend to have keen hearing because they have to rely on it so much. He could tell from the sound of your voice how kind you are.'

'He was such a cheerful old chap. In his condition, I'd be angry.'

She fell in beside Alice and they strolled on at their usual speed.

'This is just like old times,' said Iris, happily. Her face then crumpled. 'I had Jenny Jerrold yesterday.'

'That's what Gale Force told me.'

'I'm very fond of her but all she could talk about is what happened in church last Sunday. She even told me what hymns they sang. Gale Force was threatening to team the two of us together permanently, but I begged her not to. Jenny will be much happier with someone else.'

'I daresay that she will.'

'She kept wondering where you were.'

'You must have guessed that the most likely reason was to do with my brother,' said Alice. 'Did you tell that to Jenny?'

'No, I kept it to myself. It's our secret.'

'Thank you. I appreciate that.'

'Besides, Jenny is easily shocked.'

'She would have been shocked by the sight of that prisoner. He was so uncouth, Iris. I can't believe that Paul would have fallen to that level.'

'How did he get hold of your brother's papers?'

'I've been wondering about that,' said Alice. 'Somehow I don't think that man stole them. He and Paul must have exchanged their papers. There is a worrying message for us in that. My brother is somebody else now.'

Joe Keedy listened patiently as Marmion developed his theory. He had claimed earlier that the army was the connecting link between the three different murders. He now provided more detail to bolster his argument.

'Those men were not acting of their own volition, Joe,' he said. 'They were given orders to kill.'

'Who gave them?'

'Someone at the Front.'

'Dr Tindall had no connection with the North Staffordshire Regiment.'

'Yes, he did. That is why I was keen to speak to Dr Irvine again. He told me that Tindall spent time working in a field hospital during the Battle of Loos. One of the regiment's battalions was involved in that.'

'So?'

'That could be the link we need.'

'It sounds unlikely to me,' said Keedy. 'The newspapers said that it was a hellish battle for us and for the French. Casualties in both armies were enormous. If Tindall was tending the wounded, he would have been seen as a hero. He might even have been singled out for a medal. Who on earth could possibly want him killed?'

'That's what we have to find out.'

'How?'

'We must find out where the regiment is stationed and go there.'

Keedy laughed. 'Has nobody told you there is a war on?'

'We've done it before,' said Marmion. 'When we had to arrest two soldiers at the start of the war, we went all the way to France and back. We thought nothing of going into a war zone.'

'Things have changed a lot since then,' said Keedy, seriously. 'They use tanks and poison gas and bigger shells now.'

'I'm aware of that.'

'We could be committing suicide.'

'Not if we take sensible precautions.'

Keedy shook his head. 'I'm uneasy about this.'

'There's no alternative. If we want the truth about Dr Tindall's murder, we have to cross the Channel.'

'That means we could be attacked by German submarines or aircraft.'

'We'd have the protection of a convoy,' said Marmion.

'I'm not so sure.'

'We have to find out who is controlling those two assassins – because that's what they are. They escaped you yesterday, Joe. Don't you want a second chance of catching them?'

'Yes, I do,' said Keedy, eyes glinting. 'I want it more than anything else.'

'It's settled, then.'

'What about—?'

'Leave Alice and Ellen out of it,' said Marmion. 'They accept that we sometimes have to take risks. Also – they trust our judgement.'

'There's one snag, Harv.'

'I don't see it.'

'Chat would never let us go, surely?'

'He will if we supply him enough evidence.'

'But we simply don't have it yet.'

'That is why you and I are going to Bristol straight away.'

Keedy was mystified. 'Bristol?'

'Yes, Joe,' said Marmion, rising from his chair, 'and while we are there, Cliff Burge will be making enquiries in Stafford.'

'Whatever for?'

'Wait and see.'

'This is madness!'

Marmion grinned. 'Sometimes we have to resort to that.'

Claude Chatfield had finally found something that warmed his heart. As he read that morning's edition of *The Times*, he saw that he was not only quoted correctly he was praised for his record of success in solving murder cases. His eye ran down the column until it reached something that made him freeze. It was the commissioner who was quoted this time. While he applauded the superintendent's efforts, Sir Edward Henry went on to say that they depended on the brilliance of detectives like Inspector Marmion. Scrunching up the newspaper, Chatfield put it aside.

There was a tap on the door and a detective constable came in with an envelope in his hand. He gave it to the superintendent.'

'Inspector Marmion asked me to deliver this, sir.'

'Why couldn't he speak to me in person?'

'He and Sergeant Keedy are no longer in the building.'

'Where have they gone?'

'That letter may help to explain, sir.'

The visitor left and closed the door behind him. Tearing open the envelope, Chatfield was astounded by what he read. When there was another tap on the door, he was unwelcoming.

'What is it this time?' he barked.

With a look of surprise on his face, the commissioner came into the room.

'Oh, I do beg your pardon, Sir Edward,' said Chatfield, writhing with embarrassment. 'I was expecting someone else.'

The commissioner frowned. 'So it seems.'

'Can I help you in any way?'

'I sincerely hope so. I've heard disturbing whispers.'

'Pay no attention to gossip, Sir Edward. It's always unreliable.'

'That's why I came here. I'm counting on you to deny the accusation.'

'What accusation?' asked Chatfield, warily.

'Well, the story is that the suspects were identified as living in a house they had rented in Camden Town. Some of your men went off

to investigate and picked up reinforcements at the local police station.'
His eyelids narrowed. 'Does any of this sound likely to you?'

'Please go on.'

'There's not much more to say beyond the fact that the operation was
bungled. With two killers at their mercy, your men somehow contrived
to let them escape. Is there any truth in this nonsense?'

'I'm afraid that there is, Sir Edward,' croaked Chatfield.

'I refuse to believe that Marmion was involved.'

'The inspector had no part in the raid. Sergeant Keedy was in charge.'

'Then I suggest that you send for him so that I can hear the full
story.'

'Unfortunately, he is not in the building.'

'Then where is the man?'

'According to a letter from Inspector Marmion, they will be out for
most of the day pursuing a line of enquiry. What that is, Sir Edward, I
can't rightly say.'

'Then I have to tell you that I'm displeased,' said the commissioner.
'Not to put too fine a point on it, I am extremely displeased. Why was
I not informed about the failure of the attempted arrest and why are
you incapable of explaining where officers under your command are at
the moment?' He saw the newspaper on the desk. 'Ah, you have read
The Times, I see. No doubt you have been basking in the praise lavished
on you. It is as well that the reporter was unaware of yesterday's fiasco,
or you and your officers would have been pilloried. Good day to you.'

Leaving the room, the commissioner slammed the door behind him.

Chatfield buried his head in his hands.

CHAPTER EIGHTEEN

Paddington Station was busy when they got there. Marmion and Keedy noticed the prevalence of women in the uniforms of the Great Western Railway. It had become a feature of all railway stations during the war. Female porters, carriage cleaners, ticket collectors and messengers abounded. Jobs that had routinely been given to men were being done just as efficiently by women. The detectives looked on with approval. They were less impressed, however, by the long queues of passengers.

'Why is there such a shortage of trains?' asked Keedy.

'That's the wrong question,' said Marmion.

'Is it?'

'You should be asking why the price of train tickets has shot up. We're being asked to pay more for what is a reduced service.'

'That's not fair.'

'Blame the war, Joe. It's changed everything.'

The queue that they had joined eventually made its way to a platform.

'Why do we need to go all the way to Bristol?' said Keedy. 'Couldn't you have spoken to somebody by telephone?'

'That's what Cliff Burge did, and they would only release basic details of the case. The report they sent him added very little. If we want the full facts, we need to talk to a detective involved in it.'

'He got a bit more detail from the police in Stafford.'

'That's why I sent him there,' said Marmion. 'With luck, he may be able to get the full story of the murder of that publican.'

'What surprises me is that the killers were so merciless in all three cases.'

'Why is that so surprising?'

'Well,' said Keedy, 'one of them obviously has Christian principles.'

'I doubt that.'

'Think about that painting he wanted to buy.'

'I try not to, Joe. When the artist showed it to us, I thought it was revolting. Who would want to hang that on a wall?'

'John Morris – or whoever he really is.'

'Then he has a perverted idea of art.'

'You have to admit that that painting sticks in the mind.'

'It doesn't stick in my mind,' said Marmion with contempt.

'There's something else,' recalled Keedy. 'When he hired the army uniforms from Pegasus Costumes, Morris said that they'd be used in a play.'

'I know – *Soldiers of the Cross*.'

'There is no such play.'

'How do you know?'

'The woman at Pegasus Costumes had never heard of it. Nor had Mandeville.'

'What are you trying to say, Joe?'

'I wonder if that's how they see themselves.'

'Who?'

'The killers, of course.'

'You've lost me.'

'Well, we call them cold-hearted assassins,' said Keedy. 'What if they believe they are on some sort of crusade as Soldiers of the Cross?'

Having spoken to Detective Superintendent Ash on the telephone, Clifford Burge had been given a false impression of his appearance. When he met him in person at the police station in Stafford, he was taken aback.

'Is there anything wrong?' asked Ash.

'I was expecting someone bigger, sir.'

'It's the deep voice. People expect me to be fat and jolly. In fact, I'm a skinny chap with a big nose who happens to sing in the bass section of the police choir.' He laughed. 'You, on the other hand, look exactly the way you sounded.'

'Is that good or bad?'

'It's good.'

They were in a small room used for interviews. After arriving by train, Burge had gone straight to the police station and was delighted to find Ash on the premises. The superintendent was a tall, rangy individual in his forties.

'Who sent you?' he asked.

'Inspector Marmion of Scotland Yard.'

'I've seen that name in the papers.'

'You've also seen details of the case I told you about. The inspector believes there are similarities with the murder of that publican here in Stafford.'

'I'm not sure about that.'

'Exceptional violence was used.'

'I've seen quite a few cases like that,' said Ash. 'The most recent was a month or so ago. It concerned two soldiers in a military hospital. There had been a feud between them, apparently. Shortly after they were discharged, one of them killed the other with a bayonet. They counted over fifty stab wounds and both eyes had been gouged out.'

Burge shuddered. 'What happened to the killer?'

'He took his own life.'

'Let's talk about the death of that publican, Charlie Ferriday.'

'I gave you all of the details about that.'

'Not quite all,' said Burge. 'There was something you held back.'

'It was speculation rather than hard evidence. What did you make of the case?'

'I think that Molly Roper was to blame. From what you told me, she and Ferriday were close.'

'They were business partners of a sort.'

'I think there was more to it than that. If she got involved with Ferriday, she might have written to her husband to tell him. I can imagine the shock it must have been for someone marooned in the trenches. Just think,' said Burge. 'He must have been in a terrible state. His wife had betrayed him. What was there to bring him home after the war? The shame would have been unbearable. It's no wonder he decided to end it all by getting himself killed.'

'That's a good guess,' said Ash, 'but there are two things you don't know.'

'What are they?'

'Molly Roper was devoted to her husband. When she worked at the pub, she did what all barmaids do and flirted with the customers. I know because I drank there occasionally. But that was as far as it went. The only man for her was Sam Roper.'

'You said there were two things.'

'The second one was Vera Ferriday. She was Charlie's wife and kept a close eye on him. If anything had happened between him and Molly, she'd have known about it straight away and brained him.'

Burge was puzzled. 'But I thought ...'

'It wasn't Molly who told her husband she had committed adultery.'

'Then who was it?'

'We're still trying to find out,' admitted Ash. 'He did it deliberately, knowing full well how Sam Roper was likely to react. In effect, the man who wrote that letter killed Sam. Can you see what else he did?'

'Yes,' replied Burge, shocked. 'He also got the publican murdered as well.'

'Nothing happened between him and Molly Roper. The men who sliced off Charlie Ferriday's head killed an innocent man.'

When they got to the police headquarters in Bristol, they noticed how old most of those in uniform were. It was the same everywhere. Having lost so many younger men to the army, forces all over the country were compelled to supplement their numbers by asking retired officers to return to work. While Keedy was inclined to be critical of the elderly officers, Marmion admired them for responding to the call. Their experience, he contended, made up for their lack of speed and mental agility.

They were at first delighted to discover that Inspector Hugh Griggs, who had led the investigation in which they were interested, was available. When they met him in his office, however, they changed their minds instantly. Griggs was a flabby man in his forties with dark eyes set in a pasty face, and with an abiding air of resentment. Marmion thanked him for information already provided but pressed for more detail.

'Why are you bothering me?' asked Griggs. 'There's only a surface similarity between your case and the one that I'm concerned with.'

'I disagree,' said Marmion. 'We believe that Mr Tait was killed by the same two men who murdered Dr Tindall.'

'That's rubbish! What proof do you have?'

'The modus operandi is identical.'

'And there's a third case we tracked down,' said Keedy. 'It involves a cruel murder in Stafford. That followed the same pattern.'

'There is no pattern,' insisted Griggs. 'What happened here in Bristol is quite unique. Meredith Tait was killed immediately before his safe was rifled. As I told Detective Constable Burge when he first got in touch with me, it was a clear-cut example of murder for gain.'

'How close are you to an arrest, Inspector?'

Griggs glowered. 'We continue to gather evidence.'

He went on to explain that the victim was a lawyer of good reputation who had been adopted as a parliamentary candidate at the next election. Since the death of his wife, he had looked after their two children. The visitors listened to the detailed account of how and when Tait had been murdered. Marmion asked the first question.

'Mr Tait had two partners and, presumably, there were a number of others who worked in the building. How were the killers able to get close to him?'

'I don't accept that there were two of them,' said Griggs. 'One man arranged a meeting with him but, because he could not get to Bristol during working hours, he asked if Tait could possibly see him in the evening.'

'Is that recorded in the appointments diary?'

'Yes – the meeting was at 7 p.m.'

'What was the name of the client?'

'Mr James Smith.'

'Do you know why he was so keen to see Mr Tait?' asked Keedy.

'He wanted representation in a case involving a contested will.'

'Were any details given?'

'No,' said Griggs, irritably, 'but, according to Tait's secretary, a large amount of money was at stake. It was the kind of case in which he specialised. Tait was expensive to retain but he usually won any battles in court. In essence, that is it. Having inveigled himself into a private meeting with Tait, the bogus client killed him and ransacked the safe.'

'It's difficult to believe that a lawyer could be so unguarded,' said Marmion. 'Most people in his position would make sure they had someone else in the office.'

'When they spoke, James Smith obviously persuaded him that he was exactly what he claimed to be.'

'There's something you're not telling us, Inspector.'

'I sent the details to Scotland Yard. You must have read them.'

'We have. What's missing is a link between the murder and the subsequent suicide of Captain Tait.'

'We can only assume he was devastated by the death of his brother.'

'You're far too clever to work on assumptions.'

'I'm a busy man, Inspector. Instead of answering questions from you, I need to be out with my team, leading the hunt for the killer.'

'There are two of them.'

'I know this case inside out – you don't.'

'That's exactly why we need more detail.'

Gregg was dismissive. 'Well, you'll have to get it elsewhere, Inspector.'

'If you don't help us, I'll have to complain to your superior.'

'You will not solve your case by being here in Bristol.'

'No,' agreed Marmion, 'but we might be able to give you some useful information regarding your own investigation. If you assist us, we will assist you. It's called cooperation. I recommend it.'

It was good to be back on his farm again and to find that his livestock had been looked after in his absence. When he had spoken to both of his farmhands, he walked across to the large shed and unlocked it. He surveyed his workplace with pride. Sizeable pieces of timber of various kinds were stacked against one wall. The floor was covered in sawdust and there were wood shavings around the sculpture of an angel on which he had been working before he had gone to London. He was still admiring his work when his nephew came into the shed.

'They've finished milking the cows,' said Brian.

'You should learn to do that.'

'I'm no milkmaid.'

'If you live on a farm, you have to turn your hand to anything.'

'I do miss our adventure in London,' said his nephew. 'And I miss those motorbikes we stole.'

'We didn't steal them, Brian' emphasised the other. 'We simply borrowed them then returned them without a scratch on them. That means we have clear consciences.'

His nephew looked around. 'I'd forgotten what a wonderful place this is,' he said. 'Look at all these chisels. Do you really need that many?'

'Yes, I do. Each one does a separate job. I've used well over a dozen of them when working on this.' He pointed to the life-sized angel with wings spread. 'I'll have a chance to finish it now.'

'Unless we get some more instructions.'

'There is that.'

'What if we don't?'

'Then our work is done,' said his uncle. 'I start living as a sculptor again and you help me to run this place.'

'I'll miss the excitement. What about you?'

'I feel the same,' admitted the other.

'To be honest, I hope it never stops. We get the thrill of doing our Christian duty, and the world is rid of someone who deserves to die in pain.'

'That's the bit I love.'

'My favourite moment is when we say a prayer over him afterwards.'

Claude Chatfield had been tied up in meetings all morning. Still smarting from the way that the commissioner had spoken to him earlier, he went in search of the driver who had taken Marmion and Keedy away from Scotland Yard. When he finally tracked the man down, he pointed an accusatory finger.

'Where did you take them?' he demanded.

The driver was baffled. 'Who are you talking about, sir?'

'Inspector Marmion and Sergeant Keedy.'

'Oh, I see. The thing is, I've driven a lot of people about today.'

'Those are the only two that interest me.'

'Then the answer is Paddington Station.'

'Why were they going there?'

'I overheard the inspector talking about Bristol.'

'Bristol, for heaven's sake!' cried Chatfield. 'They are investigating a crime that occurred here in London.'

'I thought they were following orders, sir, and the same goes for Constable Burge. I gave him a lift this morning as well.'

'Why? Where was he going?'

'Stafford.'

'I can't believe this,' yelled the superintendent. 'Why didn't they have the decency to tell me? What use are my officers in Bristol and Stafford? I need them here, solving a murder in Edmonton.'

They had met people with the same attitude before, senior detectives in the provinces who had a grudge against Scotland Yard because of the prime position it occupied in national law enforcement. Hugh Griggs was typical of the breed. He believed that he could lead a murder investigation as well as anyone, and he hated to be diverted from it. Failing to get rid of his visitors, he was forced to give them details about the case that he had so far refused to pass on to Scotland Yard for fear of interference.

'Captain Richard Tait had been on active service for over a year,' he said. 'He was a good officer, highly rated by his superiors. He seemed to cope with the rigours of war extremely well.'

'Yet he committed suicide,' said Marmion.

'He and his wife had no children. They had always been devoted to each other. Mrs Tait wrote to him regularly. Then one day ...'

'Ah,' said Keedy as Griggs fell silent, 'I could hazard a guess what happened. Captain Tait had a letter from her that upset him.'

'That's right.'

'Did she tell him that she was pregnant?'

'Mrs Tait denies it, but I don't believe her. What is certain is that she was feeling very lonely. That made her vulnerable.'

'Vulnerable to her brother-in-law, I suspect,' said Marmion. 'That would have hurt Captain Tait more than anything. He must have felt trapped abroad in the middle of a battle while his wife was being unfaithful to him in Bristol.'

'The next thing we know,' said Griggs, 'Meredith Tait is murdered.'

'How did his sister-in-law react?'

'She collapsed and had to be rushed to hospital.'

'Did she recover?'

'Yes, she did – but she lost the baby she denied that she was carrying.'

During their beat, there were places where they stopped for a brief respite. They reached the latest of them and came to a halt. Iris Goodliffe was pensive.

'What are you going to do after the war?' she asked.

'That depends on who wins,' replied Alice.

'There's no doubt about that, is there? The Battle of Cambrai was a triumph for us. It's the only battle in the whole war for which the church bells were rung. That was a signal that the end was in sight.'

'I don't think so, Iris. According to the newspaper I read, the Germans are hitting back. They're not finished yet.'

'What a pity!'

'We've had so many false dawns in this war that I've stopped getting my hopes up. The fighting will be going on well into next year.'

'How many more British soldiers have to die before it's finished?'

'Too many, I expect,' said Alice. 'To answer your question, I think that I'll go back to teaching.'

'I'm not brainy enough to do that.'

'You've been trained to work in a pharmacy. That shows how intelligent you are. Why do you always have to belittle yourself?'

'I don't know. I just never feel good enough, somehow.'

'You do this job well.'

Iris laughed. 'Gale Force doesn't think so,' she said. 'She has a new complaint about me every day.'

'Ignore her.'

'I wish I could.'

'When the war is over, you can wave her goodbye.'

'I'll be sad to wave you goodbye,' said Iris with an edge of desperation. 'We will stay friends afterwards, won't we?'

'Of course, we will.'

'Can I come and see you at your school?'

'Maybe,' said Alice, guardedly.

'You obviously have a gift with children.'

'I love watching them grow up and develop.'

'Well, you won't be doing that for long.'

'What do you mean?'

'You'll have children of your own, surely?'

'I don't know,' admitted Alice. 'Joe and I have not really talked about it. I suppose that it will happen one day and, yes, I'd love to be a mother.'

Iris sighed. 'Being a mother is yet another thing you'll be good at.'

'I could say the same about you, Iris.'

'There's no chance of that happening,' said the other, gloomily. 'Who would want to marry me?'

Iris was back to her familiar theme. It was time to cut her short.

'Let's move on,' said Alice, leading the way. 'At our next stop, we get our free cup of tea. If we're lucky, we might even get a biscuit . . .'

After a long conversation in Bristol with Inspector Griggs, they made their way back to the railway station. On a cold, windswept platform, Marmion and Keedy reflected on what had happened.

'Griggs has got a huge chip on his shoulder,' said Keedy. 'He saw us as the enemy, not as fellow police officers.'

'We broke down his resistance in the end,' Marmion pointed out.

'He was amazed when we gave him clear proof that two men were involved in the murder of that lawyer.'

'Our big achievement was to convince him that the same killers were behind the death of Dr Tindall. He now realises that he is not dealing with an isolated event.'

'No, it's only the first of three linked murders.'

'Solve one and we solve all three.'

'I don't think Inspector Griggs would like that. He'd hate us to get credit for the capture of two people whose killing spree started in Bristol.'

'It's no time to be territorial,' said Keedy.

'Our time here was well spent. Even Chat must accept that.'

'Do you think he'll agree to our demand?'

'No,' said Marmion. 'We may have to go above his head.'

'He'd never forgive us.'

'We can live with that.' He raised his voice above the noise of the approaching train. 'Well, our work is done here. I just hope that Cliff Burge had equal success up there in Stafford.'

On the way to the sewing circle, Ellen Marmion had been wondering once again where her son was. There were periods of time when she was able to push Paul to the very back of her mind, but the trip to Shepton Mallet had changed that. Her maternal instincts were given a new intensity. She wanted somehow to assure him that they still loved him and accepted his desire to live apart from the family. They might even be able to help him financially, in a small way. With Christmas at hand and the coldest months of the year to follow, Ellen feared for his health and safety.

When she got to the sewing circle, however, all thoughts of Paul were instantly banished. She heard that one of the other women had received a telegram from the War Office to inform her of the death of her son in the wake of the battle of Cambrai. That became the main topic of conversation as they sewed or knitted garments to keep the soldiers warm throughout the winter. Ellen was grateful to be able to care about someone else's son for a change. It was a crushing blow for the family but at least they knew where he was and what fate had befallen him. There was a degree of comfort in that.

They had agreed to meet in a cafe not far from Scotland Yard so that they could pool information before reporting to Superintendent Chatfield. When they arrived, they were pleased to see that Burge was already there. They joined him at his table and ordered refreshments. Marmion gave him a highly edited account of their meeting with Inspector Griggs then it was Burge's turn.

'It was an eye-opener,' he confessed. 'On the basis of the outline facts of the case, I made some foolish assumptions …'

Referring to his notebook, he told them what had happened and how Superintendent Ash had made him look at the Stafford murder from a totally different angle. Marmion and Keedy were intrigued.

'What I didn't have,' said Burge, 'was local knowledge. He had the advantage there. He knew the people involved and was certain that nothing had happened between Charlie and Molly Roper.'

'So the publican was completely innocent,' said Keedy. 'That means the killers were acting on incorrect information.'

'Someone lied to Sam Roper. He believed them.'

'The same goes for the person who ordered the killing.'

'When we find him,' vowed Marmion, 'we'll tell him that.'

Burge was agog. 'According to you, the orders came from France.'

'Then that's where we have to go.'

CHAPTER NINETEEN

They were seated in the workshed, enjoying a glass of cider and looking back over their achievements. Their narrow escape in Camden Town had been alarming at the time but was now a source of laughter.

'I'd love to have seen their faces when they realised that we'd gone,' said the sculptor. 'They were clever enough to find us but too stupid to catch us. I really enjoyed the moment when we took to our heels.'

'Well, I didn't,' complained his nephew. 'Scarpering like that made this artificial foot of mine hurt like hell.'

'Sorry about that, Brian.'

'Last time I had to run for my life, I wasn't quite so lucky. It was during the Battle of Loos. When the bullets were flying, I didn't move fast enough, and my foot was shattered. That put paid to my army career.'

'At least you fought in a real battle.'

'You did the same in South Africa, surely?'

'No,' said the other, 'none of the battles were on the same scale as Loos. I was based outside Johannesburg as part of the 15th Brigade under General Wavell. We had skirmishes galore in the first phase of the war with the Boers but that was it. The truth is that, when it came to real action, I had far more excitement in Bristol, Stafford and Edmonton.'

'We had three triumphs in a row.'

His uncle raised his glass. 'Here's to the next one.'

'He must be delighted with our work.'

'Approval from above is more important,' said the other, looking upwards. 'Our orders really come from him. We are soldiers of the cross, empowered to wreak God's revenge.'

Claude Chatfield had had many arguments with Marmion over the years, but none had been as fierce as the one in which they were now embroiled. Every accusation hurled at the inspector was either firmly rebuffed or deftly avoided. Every demand from the superintendent was bravely challenged. At the point where Chatfield realised that he was losing the debate, Marmion issued his ultimatum.

'We must go to France,' he asserted, 'or this murder will never be solved.'

'It's out of the question.'

'Is it, sir? Because it has an interest in this case, the War Office has hounded the commissioner and he, in turn, has been hounding you. Let us exert pressure in return. If the War Office wants Dr Tindall's case to be solved, it must give us the means to solve it.'

'And what are those means?'

'Safe passage to and from north-east France and an order to the commanding officer of the North Staffordshire Regiment stationed in Cambrai, requiring him to give us all the help we need.'

'You'd be going into a war zone.'

'The sergeant and I have taken that into account.'

'I can't guarantee that the War Office will agree to your demands.'

'Then they need to be offered as polite requests,' said Marmion with a teasing smile. 'You'd do that much better than me. We leave it in your capable hands.'

Chatfield came close to frothing at the mouth.

Alice had been glad to get back to work and to see her colleagues again. When she came to the end of her shift, she left the building with Iris Goodliffe beside her, chatting amiably. They did not, however, stay together because Alice saw that Joe Keedy was waiting for her. Leaving her friend, she ran forward into a warm embrace.

'What a lovely surprise!' she said.

'Let me walk you to your bus stop,' he said, offering his arm.

'Yes, please.'

'I'm sorry to pop up like a Jack-in-the-box.'

'It's a wonderful treat for me.'

They walked on until they were out of earshot of the others.

'There's something I need to tell you Alice,' he said.

She was perplexed. 'Why are you so solemn?'

'You'll soon understand.'

Ellen Marmion replaced the receiver and rushed into the living room to sit down. Her heart was racing, and she was shaking all over. Though her husband had tried to break the news gently, it still rocked her. He was planning to go to France with Joe Keedy in the hope of making an arrest. It seemed an act of madness to her. Why risk their lives by crossing the Channel, then going to the very place where a massive battle had so recently taken place? It was an almost suicidal decision.

She gave herself time to absorb the news. From the moment she had first met him, she knew that Marmion would always put duty before personal safety. While he would exercise discretion in the face of danger, he would never walk away from it. Ellen feared that he would put his life at risk simply by sailing to France. British ships were targets for enemy aircraft and submarines. There was little defence against either. Her husband might not even reach land. Even if he did, he would be going on to an area devastated by the latest action on the Western Front.

The war had been a geography lesson for Ellen. When her son's regiment was in France, she had followed its movements with the aid of a map. As he travelled through Picardy, her husband would now be going past the Somme battlefield where Paul had fought, been wounded, and lost his best friend. It was a cruel coincidence. Her thoughts turned to her daughter. If Alice had heard the news, she would be suffering as well, terrified that she might lose both her father and the man she was due to marry in the new year. It was a frightening possibility. All that Ellen could do was to close her eyes and offer a silent prayer.

Though he had grave misgivings about their trip, Claude Chatfield sent them off with his best wishes, hoping that they would return safe and well. Notwithstanding his occasional clashes with Marmion, he admired the inspector's bravery and determination. The commissioner was even more impressed.

'I applaud their courage,' he said. 'Marmion's attitude is commendable – one has to follow the evidence, wherever it might take one.'

'I just wish it were not taking them to France,' sighed Chatfield.

'The War Office has been criticised for its slowness but that was not the case here. When I stressed the importance of their mission, arrangements were quickly made to get them across the Channel.'

'Thank you for using your influence, Sir Edward.'

'I was delighted to be able to do so. And yes, I know that they are taking a massive risk. But have faith in them, Superintendent. They have been to France before in hostile conditions and they made two significant arrests. I'm sure that they will achieve their objective again.'

It was the second time that they had been in a troop train heading for the south coast. On this occasion, however, they were not going to Brighton to conduct some interviews. Marmion and Keedy were on their way to Dover with reinforcements dispatched to repair some of the huge gaps in manpower that were the legacy of the Battle of Cambrai. The detectives could only imagine how the young and untried soldiers were feeling. Like them, Marmion and Keedy were fully aware of the dangers of joining British forces at the Western Front.

There was a lengthy wait at the port and, when their ship finally arrived, they had to let the wounded be unloaded before they could board the vessel in their place. Crossing the Channel on a cold, blustery, December night was a grim prospect, but they accepted the situation without complaint. Of more concern to them was the fear and anxiety they had created in Ellen and Alice. Until their safe return, the women would have long, anxious, sleepless nights. Both men felt guilty.

The young lieutenant tasked with looking after them had managed to find some protective clothing and helmets for each of them. Keedy joked that he would like a rifle and bayonet as well. Cabins were reserved for the officers. The remainder of the soldiers were assigned to the large public rooms. Freedom of movement was allowed but the majority preferred to stay indoors, away from the fierce wind and the stinging salt spray. Since the ship was running dark, those who ventured out on deck had to move cautiously and keep one hand on the rail. The detectives were among them.

'How are you feeling, Joe?' asked Marmion.

'I feel glad that I didn't join the navy,' replied Keedy. 'My stomach is heaving.'

'You'll get used to it.'

Marmion looked up. 'I thought I heard the sound of an aeroplane.'

'Was it one of ours or one of theirs?'

'One of theirs, I think, but it's not going to waste its bombs on a target like us that they can't see. My guess is that it's heading for London, with a lot of friends to back it up. If it drops its load over the capital, it's bound to hit something.'

'Listen to that,' said Keedy.

'Now that the German plane has flown past, all I can hear are the ship's engines and the sound of the waves battering us.'

'Listen more carefully.'

'What am I supposed to hear?'

'Someone is singing.'

It was true. When Marmion cocked an ear and concentrated, he could hear the strains of a song written the previous year and achieving almost instant popularity. Wind and waves tried to silence it, but they heard the words clearly.

> *Roses are shining in Picardy, in the hush of the silvery dew,*
> *Roses are flow'ring in Picardy, but there's never a rose like you!*
> *And the roses will die with the summertime, and our roads may*
> *be far apart,*
> *But there's one rose that dies not in Picardy!*
> *'Tis the rose that I keep in my heart!*

The invisible singer had a beautiful tenor voice, ideally suited to the sense of yearning in the lyrics. Marmion and Keedy were not the only men on deck who felt tears coursing down their cheeks.

Alice's pleasure at the unexpected appearance of Keedy had quickly dwindled into concern. The fact that he and her father were about to head for France set off a peal of alarm bells in her head. Despite Keedy's assurances, she was fearful. As soon as they parted, she decided to go to the family home to be with her mother. It was a time when they needed each other.

As soon as her daughter appeared, Ellen clung to her in desperation. Though they spent long hours together, there was little conversation. When midnight chimed, they were seated on the sofa, looking at the dying embers in the grate. Neither of them had the urge to go to bed.

'What are you thinking, Mummy?' asked Alice at length.

Ellen turned to her. 'I'm wondering where they are.'

'Somewhere safe, I hope.'

War paid no attention to the time of day. When the ship docked in Calais, they could hear the distant thunder of artillery. Men and equipment were quickly unloaded. Marmion and Keedy found themselves in the back of a car that was part of the long convoy that set off into the night. Cambrai was over ninety miles away, but they saw nothing of the countryside in the dark and besides, they slept all the way there. When they eventually woke up, they had reached the British encampment. They got out of the car in the gloom to see a vast array of tents and a haphazard display of tanks, armoured cars and ambulances. Soldiers were moving about everywhere. There was no sense of triumph after their success on the battlefield. What the detectives felt was an abiding sense of fatigue.

Someone was ordered to take them to the area where the North Staffordshire Regiment was based. Once there, Marmion handed over the letter he had been given by the War Office. It earned them enough time to have a wash and shave to smarten themselves up. They were then given breakfast and shown to the quarters of the commanding officer and told to wait.

After an hour of twiddling his thumbs, Keedy became restive.

'They've forgotten us,' he complained.

'We have to be patient, Joe.'

'But we are on serious business.'

'Nothing is more serious than war,' said Marmion. 'We're here to talk about three murders. Compare that to the huge losses in the Battle of Cambrai. They run into thousands. We have to keep things in perspective.'

'Are they just going to ignore us?'

'There's no question of that happening,' Marmion assured him. 'The letter from the War Office will open doors for us. That is why I handed it over straight away. It not only demands that we are given cooperation, it gives exact details of why we are here. It will save a lot of explanation.'

Keedy was unmoved. 'I still think they've forgotten us – on purpose.'

Ten minutes later, a tall, stately man in the uniform of a Lieutenant-Colonel came into the tent. Now in his late fifties, he had deep-set eyes and a black moustache fringed with grey hairs. Julian Fulton introduced himself and studied them in turn.

'I'm not sure that we can help you, Inspector,' he said. 'The battle we have just fought comprised ten days of utter carnage. It's more than possible that the person you seek is now buried in a war grave.'

'We believe him to be an officer,' said Marmion.

'Officers fell in profusion along with their men.'

'It's the relationship between the two that interests me, sir.'

'It rests firmly on discipline, Inspector.'

'Is it true that, when men are killed in action, the officers who commanded them often write to their families to offer sympathy? That was certainly the case,' Marmion went on, 'in my son's regiment. He fought at the Battle of the Somme.'

'I'm sorry to hear of his loss,' muttered Fulton.

'He's not dead,' explained Keedy. 'He was only wounded.'

'Ah, I see. To answer your question, Inspector, it is the practice for officers to contact the families of those who fall in battle. In this regiment, they are sometimes helped by our chaplain, the Reverend Wilshaw. He has a gift of offering a few comforting words to grieving families.'

'Then the chaplain may be a good place to start,' said Marmion. 'May we speak to him, please?'

'I'll send someone to find him, but you may have to wait. He is always in demand. Harry Wilshaw is an inspirational man,' said Fulton. 'You will never have met anyone quite like him.'

Braving the icy wind, the Reverend Harold Wilshaw finished conducting the latest of a long line of burial services. After a brief chat with those beside him, he headed briskly for his quarters. He was intercepted by a messenger.

'Lieutenant-Colonel Fulton sends his compliments and asks you to join him.'

'Do I have time to change?' asked Wilshaw, indicating his surplice.

'It's an urgent summons, Reverend.'

'Then I'll come at once.'

* * *

While they waited for the chaplain to arrive, Marmion and Keedy learnt something about the battle. Lieutenant-Colonel Fulton was honest with them.

'Cambrai is a an important rail town for the Huns,' he said, 'and an essential part of their supply line. Attacking it was vital.'

'And you did just that,' said Keedy, impressed.

'It was a pyrrhic victory,' admitted the other. 'We smashed a hole in the German defences and shattered the myth that the Hindenburg Line was impenetrable, but there was a terrible price to be paid. We sent 476 tanks into battle plus six infantry and two cavalry divisions. They cut through the Huns like a knife through butter.'

'How many of the tanks did you lose?' asked Keedy.

'About two-thirds of them. Many of those that survived need repair.'

'But you made big territorial gains,' noted Marmion.

'We did indeed,' said Fulton, 'and we were rightly praised. But we were not, alas, able to hold all the land we occupied. Success can bring problems. In this case, it exposed our lack of manpower. We captured some 11,000 prisoners, giving ourselves the headache of keeping them safely locked up.'

Before he could elaborate, he saw the chaplain enter the tent. Clutching his Bible, the newcomer shared a benign smile among all three of them. Wilshaw was a slim, striking man of medium height with a luminous face that made him seem ten years younger than he really was.

'Thank you for coming, Harry,' said Fulton, amicably. 'These gentlemen believe that you may be able to help them.'

As the detectives were introduced, Wilshaw gave each of them a firm handshake, looking them in the eye as he did so. Fulton then withdrew, leaving the others to sit down and exchange a few pleasantries. Marmion then took charge.

'We are investigating three murders that occurred back in England,' he explained, 'and they are linked together by this regiment.'

Wilshaw was surprised. 'Really?'

'We wondered if you knew any of the victims.'

'It's possible, Inspector. What were their names?'

'The first one was Captain Tait – that's Richard Tait.'

'No,' said the chaplain, shaking his head. 'That's not a name I recall.'

'Lieutenant-Colonel Fulton assured us that you had an amazing memory.'

'It's kind of him to say so, but I have met thousands of soldiers during the years I have been chaplain. You can't expect me to remember all of their names.'

'You ought to remember this one,' said Keedy.

'Why?'

'He committed suicide by shooting himself.'

'Then you are quite right, Sergeant,' said Wilshaw, seriously. 'I should have remembered him. I wish that he had turned to me. I am trusted to keep secrets, you see. Officers are there to lead, not to show sympathy. Men find it difficult to reveal any worries or weaknesses to those in command. If they come to me, they are able to open their hearts.'

'That must be a consolation,' said Marmion. 'As a man of the cloth, you are more approachable.'

Wilshaw chuckled. 'Not everyone thinks like that,' he conceded. 'To some of the coarser types, I am a figure of fun. I endure their mockery without turning a hair because I know that the majority trust and respect me. What they are desperate for is someone who will listen instead of merely barking orders at them.'

The detectives were impressed by him. Wilshaw embodied dedication.

To maintain a Christian presence in the regiment, he was ready to undergo multiple dangers and discomfort. Marmion remembered that his son had spoken well of the chaplain in his regiment. Such men were priceless assets.

'Even the atheists turn to me sometimes,' said Wilshaw. 'They rail against the sheer futility of this war and ask me why God is allowing it to happen. I usually manage to convince them that there is a sense of purpose in what he is doing.'

'I wish you could convince me,' murmured Keedy.

'Let's go back to Captain Tait,' said Marmion.

Wilshaw nodded. 'I'm trying hard to place him.'

'He came from Bristol.'

'Then that makes him unusual. For obvious reasons, we recruit largely in Staffordshire. It may be that the captain had a prior connection with the county, of course, but I've no idea what it was. And I still have no memory of him, I fear. Why did you bring up his name in the first place?'

'His brother was brutally murdered.'

'Good heavens!'

'It's the reason we're here,' explained Marmion. 'The death occurred in Bristol, but we believe that it was ordered by someone in his brother's regiment.'

The chaplain blenched.

Having made the effort to arrive early on the previous day, Alice Marmion turned up for work fifteen minutes late. She knew that explaining that her bus had been delayed was not an adequate excuse. If someone were a mere five minutes late, Inspector Gale would seize on the opportunity to berate them. As she entered the building, therefore, Alice gritted her teeth in readiness.

The inspector swooped down on her and took her into a side room.

'I'd like a word with you,' she said, quietly, 'and you don't need to tell my why you're late today. To be candid, I didn't expect to see you at all.'

'You've been speaking to Superintendent Chatfield,' guessed Alice.

'He felt that it was important to explain your situation.'

'I'm grateful to him.'

'You seem to be displaying the courage I expected of you.'

'I have duties to perform. It never occurred to me to let you down.'

'My thoughts are with your father and Sergeant Keedy,' said the other, 'but my principal concern is with you, Alice.'

'Thank you, Inspector.'

'Let me give you some advice. It is only natural that you wish to confide in Iris Goodliffe. In this case, I feel that would be unwise. She would fear the worst and talk endlessly about the danger they face.'

'I'd already decided to say nothing to her.'

'That's very sensible of you.'

'I'm here in the hope that work will keep my mind off the situation.'

'That's the second time this week that you've told me that,' said the other, smiling. 'I hope that it doesn't become a habit.'

'So do I.'

'Two crises in one week are enough for anybody.'

'I agree.'

'How do you feel?'

'I feel that I'm ready to do what I've been trained to do,' declared Alice. 'I will not be distracted, I promise you. Today will be just like any other.'

When he gave the chaplain the outline details of the case, Marmion watched him carefully. Wilshaw seemed genuinely horrified and tried to probe for more information. Marmion suggested that he might not wish to hear exactly how the lawyer had been killed.

'A strong stomach is a necessity in my job,' said Wilshaw, stoutly. 'I have seen death in many forms and know how hideous it can be. In this case, I am sorry that Captain Tait did not seek me out. I might have been able to still his demons.'

'What we can't understand,' said Keedy, 'is why the brother was killed and the wife was spared. Both were at fault.'

'Indeed, they were. Marriage is sacred. It must be respected as such at all costs. The brother may have died but Captain Tait's wife has not escaped punishment. For the rest of her life, she will suffer torments of loss and regret. Unhappily,' the chaplain went on, 'the situation is all too common.'

'In what way?' asked Marmion.

'Well, I could cite dozens of cases where a wife's adultery has driven men in this regiment to extremes. Mail from their home is vital to the morale of our soldiers. They like to know that they are loved and remembered. However,' explained the chaplain, 'we do not filter bad news out of any letters. If something serious has happened at home, men are entitled to know what it is.'

'We can imagine their situation.'

'It's heart-rending to see at close quarters, Inspector. Soldiers feel trapped and helpless. When they hear of wives or girlfriends who have gone astray, they are at their wits' ends. And there are other shocks sometimes. Only a few weeks ago,' recalled Wilshaw, 'I was shown a letter by an officer in which his wife told him that the house had been burgled and that his precious collection of Roman coins had been stolen. Worse still, his beloved dog had been shot.'

'He must have been so frustrated,' said Keedy.

'That's an understatement, Sergeant.'

'What happened to him?'

'He is still here, haunted by the thought that he was not at home to protect his wife and property. We simply can't grant compassionate leave in such cases.'

'No, I suppose not.'

'My apologies, Inspector,' said Wilshaw. 'I was digressing. You spoke of three murders. Which was the second one?'

'It concerns a Private Samuel Roper.'

'Ah, now that's a name I do remember.'

'Did you know the man?'

'Oh, yes. He confided in me that his wife had been unfaithful. What really upset him was that the man in question had been a close friend of his, the landlord of his local pub. They had grown up together. Roper told me that – until he got the news – the first thing he had wanted to do when he got home was to go fishing with this friend, Charlie Ferriday. I gave Roper what little advice I could,' said Wilshaw, 'and he went back to the unit. Foolishly, I flattered myself that I had taken some of the sting out of his pain. The next day, I was told that he had suddenly clambered out of his trench and run directly towards enemy lines. He was cut to ribbons by German machine guns.'

'Charlie Ferriday was hacked to death in Stafford,' said Marmion.

'I deplore what he did,' said the other, 'but I am shocked to hear that he was murdered as a result. How did you get to know of this, Inspector?'

'We looked into cases that had elements in common with the one we were investigating.'

Wilshaw was startled. 'That was enterprising of you.'

'The sergeant and I went to Bristol and talked to the officer in charge of the case involving Captain Tait's brother. While we were doing that,' Marmion went on, 'a colleague of ours went to Stafford and spoke to someone with a detailed knowledge of this second case.'

'What makes you think that the cases are connected?'

'The similarity is unmistakable. Mr Tait was dismembered, and Ferriday was decapitated.'

Wilshaw was horrified. 'How gruesome!'

'The two killers left their autograph on both victims.'

'How do you know that there were two of them?'

'We have clear evidence of that,' said Marmion. 'We know their names or, to be more exact, the aliases they use.'

'John Morris and Anthony Brown,' said Keedy.

'The sergeant even found out where they were hiding.'

'It was a house in Camden Town. We came close to catching them there.'

'Your detective skills are quite remarkable,' said Wilshaw, looking from one to the other. 'Who was the victim in this third murder?'

'We'll come to him in a moment,' said Marmion. 'There's something about the case in Stafford that we need to explain. When we first heard about it, we concluded that Ferriday, the publican, had seduced Samuel Roper's wife.'

Wilshaw nodded. 'That's exactly what Roper himself told me.'

'He was wrong.'

'How could he be? He had a letter from Stafford.'

'Was it written by his wife?'

'Well, no,' said Wilshaw, 'it was not. It was sent by a friend of Roper's, who felt that he ought to know what was going on behind his back.'

'Did he show you the letter?'

'It no longer existed. Sam Roper was so angry that he burnt the letter with his cigarette as soon as he had read it. By the time he came to me, he was in a manic state. The next day,' said Wilshaw, 'he decided there was no purpose to his life, so he put an end to it.'

'What action did you take?'

'I felt obliged to write to his wife and tell her what happened. It was not for me to chastise her for what she had done. I merely offered my sympathy and gave her the facts, knowing that she would draw her own conclusion.'

'You gave her the facts as you saw them,' corrected Marmion, 'but they were false. Roper did not die because his wife had slept with Charlie Ferriday. The police in Stafford are absolutely certain that the publican had not seduced Mrs Roper.'

'Then why was Roper so certain that he had?' asked Wilshaw.

'His letter came from someone who wanted him to suffer by making him believe that the wife had betrayed him. The police in Stafford have yet to identify the man but they believe it was someone with designs on Molly Roper herself.' The chaplain was stunned. 'You see how malign a letter of that kind can be. It led to the death of a decent man and the misery of an honest woman. Mrs Roper lost a husband she worshipped and a man with whom she had worked happily for years, and whose own wife is still wondering why he was butchered to death.'

'You can see why we are so keen to catch the men responsible for the murder,' said Keedy. 'They have killed three victims to date. We are determined to prevent them from adding another name to the list.'

'More power to your elbow, Sergeant,' said Wilshaw, sternly. 'What was the name of the third victim?'

'Dr George Tindall.'

'And you say that he was linked in some way to this regiment?'

'He is a renowned surgeon, by all accounts,' said Marmion, 'and felt the urge to help in the war effort. He worked in a field hospital near your regiment when they were engaged in the Battle of Loos.'

'That was rather a torrid time,' sighed the chaplain.

'Did you ever meet or hear of Dr Tindall?'

'I'm afraid that I didn't.'

'Yet you must spend a lot of time among the wounded and meet large numbers of the medical team.'

'I do, Inspector. It is an aspect of my work that is important to me. It means that I have rubbed shoulders with countless patients, doctors, nurses and stretcher-bearers. This surgeon, George Tindall, may well have been in the field hospital when we fought at Loos, but I have no memory of the man.'

Before the chaplain could say anything else, an orderly came into the tent, apologised for the interruption, then explained that Wilshaw was needed desperately.

'I'm sorry,' he said to the detectives, 'but I must go. Someone else is on the point of death and asking for me. I don't expect to be long.' A thought struck him. 'Why don't you come to my quarters in twenty minutes or so. I have a record there of all the soldiers I have advised or helped in the past. Captain Tait's name may well be among them. If I am not there, just step inside.' He moved off. 'Please excuse me.'

Wilshaw left with the orderly. Marmion turned to Keedy.

'What did you make of him, Joe?'

'I think he's the nearest thing to a saint that I've ever met.'

'He's certainly found his true calling,' said Marmion, 'but I'm surprised that he couldn't remember two of the names I put to him.'

'I can suggest why he didn't recall Dr Tindall.'

'Can you?'

'Yes,' said Keedy. 'Perhaps the doctor was using a different name.

I'm thinking about that second wife of his. She knew him as Michael Langford.'

Marmion was dubious. 'Would he dare to give the army a false name?'

'He had the cheek to do anything.'

They were together in the workshed again. While the sculptor continued to chip away at the wooden angel, his nephew looked at the one bare wall.

'That would be a perfect place to hang it,' he said.

'What are you talking about?'

'That painting I wanted to buy.'

His uncle glowered. 'I wouldn't have it anywhere near me,' he said, breaking off from his work. 'Every time I looked up at it, my toenails would curl.'

'But it's a religious painting.'

'It's the work of a bungling amateur. He should stick to selling fruit and veg in the market and leave real artistry to people like me.'

'You know,' admitted the other, 'I never really took your work seriously until I was saved. And that only happened because I was stuck in a field hospital in Loos. It was pandemonium in there. Doctors and nurses were darting about everywhere as new patients came in. The only person with the slightest interest in me was the chaplain.'

'He did you an enormous favour. Before you joined the army, you were turning into a real criminal.'

'I couldn't help it,' pleaded the other. 'After my apprenticeship as a locksmith at Chubbs, the temptation was too great. I had a knack for opening just about every lock I came across in Wolverhampton. So why not make use of it?'

'It was against the law, that's why. Frankly, I was ashamed of you. It's why I urged you to enlist. I thought it might bring you to your senses.'

'A German bullet did that. You can't make a quick getaway with an artificial foot. I was at a low ebb in that field hospital. And then,' he went on, face brightening, 'I met a miracle worker. He wiped away my former life as if it had never existed and gave me a better one.'

'Serving God and doing his bidding.'

'That's when I came to work for you and realised what amazing skill you had. I understood why you did so much work for churches.'

'And the occasional monastery,' boasted his uncle. 'I carved a new lectern for one of them. It was the most satisfying commission I ever had.'

'The most satisfying things I've ever had were the ones I shared with you. It all started when the chaplain came into my life. I swore to him that I would do absolutely anything he asked me,' said Brian, 'if it involved serving God. He took me at my word.'

'And he put you to the test, Brian. After keeping in touch with you by letter, he was ready to trust you. That's why he asked you to go to Bristol on a mission. You had the sense to involve me.'

'I knew that you had strong religious principles,' said Brian, 'and I needed to have your advice. You not only encouraged me to do what I was asked to do, you agreed to help me. That made all the difference.' He smiled. 'It's funny, really, isn't it?'

'What do you mean?'

'Well, you saved me from a life of crime and gave me a job here – yet you urged me to commit three murders.'

'They were not crimes, Brian.'

'Other people would say that they were.'

'They don't understand. We were God's executioners, obeying his command and ridding the world of sinners who had no right to live.'

* * *

Having taken directions, they went to the chaplain's quarters. When they entered, they found him on his knees in prayer in front of a crucifix that stood on a small cupboard. Marmion and Keedy felt embarrassed at having interrupted him. Before they could step out of the tent, however, Wilshaw got to his feet to give them a welcome.

'Don't go,' he said. 'I always pray after I've just watched somebody die. Thankfully, I was in time to say a few parting words to him before he slipped away.'

'You talked about checking your records,' said Marmion, 'to see if the names of Captain Tait and Dr Tindall were there.'

'I'll do that in a moment, Inspector. First, I must ask you to confirm what you told me about the person I did remember – Samuel Roper. Is it true that the man who, allegedly, seduced Roper's wife was, in fact, innocent of the charge?'

'He was completely innocent,' said Marmion.

'How can you be so sure?'

'One of the detectives involved in the case knew Ferriday and went to his pub occasionally. The publican and his wife were a devoted couple. Mrs Roper had worked happily with them for years. She was equally devoted to her own husband and proud that he had enlisted in the army.'

'I see.'

'Ferriday was killed in the same way as the others,' said Keedy. 'It's the reason we've been able to link all three cases.'

'And you came close to catching the killers, you say?'

'Extremely close.'

'We've gathered a lot of information,' added Marmion. 'We have a good description of each of them and it has been passed to police stations throughout the country. It's only a matter of time before we catch them and find out who has been giving them their orders.'

'And what sort of person do you imagine he would be?' asked Wilshaw.

'He's a man to whom adultery is an anathema.'

'It's one of the Ten Commandments – "Thou shalt not commit adultery".'

'There's a commandment that comes before it – "Thou shalt not kill".'

'There are exceptions in some cases,' argued the chaplain.

'Someone obviously believes it,' said Keedy. 'He thinks that adultery has to be punished by death, as if it's a crime.'

'It's more than a crime, Sergeant – it's a sin.'

'We suspect that one of the killers had military experience,' said Marmion. 'It's highly likely that he served in this regiment.'

'Then why isn't he still in uniform?' asked Wilshaw.

'He could have been invalided out of the army,' replied Marmion. 'People who actually met him told us that he has a pronounced limp. It might be the result of a war wound.

'I see.'

'One person did more than simply describe him,' said Keedy. 'He actually drew a portrait of the man.'

'I have it here,' said Marmion.

Taking it from his pocket, he unfolded it then showed it to the chaplain. Wilshaw's face whitened and he turned away.

'I've never seen this man before.'

'Are you quite certain?' asked Marmion, watching him closely.

'Yes.'

'Look me in the face and tell the truth.'

Wilshaw forced himself to look at Marmion. As he met the inspector's gaze, he began to wilt. He ran his tongue over dry lips. Tears formed in his eyes.

'When you came in,' he confessed, 'I was not praying for the man who died while I crouched beside him. I was praying for forgiveness.'

'That's what I guessed. We like to think that our detective skills guided us to you, but I daresay you view it differently. You believe that God brought us here.'

Wilshaw shivered. 'When did you suspect me?'

'You gave yourself away when you realised how painstaking our work had been. We not only tracked down your accomplices, we came very close to catching them. I saw your face twitch when you learnt that.'

'The mistake was accidental,' pleaded Wilshaw. 'I swear it. Mr Ferriday should still be alive. I could not believe it when you told me that he had been beheaded. That was not what I instructed. What sort of monsters have I let loose?'

'The kind that kill for the sake of it,' replied Keedy. 'And they got a weird religious thrill out of it.'

'You did know Captain Tait, didn't you?' said Marmion.

'Yes, I did,' confessed the chaplain, 'and I had no qualms about what happened to that brother of his. He deserved to die for such an act of betrayal,' he went on, voice rising. 'And Dr Tindall deserved to die as well.'

'You had no right to make those decisions,' said Marmion.

'God directed my hand. Don't you understand? Holy matrimony had been abused. The sinners had to be punished.'

'Ferriday was no sinner,' Keedy reminded him. 'He was wrongly accused.'

'I freely admit it,' said Wilshaw, 'and I'm ready to accept my punishment.'

'And what about Dr Tindall? Why did you order his assassination?'

'Tindall was a scourge. Brilliant as he was, he had a darker side to him. One of the nurses he seduced became pregnant by him and the other, a faithful wife, was tricked into betraying her marriage vows. It destroyed her. I remember her weeping piteously. Unable to face her husband, she drowned herself.'

'Why didn't you challenge Dr Tindall?' asked Marmion.

'He'd already gone back to England,' said Wilshaw, scornfully. 'He told me that he was desperate to see his wife – a woman he had betrayed at least twice.'

'So you gave orders for him to be tracked down.'

'It took time,' said Wilshaw, 'but I had two men at my command, imbued with the same beliefs as me. They found him in the end. Tindall exploited women at will and treated marriage as if it were meaningless. He had to die.'

'The same is true of you,' said Marmion.

Before he could seize him, Wilshaw began to cough violently, bending forward as if he were about to vomit. Taking out some keys, he unlocked the cupboard and extracted a bottle of pills. He removed the cork and tipped the pills into his hand. When he tried to put them in his mouth, however, he felt Marmion's strong hand on his wrist.

'Let me go!' he cried

'You won't escape that way,' said Marmion, shaking the chaplain's wrist until he dropped the pills. 'Handcuff him, Sergeant.'

Keedy stepped in swiftly to obey the order. Though he did not resist, Wilshaw kept pleading with them.

'Let go of me,' he begged. 'I acted in good faith and made a ruinous mistake. I'm prepared to suffer the consequences. If I swallow those cyanide pills, I will not only die, I'll do so in excruciating pain, as did Meredith Tait and George Tindall.'

'And Charlie Ferriday,' said Marmion, bitterly.

'That is what I regret most. I had an innocent man killed.'

'What will your regiment think about you when they realise what you did?'

'I shudder at the thought, Inspector. I beg you to give me those pills. You will save yourselves the trouble of taking me back to face trial. It's the best way.'

'Let me ask you one question, Reverend. Are you married?'

Wilshaw reacted as if he had just been punched in the stomach.

'I was,' he whispered.

Seated in the superintendent's office, Sir Edward Henry listened to the report with an amalgam of admiration and horror. While he was impressed at the way that Marmion and Keedy had solved the case, he was sickened by the behaviour of the chaplain.

'The man was a veritable monster,' he said.

'According to the inspector,' Chatfield told him, 'the Reverend Wilshaw was held in the highest regard.'

'How could anyone look up to an ogre like that?'

'He did good work, Sir Edward, there's no denying that. On first meeting him, Marmion and Keedy thought that he was a species of saint.'

'A saint!' exclaimed the commissioner.

'He will never be able to instigate murders again.'

'What about his two assassins?'

'I am confident that we may soon hear of their arrest,' said Chatfield, beaming. 'I will then have the pleasure of informing the police in Bristol and Stafford respectively, that we have solved a murder case for them.

Conscious that the men they were after would not surrender easily, Marmion asked for two armed officers to be assigned to him. He had found the address of the farm in the chaplain's diary along with the names of the killers who had been his henchmen. The driver took them out of the maelstrom of the capital and off into the wilds of Herefordshire. When they eventually reached the property, they parked a short distance away and walked up the path. The first person they met was one of the farmhands, a stocky, middle-aged man in the process of mending a fence. He told them where they would find the owner and his nephew.

'I didn't realise they were related,' said Keedy.

'You take the nephew,' ordered Marmion, 'and we'll tackle his uncle.'

When they split up, Keedy and one of the supporting officers went off to a row of pigsties. The man feeding the pigs from a large bucket moved with a limp. When Keedy nudged his companion, the latter took out his revolver. They closed quickly on the suspect.

'Brian Gullard?' said Keedy.

'Who are you?' asked the other, turning to face him.

'I'm Detective Sergeant Keedy from Scotland Yard and I've come to arrest you for the murder of Dr George Tindall.'

The man blinked in surprise. 'I don't know what you're talking about.'

'I think you do,' said Keedy, taking out a pair of handcuffs.

Gullard responded by hurling the remains of the pig swill at him before taking to his heels. Angered by the mess over his coat, Keedy went after him. Gullard was determined to escape but his artificial foot hampered him badly. The detectives soon caught up with him. When he saw a patch of thick mud ahead, Keedy timed his dive to perfection. He landed on Gullard's back and sent him head first into the mire. Before he could move, Gullard felt his arms being pulled behind him so that the handcuffs could be clipped on to his wrists. He writhed madly.

'Look at the mess on my coat,' said Keedy, standing up. 'I ought to send you the bill from the cleaners.'

Marmion, meanwhile, had entered the shed with the other armed officer and saw the sculptor working at his bench. The man guessed at once who they must be and why they had come. Turning to face them, he had a thick chisel in one hand and a mallet in the other. He was clearly prepared to use them as weapons. Marmion's companion drew his gun.

'I'd advise against it, Mr Hooke,' said Marmion, quietly. 'Detective Constable Neill is an excellent marksman.'

'What do you want?' grunted the other.

'First of all, I need to pass on some news. Your good friend, the Reverend Wilshaw, was arrested when we confronted him recently in Cambrai.'

Hooke was shaken. 'I don't believe it.'

'There will be no more orders to kill for you and your nephew.'

'Who are you?'

'My name is Detective Inspector Marmion and I've been leading the investigation into the murder of George Tindall. He was the third of your victims after Meredith Tait and Charlie Ferriday.'

'They deserved to die!'

'The same, I fear, may be said of you and your nephew.' He looked at the wooden angel. 'That's a wonderful carving. It's a pity you won't be able to finish it.'

The man reacted instantly, hurling the mallet at Neill, and knocking the gun from his hand. With the chisel raised, he ran towards Marmion, but the inspector had anticipated an attack. Swooping up a handful of sawdust, he threw it into his face and blinded him momentarily. All that the sculptor could do was to slash away wildly with his weapon. Marmion and Neill moved in swiftly to overpower him and take the chisel from his hand. The prisoner was soon handcuffed.

Keedy came into the shed with the other prisoner.

'We did God's work,' said Gullard, defiantly. 'We were soldiers of the cross.'

'Yes,' added his uncle. 'Our orders came from above.'

'So did ours,' said Marmion. 'You'll be able to meet the superintendent.'

It was Saturday evening and all four of them were enjoying the luxury of a meal together. Now that the murder of Dr Tindall had finally been solved, Marmion and Keedy were able to relax slightly. When the meal was over, they moved to the living room. Ellen and Alice wanted full details of the arrests and how the killers had tried to justify what they had done.

'We have had difficult cases before,' said Marmion, 'but this was the most testing. I hope we never have to go into a war zone again.'

'I found our visit to Herefordshire more dangerous,' said Keedy. 'My overcoat will have a permanent smell of pig swill.'

'It will remind you of an important arrest you made.'

'The most important arrest was that of the chaplain. He set himself up as judge and jury. And he had two executioners at his beck and call.'

'The Reverend Wilshaw had been married,' said Marmion, 'but his wife was unfaithful to him. It was a wound that would never heal. It warped his mind. He found solace in ordering the deaths of men who had seduced married women.'

'It's all over now,' said Keedy. 'We can actually have free time again.'

'Oh,' said Alice, 'I'm so glad about that. We can start looking forward

313

to Christmas. I feel that it's going to be really special this year.'

'So do I,' said Keedy. 'We deserve a treat.'

'It won't be such a treat for Ellen,' Marmion pointed out. 'There's all the cooking and preparation to do.' He turned to her. 'That's right, love, isn't it?'

'What?' she asked, coming out of a daydream. 'I'm sorry. I didn't hear what you said.'

'We were talking about the wonderful Christmas we'll all have.'

'It won't be wonderful for all of us.'

'What do you mean?'

'There'll be an empty chair at the table,' she said, quietly.

After thanking the driver for the lift, Paul Marmion jumped off the cart, pulled on his haversack and began to trudge towards the nearby village.

EDWARD MARSTON has written over a hundred books. He is best known for his hugely successful Railway Detective series and he also writes the Bow Street Rivals series featuring twin detectives set during the Regency as well as the Domesday series and the Home Front Detective series.

If you enjoyed *Orders to Kill*, look out for more books by Edward Marston . . .

To discover more great fiction and to place an order visit our website
www.allisonandbusby.com
or call us on
02039507834